Ride Me

rebecca brooke

Cover Design by Sommer Stein of Perfect Pear Creations

Editing by Emily A. Lawrence of Lawrence Editing

DEDICATION

To everyone who never thought they could have the one person the always wanted.

TABLE OF CONTENTS

Love

is

Love

SAWYER

“Jesus fucking Christ. I’m coming.”

I threw my legs over the side of the bed, blinking my eyes into focus, the sunlight reflecting off the white walls burning them. Why was someone banging on my front door before nine in the morning and where in the hell had Heath gone? He should’ve been dragging his ass out of bed to see who’d been banging on it for the last fifteen minutes since I only went to bed a couple of hours ago, after reworking the lyrics for our latest song. Even as the drummer of Jaded Ivory, I did my fair share of songwriting.

I tugged on a pair of shorts and ran a hand over my face. The pounding started again and I forced myself to leave the room to answer the door. I noticed Heath’s door open, the room empty as I passed by. No wonder he hadn’t answered the door. I hadn’t heard his car leave, but that didn’t mean anything. The minute my head hit the pillow I was out cold.

By the time I reached the door, the person on the other side had started yelling and I couldn't stop my eyes from rolling. A voice I'd know anywhere. I yanked the door open.

"Why didn't you use your key?"

Mari stood on my porch. Her one hand still raised to knock, the other settled firmly on her hip. She dropped her hand and shrugged. "Because I forgot it. What took you so long?"

"I was sleeping, like most people would if they were up all night."

Mari was the lead singer of our band, Jaded Ivory, and my best friend. We met in college freshman year. We were both trying to escape the memories of home and grew close pretty quick. She'd been bullied by the jocks in her class. They'd flat out tortured her. Over the years, I watched her shake off that shell and become a brand-new person. Someone with self-confidence.

Mari stepped around me and into the house, her eyes moving around the room, no doubt taking in the pizza boxes and beer cans scattered throughout it. She looked back at me and lifted a brow as I shut the door. "How many all-nighters have you pulled lately?"

The woman knew me better than anyone else in the world. Well, maybe there was one other, but it had been seven years since the last time I saw him. Even if I did, I'd highly doubt he knew or would want to know anything about me now. Not with the way I left.

"More than I can count."

Mari flopped onto the couch, her nose scrunched up, and she leaned forward, pulling something out from behind her. She lifted a brow, holding up a drumstick. "Nice to know Heath suffers like I used to." She tossed the stick at me and laughed.

I caught it mid-air, then dropped into the seat next to her. "Very funny. What are you doing here this early?"

"It's not early."

"For you it is. We're talking about a girl who thought that anything before eleven in the morning might as well be dawn. You'd get up and swear no one should have to get up before it was time to eat lunch."

Mari held up her hands. "Okay. Okay." She lifted my arm over her shoulder and snuggled into my chest. I couldn't help but hold her close. It seemed so long since either of us had the time to sit and talk the way we used to.

"I missed this," I whispered into her hair.

She snuggled closer. "Me too."

"You still haven't told me what you're doing up so early."

She sighed. "I was lonely."

I couldn't stop the chuckle that escaped my lips. "You're lonely? I'm pretty sure all you have to do is look at Cole and he's trying to get your clothes off."

"Pretty much. Except he's not home. Cole left last night. Hayward has an away game this weekend."

Cole was Mari's boyfriend. As a star football player, he had plans to play professional football. At least until he broke his leg. When he couldn't play anymore, he began coaching. Last year he'd been hired by Hayward, the local university, to coach their offensive line.

"So I'm the backup plan?" I tried to keep the amusement out of my voice, but I should have known she'd see right through me.

Mari sat up and smacked me in the chest. "You're never the backup plan." She settled back down against me and whispered, "But I miss seeing you all of the time."

"I miss you too, but we do see each other almost every day."

"It's not the same."

"I know it's not, but you're happy, right?" I asked, a part of me a little jealous, wanting the same happiness for myself.

"So happy." Mari glanced up at me. "I'm still waiting to hear you found your Prince Charming."

"I think you'll be waiting a very long time for that to happen."

"There's no one you have your sights set on? We're in a whole new city. Have you even bothered to look around?"

"I've looked," I said, hoping Mari would leave it alone. Sure, I'd noticed guys throughout the city, but it wasn't exactly easy to pick them up when you were hiding the fact you were gay from everyone, except your two best friends and Mari's boyfriend.

"Sawyer, be honest with me."

"Even if I were looking, how in the hell am I supposed to go on a date without the world finding out?"

She squeezed my waist tighter. "We're in a bigger city. There's got to be a way."

"You know that's not the way it works. Someone will always be looking to make money off the story if they can."

"I wish it didn't have to be that way."

I tucked my finger under her chin and lifted her face to mine. "It doesn't have to be. At some point, we'll have made our way to the top and I won't have to hide anymore." At least I had to hope it would be that way, or I'd have to wonder what the point of it all was.

"You shouldn't have to hide who you are for Jaded Ivory."

"No, but you have to remember there are two sides to that coin. There are enough bigots in the world. I'd have to worry about it impacting our sales. On the other side, I don't want to become one of the poster boys for gay musicians everywhere and our sales jump because of who I want to sleep with."

"That wouldn't—"

"Yes, it would."

She huffed and I pressed a soft kiss to her forehead.

"I know you want to make everything right in the world. This may not be something you can fix."

She narrowed her eyes at me. "You doubt my abilities? I'm gonna figure this one out if it kills me."

Oh, Christ. Who the hell knew what she had up her sleeve. When Mari focused on something, she didn't let it go until she got it. At least this Mari did. *Fuck, I've helped create a monster.* Or at least someone who was going to get me into a boatload of shit. The first time I met Mari, she hid behind long locks of blond hair. Afraid of the world. I thought bringing Mari out of her shell might help us both. Maybe it made me a dick, focusing on her to forget all I'd walked away from. In the end, she'd become the woman sitting beside me, ready to take on the world so I wouldn't be lonely.

And for years, I hadn't been. Neither one of us was interested in finding love. We both wanted someone in our bed for the night and that was enough. I had a feeling Mari's goal was to prove she came out stronger than before. Mari's bullies had taken their toll on her. Especially when Cole showed up in her life. He'd been part of the crew that made her life a living hell. Since he'd found her again, he'd been going out of his way to make her happy and atone for everything he'd done to her.

Nobody was going to tell her she wasn't good enough again. Me? I just wanted to fuck him out of my head. Not an easy feat when you were hiding who you were from the world. I spent plenty of nights in college driving an hour or two away from campus to find a guy to hook up with. All to keep my secret. Even from the band. At least most of them.

Heath had been my roommate all through college. It would have been impossible to keep something like that from him. Then again, I didn't want to try and hide that part of me in college. In my mind, three years should have been enough time in the closet. Never once did I consider the implications of being in the band. Like I told Mari earlier, I didn't want who I chose to sleep with to impact Jaded Ivory.

"Don't hurt yourself trying. I'd hate to get Cole pissed at me."

She rolled her eyes. "That would never happen."

"You have that much control over the poor guy?"

She laughed. "No. He's glad that you and I were never together."

"Please tell me he's not still worried about that."

Mari's boyfriend, Cole, had gotten into his head that we were sleeping together. She begged me to tell Cole the truth. Not wanting to be the one thing that drove them apart, I gave in and told Cole my secret.

"Not at all." She moved to sit farther on the edge of the couch and patted my leg. "Now, you're going to get dressed and come to breakfast with me."

"Nope. I'm going back to bed. We have that meet and greet tonight."

It wasn't something we could miss. Jaded Ivory had worked too hard to get to this point. Once Mari joined the band, our popularity had exploded, leading to our first recording deal with LiteStar Records.

Mari poked me in the chest. "And you can take a nap later. Now go get dressed. We're going to get pancakes and figure out how to get you a man without anyone finding out."

"Mari," I warned, even though I knew it wouldn't do any good.

"Don't even try it, Sawyer. Go. Get. Dress." She pulled her phone from her bag. "I'll wait here."

There was no point in arguing with her. Even if I tried to go back to bed, she'd find a way to wake me back up. "Fine," I grumbled.

"Just remember, the faster you get changed and we leave, the faster you can get back here and grab a nap before the meet and greet."

I walked into my room and eyed the bed. Sleep or breakfast with Mari? She had a point. Most of the time we spent together anymore was with the whole band. With her moving in with Cole, we lost that extra time alone. I pulled the T-shirt over my head and tossed it on the bed. I'd sleep later. I may not want to deal with finding a guy for a random hookup, but I'd still take Mari's company. By

Sunday, Cole would be back. No reason to not sleep then.

After a quick shower, I threw on a clean T-shirt and jeans. Mari was still sitting on the couch with her phone in her hand when I went back to the living room.

She looked me over. “Ready?”

I gestured to the door. “Let’s go.”

SAWYER

It seemed as if we'd been sitting at the meet and greet forever. I honestly never thought that many people would show up, but the excitement of it all was weaning the longer we stayed, the exhaustion from the last week of no sleep slowly taking its toll. By the time we'd gotten back from breakfast, Heath was home and all hope for sleep went down the drain. I handed back the poster with a forced smile, hoping the fan in front of me didn't notice. My eyes landed on the poster in the next person's hand. Without bothering to look up, which I knew made me an asshole, I kept the smile plastered on my face as I took the poster and began signing my name.

"The least I could get is a real smile."

Shit.

My first thought was that I'd been caught faking it, when the words played over and over in my head. *I know that voice.* Afraid to have my suspicions confirmed, I lifted my head slowly to meet green eyes I never thought I'd see again. I opened my mouth to speak, but nothing would come out. It was as if my tongue was tied in knots, not to mention that my brain wasn't firing correctly. I just sat and stared.

Reagan.

Of course the man was as sexy as ever. The T-shirt stretching across his chest to pull tight on the well-defined muscles of his biceps. The clean-shaven face of my memories was no more, a slight five o'clock shadow in its place. I swallowed hard, trying to push down the nerves at seeing him again. It'd been almost seven years since I'd left Reagan at home. The day I parked my car down the street from his house, I sat there for hours mustering up the nerves to tell him the secret I'd kept from him for years, only to drive away long after midnight without ever having knocked on his door.

Now, he stood before me, watching me, waiting for some type of reaction, that I apparently was almost incapable of giving. But this man had been my best friend since we were seven years old. There was no reason I couldn't talk to him. Eleven years was a lot of time to throw away.

"What are you doing here?"

One brow quirked up. "Friends eleven years and that's the best opening line you can give me? I was hoping for something more along the lines of hi, how have you been?"

I shook my head. "Sorry about that. You took me by surprise, is all. Hi, how are you?"

The corner of his lip turned up in a smile so familiar, a bit of the tension left my shoulders. "That's better, but I don't mind answering your question first. I went to law school at Hayward. Got a job in the city and saw you'd be doing a meet and greet in the area. Figured I'd come and see you."

"A lawyer?"

"Yeah, one more—" The sound of a throat clearing came from behind me. Reagan looked over his shoulder and back at me. "Sorry, I don't mean to hold up the line."

"Don't worry about it." I noticed the line behind him getting longer. That was the thing about sitting directly to the left of Mari. The people usually got their stuff signed by her, then jumped in your line.

"I'd really like to catch up. Think we could meet up for a drink after you're done?"

My head screamed at me to come up with some kind of excuse why I couldn't meet him, but my dick, which had perked up at the sight of him, and my heart were leading the charge. I'd been in love with Reagan since I was sixteen years old. Now with him standing there in front of me, I knew if given the chance I would be again. My dick was half hard with him simply being in the room. Somehow I knew sitting down with him, even for only one drink, was going to screw with my head. Always a glutton for punishment, I nodded. "Yeah, that would be good. We have another half an hour, if you don't mind waiting."

"Not at all." He threw his thumb over his shoulder. "I'll let you get back to it."

"I won't be long."

"Take your time. I can wait."

I knew his words had their own double meaning. He'd had to wait for seven years for a chance to talk. There was no doubt in my mind he'd want to know why I'd disappeared without a word all those years ago. I knew he'd checked in with my parents more than once over the years, and it had to be frustrating for him when they wouldn't give him any hint of where I went. Before I'd left I told my parents I was gay, completely prepared for them to kick me out. What I hadn't expected was for them to tell me they loved me no matter what and promised to keep my secret.

I pasted a smile on my face, more than aware that Reagan watched me from the other side of the room. My stomach clenched into knots, getting tighter and tighter as time ticked away on the clock. Each signature meant another minute closer to sitting down with Reagan. And I had no idea what to tell him. Besides my parents, three other people knew the truth and it wasn't the whole band. Was I ready to tell Reagan? Was he ready for the *entire* truth? Something told me the answer was no.

Out of the corner of my eye, I saw Mari watching me. Besides Reagan, she could read me better than anyone else. She'd be able to see the fake smile on my face. No doubt in my mind, she'd pull me aside later and demand answers.

As I got closer to the end of my line, my heart pounded so hard in my chest, I wondered if everyone in the room could hear each beat. Tom, our manager from the label, stepped into the room, probably getting ready to escort out the last few people. Before he had a chance to say anything, I waved him over. He bent down close to keep the fans from hearing what he had to say.

"What's up, Sawyer? Ready to call it a night?"

"More than you know," I whispered. "Look, see that guy leaning against the wall?"

Tom glanced over his shoulder and nodded. "What about him?"

"He's a friend of mine. Let him wait here while we get packed up?"

"Sure. Not a problem. I'll work on getting everyone else out of here. I imagine you guys need a break before tomorrow."

A part of me wanted to scream *no*, tell him to keep letting people in. Anything to avoid a moment I'd dreaded since the moment I left. Seeing Reagan again was already beginning to wreak havoc on me. I knew I'd have to build one giant ass wall around my heart if I was going to keep it safe. Whether I liked it or not, I needed it to be that way. Jaded Ivory was working its way up the charts and I wouldn't let my personal life get in the way of that.

Tom started to clear the room and I stood, stretching my legs for the first time in hours. Reagan came over to the table, twirling his cell phone in his hand.

"Ready?"

"Give me a minute. I need to grab my stuff. I'll be right back."

Reagan nodded. "I'll wait here."

I moved through the door on the other side of the room, only to run directly into Mari. Time for round one of questions.

"I thought you said you didn't have your eyes on anyone. Who's that guy? You've been sitting there for the last half an hour with a fake smile plastered across your face." She crossed her arms over her chest. "Well, are you gonna answer me?"

I mimicked her stance. "Maybe if you take a breath long enough for me to answer."

She rolled her eyes and made a go ahead gesture with her hand.

I glanced around, making sure no one was within earshot. When I was sure we were alone, I moved my gaze back to hers. "I don't have my eyes on anyone. That's Reagan."

"Reagan?"

I didn't say anything, just waited for the light to go off. It only took a few seconds for her jaw to go slack and her eyes to widen.

"That's Reagan?" she whispered when she managed to get her voice back.

I dropped my arms by my sides and sighed. "That's him."

"What's he doing here? How did he find you?"

"Honestly, I don't know. I'm sure he saw our poster somewhere. It's not like we could keep a low profile forever."

"Oh my God." She rubbed her temple with her fingers. "Are you okay with him being here?"

"I don't know that either."

"What are you going to tell him?"

It was like freaking twenty questions and I didn't have an answer to a single one. "I have no idea. I'm not sure what to say in front of him."

Mari took the pendant on her necklace between her fingers, moving it back and forth around her neck, her eyes pointed toward the ceiling. I knew it meant she was thinking of what would be the right answer. Suddenly, she stopped and brought her gaze back to mine. "I think you need to tell him the truth."

I ran a hand through my hair, pacing the small hallway in an attempt to burn off the nervous energy flowing through me. "Yeah, I'm sure that'll sound great. Hi, Reagan. Yeah, I left because I'm gay and have been in love with you since we were sixteen, but you're into girls. Not sure that's gonna work."

Mari stepped in front of me, stopping me in my tracks. “You know that’s not what I mean.” She’d been my best friend since we met in college seven years ago. Right around the time I’d walked away from Reagan. I was looking for someone to replace that easy camaraderie I had with Reagan. Mari was closed off and I made it my mission to get her to open up. It helped us both. Mari came out of her shell and became the person I knew she could be. For me it was the perfect distraction from what I left behind.

I scoffed. “I’d like to avoid the subject altogether.”

“I’m not sure that’s really possible at this point.”

“I know. But how the hell do I tell him that?”

“Just like you told me. Be honest.”

“It’s different with him.”

Mari gripped my shoulders and shook her head. “It’s only different if you make it different.”

Deep down I knew she was right. My reaction to the way I told him was the only thing that would make it different. When all was said and done, I was more afraid of his reaction. “And what if he can’t handle who I am?”

Mari moved her arms up and around my neck, pulling me tight to her. “Then he’s not the man you thought he was and isn’t worth your time,” she whispered in my ear.

My heart rate slowed and I could pull in a full breath. I held her tighter and placed a brief kiss on her head. “Thank you. That was exactly what I needed to hear.”

She leaned back, a smirk lifting the corner of her lips. “I know. It’s my turn to hold you up. You’ve been doing it for me for years.”

"Love you, Mari. Not sure what I would have done without you all these years."

"Love you, too. I think it's the other way around, though, but we can worry about it later. Right now, I think Reagan has waited long enough."

I stepped back out of her embrace and nodded. "I think you're right."

I backed toward the door when Mari called out, "Text me later."

"Don't worry. I'm sure they'll be plenty to tell."

I turned on my heel and went to face the secrets of the past. Hopefully, they weren't too big to keep me buried under them.

Chapter Three

Reagan

I watched Sawyer as he continued to sign item after item. The moment I found out about this meet and greet I bought tickets. It wouldn't have mattered to me how much the tickets cost. I was going to be here. For years I wondered what had happened to Sawyer. We'd always planned on going to different schools, but I never expected the night before we left for college to be the last time I saw him. I'd counted on texts, Skype, and holidays to get us through to the next summer.

Except, one night he was there and the next he was gone. The only thing I knew was the name of his college. Nothing about what dorm he was staying in or who his roommate might be. Otherwise I would have hunted his ass down and demanded an explanation. He'd disconnected all his social media and changed his number. Sawyer basically disappeared off the face of the earth and I had no way to find him. His parents wouldn't give me a single hint about where I could find him either.

It amazed me how, after all this time, I still needed to know why he walked away. Our friendship had survived the four years of high school where our interests pulled us in different directions. I had to know why it never got a chance to survive college.

I watched as woman after woman practically threw themselves at him, trying to get him to notice them. Nothing had changed since we were in high school. Every girl in our class wanted to snag Sawyer, but none of them ever did. Something about this rubbed me the wrong way. The entire time, he kept that fake ass smile on his face. Knowing I was the only one in the room to get a real smile left a strange feeling in the pit of my stomach. The same one he had whenever he wanted to be somewhere other than where he was. I had a feeling my being there didn't help the situation, but that was tough shit. He was the one who walked away without a word. For the longest time I wondered what I'd done to push my best friend away. At some point I gave up trying to reason it out and hoped one day I'd get my chance to get some answers.

Another guy stepped into the room a little bit later, and after talking to Sawyer, began to clear the room. Honestly, I was surprised when I wasn't asked to leave. The bitter part of me figured it wouldn't be a shock if he used some other guy to give me the boot. Once the room was empty besides me and the members of the band, I walked over to the table to give Sawyer a quick reminder that I was still waiting. He promised he'd be back and disappeared through another door, following the lead singer of Jaded Ivory. She was tiny, with shoulder-length, curly blond hair. I thought her name was Mari, but it wasn't like I paid a lot of attention to anyone else in the band once I realized who sat behind the drums. Sawyer's playing style was distinct. It would have been hard to miss the first time I saw them play.

Seconds then minutes passed and a part of me started to wonder if Sawyer had gone out another door to avoid me. He knew I'd want an explanation for the way he disappeared. The Sawyer I knew wouldn't run from the consequences of his decisions. Then again, he'd run from something when he left. The door opened and relief drew the tension from my shoulders when I saw his brown, shaggy head step through. He shut the door behind him, keeping his back to me longer than necessary. It wasn't until he finally turned around that I noticed the stiff set of his shoulders, the way he kept his hands shoved into the front pockets of his jeans.

Time hadn't changed Sawyer much. The gauges in his ears had gotten larger and I could see ink peeking beneath the sleeve of his shirt. Besides music, it looked as if he'd gotten some time in the gym. His arms and chest were bigger than I remember them, but the longer hair and inquisitive green eyes, which were currently focused somewhere over my shoulder, hadn't changed a bit.

"Anywhere specific you wanted to go?" he asked, still standing across the room. He lifted his hand to run it through his hair and I couldn't help but notice the way his hand shook.

Maybe more had changed than I originally thought. Sawyer wasn't usually nervous. He'd always faced every challenge head-on. Not that I really knew him anymore. An invisible barrier had been resurrected between us. A wall I hadn't built and had no idea how to tear it down.

"Doesn't matter to me. I can drive if you want, though."

"Yeah." He nodded. "Yeah, that works. Heath drove us here tonight. There's a sports bar down the street."

"McGillian's?"

"That's the one."

"I know the place." I gestured over my shoulder. "My car's parked out front in the lot. Are you good to go out that way?"

"The crowd should be gone by now." Sawyer reached for his back pocket but shook his head, shoving his hand into his front pocket. At least one thing hadn't changed. Sawyer had a habit of twirling his drumsticks in his hand. He walked forward and grabbed the handle of the other door. "Let's go."

I followed him into the hall and wondered for the millionth time what I was doing. Did he plan to spend the whole night saying as little as possible? I wanted answers, except with the way the conversation had gone so far it didn't seem I'd get them.

This was a man I spent every single day with since the time I was seven. He knew all my secrets. From the first time I got drunk and puked to the time I lost my virginity to Bridget Wilson sophomore year. He knew it all. A few years shouldn't make a difference. Yet, there we'd stood and it was like he didn't know how to talk to me.

Once we stepped out into the cool night, I pointed to the left side of the lot. "My car's this way."

I led the way, unlocking it and climbing in as Sawyer shut the door behind him and fastened his belt. He glanced around the car and chuckled.

"Guess your need to be a neat freak hasn't changed in all these years?"

While I knew he was trying to break the ice with a joke, the comment rubbed me the wrong way. The reality was we didn't know each other anymore. And I blamed him for that. He was the one who disappeared without a word, leaving us both in this completely uncomfortable situation. Something I planned to push aside. If anyone should feel uncomfortable it was Sawyer. He'd made a decision that affected us both. The least he could have done was say goodbye. The lack of explanation would have made me crazy, but I would have known when I woke up the next morning not to run around trying to find out what had happened to him.

"Guess not." I tried to shrug it off. Not that it worked. The more I thought about the day he disappeared, the more my muscles tensed.

"Reagan..." Sawyer started.

"Let's wait till we get to the bar. I think we both have a lot to say to each other and I'd rather not do it while driving down the road."

Out of the corner of my eye I could see him fidget in his seat.

"Fair enough."

The tension filled every available space in the car, almost choking me under its weight. I wanted to take back my words and demand answers. More than that, I wanted to see the look in his eyes when he answered me.

The rest of the drive was silent. Not even the low sound of the radio penetrated my senses. The man next to me held my whole focus, which made me glad when I pulled up to a metered spot along the curb. Sawyer practically leapt from the car. Not that I could blame him. It seemed we both needed a second to breathe.

I watched as Sawyer walked inside without looking back and dropped my head onto the steering wheel. *What the hell am I doing? Why do I need these answers so bad?* Things had been going so well in my life. I'd finished my undergrad with honors and was accepted to one of the most prestigious law schools in the country. And after once again graduating at the top of my class, I'd been hired at one of the most highly respected law firms in the city. One little song on a radio station led me down this rabbit hole. Who knew when I went to download the song I'd find Sawyer's face staring back at me. Yet, there I sat in my car, hiding from my closest friend from childhood, while he sat inside the bar.

What was the big deal?

The big deal was the moment I realized Sawyer's dream had come true and I'd seen him play, acid ate at my insides. I wondered what had made him walk away from our friendship. What had I done? I may have been the jock while he called himself the band geek, even if he played his own sports, but it had never gotten in our way before. I would've cheered him on, like he'd done for me so many times.

It was fucking ridiculous. We were both grown adults. All I could do was say my piece and let him say his. No reason we couldn't sit down to hash out the problem and move on. Whether that was as friends or acquaintances living in the same city. Either way, after tonight I'd put all the questions behind me.

With my new resolve, I climbed from the car and dropped some change in the meter before heading inside. The place was crowded, people standing back to back. Hell, I was lucky to have found the spot out front considering the number of people inside. Then again, luck always seemed to be on my side when Sawyer was around. The dim lighting made it difficult to see where he'd gone. I moved farther into the room, scanning the tables, hoping he realized this was not a conversation I wanted to have sitting at the bar with an audience. I craned my neck to the left and found him seated at one of the booths in the back, facing the door.

When our eyes locked, he quickly looked down at the paper on the table. Did he think he could hide behind a menu? Slowly, I made my way through the crowd and dropped into the seat across from him. He glanced up for a brief second before moving his eyes back down. He had the beer menu out. *Good.* I needed a drink.

I reached for the other menu sitting behind the napkin holder. If I could have kept a straight head, I would've ordered a double shot or two of tequila. Knowing my tolerance for the shit over the last few years, I knew I wouldn't. A beer would have to do to calm my nerves. I found one I liked and shoved the menu to the side. Sawyer scanned the menu as if he'd never seen the choices. When he made no effort to look at me again, I decided enough was enough.

"Find what you want?"

His head snapped up. A hint of color stained his cheeks. Guess he figured out his ruse wasn't working. It was time to face the music. "Um...yeah."

He pushed the menu aside, thumbing its corner. Silence descended over the booth. Ironic considering the noise level in the bar. It was like we were an old married couple who'd run out of things to talk about. There were so many things I wanted to say to him, but I knew he had to be the one who started the conversation. I'd taken the first step by showing up tonight, now it was his turn.

"Reagan..." he began again like in the car.

"Hey." A sweet voice came from beside me.

The interruption annoyed the hell out of me, but I couldn't fault the poor girl for doing her job. I glanced up to see a petite brunette standing at the end of the table. *Fuck.* She was gorgeous. Caramel-colored eyes focused directly on me. I couldn't help the way my eyes followed her jawline down to where the neckline of her shirt was ripped to reveal more of the creamy skin beneath. She pulled two coasters from her apron. "What can I get you guys?"

I flashed her a smile. "Heineken."

Her cheeks pinkened as she smiled back. She turned to him. "Got it. And you?"

He didn't bother looking over, his focus locked on me. The way his eyes watched me made me shift in my seat. Something was there, except I couldn't place it. Then again, I hadn't seen him in so long, I could just be imagining things.

"Guinness."

The waitress moved her gaze between us. When she looked back at me, I could see an uncomfortable smile cross her lips, like she didn't know what she'd walked in on. She wasn't the only one. That look had me confused as hell.

She tucked the pen and pad back into her apron. "I'll be right back with those drinks."

Apparently, whatever Sawyer had to say made it impossible to even try and put on a friendly face. Although, I'd watched him do it for hours tonight. I could only imagine the toll that would take on someone. It had to be exhausting to be happy and enthusiastic for hours at a time. Constantly being in the spotlight.

Silence fell over the table again. I forced my ass harder into the vinyl seat to keep from getting up and shouting to break it. I kept my eyes glued to his, waiting for the moment he'd explain everything. His thumb and forefinger tapped out a beat on the table, something I was pretty sure he wasn't aware of doing. A part of me wanted to do something to calm his nerves, except he put himself in this situation and he'd have to dig out of it himself.

He chuckled humorlessly and I narrowed my eyes at him. "Why the hell are you laughing?"

A sigh left his lips. "I find it completely ironic that after being friends for most of our lives, I have no idea what to say to you."

I wanted to yell 'tell me why you left,' but the words stuck in my throat and I bit the inside of my cheek hard enough to draw blood. Instead, I waited.

He picked the spoon up from the table and began twirling it around. His gaze roved over me once again and a tingle started at the base of my neck. "Honestly, I don't think much about you has changed in all these years, and I can guess you want to know why I left. And I don't know how to explain it."

Apparently the years had made Sawyer less straightforward. My hand clenched and unclenched as I tried to control my annoyance. "How 'bout the beginning?"

SAWYER

I could see the way his jaw tightened and his hand flexed against the table. Reagan was annoyed at my bullshit answer. Even I knew it was crap. I had no idea what to say to this man. A man I loved since we were sixteen years old. Deep down, I had a feeling it wouldn't take much for me to fall for him all over again. Mari would be pissed, but I couldn't bring myself to do it. I wanted to give Reagan as much of the truth as possible without laying it all on the line. In the end, whether or not Reagan and I were friends, he didn't need to know about me being gay. Nothing good could come from it. Exactly why I'd kept it under wraps for so long. Until I found someone worth coming out for, I was keeping that shit locked up tight in the closet.

"The beginning, huh? You still don't beat around the bush?"

"Not when I've been waiting years to hear the answer so I can stop questioning how I fucked up."

"Is that what you think?" My hand itched to reach across and take hold of his. Never in a million years had I wanted Reagan to blame himself for the way I left. I hoped he would have put it all on me.

He scoffed. "No, most of the time, I assume you were being an asshole. But we both know what happens when you assume things. Then there's the small part of me, the nagging voice in the back of my head that makes me question what kind of person I am to push away my best friend."

"You didn't push—"

"Here you go." The waitress placed the beers in front of us.

For the second time, I couldn't help but notice the way his eyes drifted over her. How for one brief second, I wished he'd look at me that way. That somehow, he'd find me sexy the way I found him. The strong biceps expertly defined by the tight shirt covering his torso. I wondered how his abs would feel beneath my fingertips, at least until I forced myself back to reality. Reagan was straight and would never see me like that. That kind of thinking would get me in trouble. Before he caught me staring again, I moved my gaze to the pint glass in front of me. Picking it up, I swallowed back a few gulps, letting the smooth but bitter liquid warm me from the inside out.

"Thanks," he said, flashing her his dimpled smile. The one that had girls tripping over themselves to get to him. If I thought for one minute it would do me any good, I'd be at the head of the pack.

He picked up his own beer and I tried not to be envious of the bottle as it touched his lips. I watched the way his Adam's apple bobbed as he swallowed it down. *Get it together*. It was like I'd suddenly lost my head and didn't know how to keep myself on track.

He gestured toward me with his bottle. "Go on."

"It wasn't your fault I left. I had a lot of shit going on that I wasn't ready to share with anyone."

"Why does this sound like one of those bad breakup speeches? *It's me, not you.*" He laughed, but it didn't reach his eyes.

"I guess it does, but it's the truth. My head was a mess before I went to school. Shit I kept buried way down deep. I had no idea how to deal with any of it, so I ran. I ran from you. Ran from my parents. Ran from everyone."

He twisted his thumb around the neck of the bottle, his gaze never moving from the table. The rest of the bar faded away, as the pounding of my heart became the only thing I could focus on.

He set the bottle on the table and brought his head up. "You know, it pissed me off after a while. For my entire freshman year of college, I questioned myself. Questioned what I'd done to push you away. We weren't two chicks having a cat fight, but it didn't stop me from wondering."

"That was never my intention."

"Even when I asked your parents how to get in touch with you, they refused to tell me."

I dropped my gaze, afraid of how much to let him see. "I asked them to. They had no idea why I left without a word, just that I didn't want anyone to get in touch with me. I didn't want to drag you down with me, not when I wasn't ready to explain."

Which was partially the truth. There were only two outcomes I could see if I told him the truth. One he'd be completely disgusted by my choices and quickly run the other way. Or he'd feel sorry for me, but slowly create distance between us until there was nothing left of friendship to salvage. I just made the first move.

"You wouldn't have taken me down with you. I would have done anything I could to pull you out of the hole you were in. That's what we did for each other."

His words set off something inside me and I wanted them to be real more than anyone could ever imagine. For him to want to hold me up no matter what, but with my secret there were always exceptions. I shook my head. "I didn't give you the chance to try. Whether either of us like it, this was something I had to deal with on my own."

"So you're still not going to tell me what it was."

I twisted the glass beneath my fingers. "It took me a long time to climb out of that hole and it's not one I'd rather fall back into."

Reagan nodded. "Fair enough."

I could tell he was frustrated by my answer. The tight crease of his brow always gave him away. I wanted to reach out and smooth my fingers over the lines. If I thought eighteen-year-old Reagan was attractive, I had no idea what I'd been missing all these years. The man before me set my blood on fire. A light scruff along his jaw line accentuated lips I dreamed about for years. His muscles now stretched the fabric of his shirt. His arms had been well-defined from years of playing football, but this went beyond definition. I gave myself a mental shake. I didn't need Reagan to ask any more questions I didn't want to answer.

"I know that's not the answer you wanted to hear. Maybe someday I'll be ready to tell you, but today's not that day." I picked the glass up and drained half of it.

Reagan sighed. "You're right, it's not fair for me to ask."

I shook my head. "No. It is fair. I'm just not ready for that and it's on me."

An awkward silence engulfed us once again, neither of us satisfied by the conversation. With only half the truth on the table, who would be? If we were going to get past this, we needed to find common ground again. Reagan finished his beer and I was surprised when he asked for another instead of the check. Maybe I wasn't the only one looking for a way to mend things.

"So, law school?" I finally asked, hoping to push the conversation forward. "I thought you wanted to be a doctor."

He shrugged, bringing the bottle to his lips. I forced myself to look away from his and the way they wrapped around the bottle. Getting a hard-on wouldn't be the wisest way to keep my secret. Somehow, I needed to force my desire for him aside. Reagan was the one person I couldn't have and if I didn't remember that I'd lead myself down a path I couldn't afford to go. One that would only lead me to heartache again.

"I did until my second semester in undergrad. The stress of trying to get into the best program was insane. I took a forensic science class as an elective and realized how much more relaxed they all seemed. The lab science didn't interest me, but I found the process of evidence did. After that I decided to look into other fields similar to that."

The waitress set his beer on the table and Reagan immediately picked it up and took a sip.

"Criminal justice was perfect. After that I started looking at law schools."

I leaned back in the booth, my knee accidentally grazing his, and I had to swallow the groan that threatened to leave my throat. "So you work in criminal law?"

He twirled the bottle in his hands, the muscles in his shoulders and arms finally beginning to relax. "Nah, I thought about it for a second, but I'd never be able to defend someone I knew was guilty. My firm deals with business and contract law."

All of that made sense. Reagan was a defender of innocents and I couldn't imagine him trying to protect someone who might be guilty of hurting another person.

"Guess you could be my lawyer someday."

The bottle in his hand stopped moving and a brow winged up into his hairline as he stared at me. For a moment, I wanted to shrink into the seat. Maybe find a way to reverse time and cover my mouth with my own hand. Either way, anything would work as long as I didn't get a chance to jump headlong into crazy ideas. It had been years since we'd seen each other and I expected no repercussions for my actions? That Reagan would just jump at the chance of being my friend again? Though, it was hard not to think that way. We slipped into an easy, comfortable conversation without a problem, which made it so hard to remember all the time that had passed. It was like we were teenagers again. Stealing beer from one of our parents and sneaking out into the field to drink it.

The more I thought about it, the more I realized that was probably when I started falling for Reagan. Those quiet nights, lying on the hood of his truck, not a care in the world. As if no one else existed. It took me years to realize when it started to happen. I'd thought it was because we'd been so close. Now, he sat across from me, sexier than ever. Never once did I imagine a world where I'd still want my straight best friend.

"You...ah...you know what I meant." I twisted the glass in my hand.

"Sawyer?" The tone of his voice no longer held the same detached sound to it. I lifted my head to look into his eyes.

"Yeah?"

"It means a lot that even after all these years, you'd trust me with your career."

I'd trust him with more than my career. I'd trust with my heart, my happiness, my life. "I've never not trusted you. It was me I didn't trust."

"I'm starting to see that."

He polished off the rest of the beer and signaled the waitress for a new one. He settled into the seat, resting his arm along the back. That was when it hit me like a freight train moving at top speed. The time for excuses and apologies was over. I could have my best friend back. It might take a little bit of work, but I was willing to put the time in.

I ordered another drink for myself and got comfortable. "How are your mom and dad?"

He smiled. As an only child, Reagan was really close to his parents. They were a very tight-knit family. Not that my family wasn't, but things were different when you had a sister.

"Mom and Dad are good. My mom's still teaching, but Dad retired last year."

"She still in the same classroom?" His mom had been my teacher.

"Well..." he trailed off.

"Oh God." I covered my eyes with my hand. "Don't tell me she's still in the same classroom."

"Yep." A mischievous glint lit his eyes.

"She found it, didn't she?"

A booming laugh fell from his lips, causing a few people at other tables to look over at us.

"Dammit. Was she pissed?"

"Put it this way, if we were still in school she probably would have kicked our asses. But—"

The waitress dropped off our drinks. He kept his gaze on me as he tipped his head back, draining a quarter of the bottle. Asshole set it down and sat there like he hadn't just stopped in the middle of his story.

I picked up my own glass and pointed it at him. "Don't be an ass and leave me hanging. What did she say?"

Reagan's mom was like a second mother to me before I left. Even afterward, I knew she asked my mom about me on more than one occasion. Even told my mom how proud she was of me when our contract got picked up. Not that we were always so well-behaved and appreciative. Mrs. Setton was our teacher in fifth grade. Our school didn't always put students in their parents' classes, but for Reagan, the school made an exception. We'd tortured our fourth grade teacher. Both the guidance counselor and Mrs. Setton thought she'd be the best choice to keep us in line. For the most part she did. We'd figured out real quick the consequences for acting up in her class. Extra homework and a weekend grounded. After that we played little tricks. Stuff that didn't disrupt the class. Things she found later on. We were two ten-year-old boys who thought they were the smartest kids to ever run the school.

"She laughed her ass off and now has the book on display in front of her room with a sign above that says 'how not to act in my class.'"

We decided it would be funny if we printed pictures of ourselves and glued them over every picture in one of her textbooks. It was one of the extra ones that sat on the shelf the whole year. God, were we idiots. When the next school year started, we waited to see who would get our book. No one did. And so it went the next year. By the time we got to be seniors, his mom hadn't gotten new textbooks. We figured there was no reason to fess up about what we'd done and kept our mouths closed, hoping she'd retire before she found it. Apparently, we hadn't been so lucky.

I made a show of wiping the non-existent sweat from my brow. "Well, thank God for that."

Our laughter settled something inside me. I missed being able to laugh and joke with him. A weight I hadn't noticed since I'd left began to lift from my chest. I was finally beginning to believe we could get past the choices I made.

"What about your family? Have you been home to see them lately?"

"A few months ago. Mom and Dad are both retired. They told me they talked to you the last time you were home on break."

"I went to see them." He tilted his head. "They didn't tell you what we talked about?"

I shook my head. "Nope, just that they saw you."

"Did you have any idea I was living in the same city as you?"

"Uh-uh. Mom stood her ground on that. If they weren't allowed to tell you where I'd gone, I wasn't allowed to know what you were up to."

That made him chuckle. “I knew there was a reason I loved your mom. She was always the fair one.” He paused for a moment. “I’m guessing your sister didn’t have the same holdup?”

“You’d be surprised at how much she didn’t tell me. I only knew when you were home and other small details, but nothing more. She refused to tell most things.”

A whistle left his lips. “I’m impressed. I’ll have to remember that the next time I see her.”

Julia was the first person I told once I realized I was gay. I knew she’d be supportive of me and even sat and held my hand while I told my parents. In the end, she was the one to convince me to go to college and start over. She loved Reagan like a brother, but she knew me enough to see I’d never move on and find someone for myself. That I’d bury that shit as deep as it would go to make sure Reagan was happy. She was right, I had to learn to love me if I was ever going to be able to accept someone else in my life and not break apart when Reagan did the same with his. I thought I’d finally gotten to that point, but the more Reagan and I settled back into the friendship we once shared, the more I realized nothing had changed. The connection that had always been there flared to life.

Lust burned through me. I had to hope that was it, and not a prelude to falling in love with him.

SAWYER

Hours passed by in a blur as we caught up on the last few years. He'd been much more serious in college than I'd expected. Maybe it was being all alone at a new school or maturity. Who knew? Deep down, I had a pretty good feeling it was my fault. Not that it was a bad thing. Reagan had managed to get on the dean's list and eventually accepted to one of the most prestigious law schools in the country. He graduated with honors and became an associate at his firm two years ago.

The crowd in the bar had begun to thin out when Reagan glanced down at his phone. "Shit. I have an early meeting tomorrow."

He shoved his hand into his front pocket, pulling out enough cash to cover the beers. I rolled my eyes and followed suit, throwing down an extra twenty and giving one of his back.

"You don't have to get my beer."

"I'm the one who dragged you out for a drink."

I waved his twenty at him. "And I'm the one who owes you one."

He eyed me up and down, snatching the money out of my hand. "Fair enough."

"Now tell me where you live and I'll drive us home."

I gave him the address and followed him out of the bar, hoping we could hang out again. And before I could stop myself, the words were out of my mouth.

"We're playing at the Pinnacle Arena tomorrow night. It's down near the harbor."

"I know where it is. I've been here for four years."

And just like that, the joking banter seemed to come to a halt. Another reminder of how close, yet how far we'd been from one another. The walk to his car was silent as I tried to think of the right thing to say. It seemed as if I was constantly stepping in it when it came to Reagan. Always saying the wrong thing. We climbed in, but before he had a chance to start the car, I turned to face him.

"You know I didn't know where you were once you graduated, right?"

"You knew my number and never used it." He started the car without looking at me and pulled away from the curb.

I ran a hand down my face and around the back of my neck. "Honestly, I didn't know if you'd want to talk to me after all this time."

He slowed down and turned onto a side street. After putting the car in park, he leaned his head back against the seat. "Sorry. I didn't mean to snap. I may not like what you did, but I get it. Doesn't make it easy to forget all the times I wondered what I did to ruin our friendship."

"It wasn't—"

He held his hand up to stop me. "I know that now. It's just gonna take time for that to not be my first reaction. So I'm apologizing now."

I shook my head. "You don't need to apologize to me. I'm the one who caused this mess."

"And you've already apologized. We'll figure it out."

I couldn't stop the way my heart stuttered in my chest at the *we'll*. If only he knew how much more that actually meant to me. My need for him hadn't faded or died after all these years. In fact, seeing him again seemed to spark it back to life. I forced myself to breathe. "We will."

The corner of his mouth curved into the half smile that had always caught my attention. Cocky, yet self-assured. That one smile said everything that drew me to Reagan in the first place. Thankfully, I kept myself under control and gave him a slight shove to the shoulder.

"All right, now take me home. You have work in the morning."

He scoffed. "Yeah, like I never pulled an all-nighter before. It's not my fault you need your beauty sleep. I'm fucking hot whether I'm tired or not."

Oh, fuck me. He had no idea about the truth to that statement. Damn, if I wasn't careful, I'd be in big trouble with him and his mouth.

I rolled my eyes. "You're still a conceited bastard, I see."

A full belly laugh burst from him. He put the car in drive and made a quick U-turn back onto the main road. "I'm just honest to a fault."

That had me laughing. "Yeah, so I guess you've always been honest. I'm pretty sure I can think of a few situations where that's definitely not true."

"Really?" he challenged. "Like what?"

"Senior prank."

Reagan had convinced a bunch of guys in our senior class to collect all the lawn gnomes from houses in town and 'plant' them all over the front yard of the school. When the press showed up to take pictures, one of the guys accidentally gave up Reagan as the man with the plan. The reporter asked him about where he got the idea to take lawn gnomes. Reagan looked the reporter right in the eye and said he couldn't imagine why the reporter had asked him that question. As a law-abiding citizen he would never consider stealing from anyone and was insulted that the reporter thought he would. Needless to say, he left the reporter staring at him mouth agape. The next day the headline read, "High School Seniors Falsely Accused of Stealing Garden Gnomes." He'd also gone as far as setting up a group to return the gnomes to their rightful owners.

The streetlights illuminated the rapid shaking of his head. "Nope. Doesn't count."

"And why doesn't it count?"

"'Cause I say so."

I chuckled. "Yeah, I'm not sure that's going to work out so well for you when you try to use that in court someday."

He shrugged. "Maybe not, but it's always worth a try." He glanced over and winked at me.

The front light illuminated the drive as we pulled up to the curb. We sat in silence for a few moments. There was still an awkwardness that stayed with us from the bar, but it was nothing compared to the silence when we first arrived there.

Knowing we couldn't sit there all night, I turned to Reagan.

"You'll come tomorrow, night?"

"I'll be there. I've waited a long time to see you play in person again."

The simple comment made me think with a little work we'd be able to repair the friendship I'd broken. At least until he found out the whole truth. I opened my bookbag and took out the lanyard with a small badge attached and handed it to Reagan.

"When you get to the arena, use this to get into the back lot and through the VIP entrance. I'll let them know you're coming and have someone show you to my dressing room."

Our fingers brushed against one another as he took the badge from my hand. I did everything in my power to suppress the shiver that wanted to race down my spine.

"I have a client meeting at four, but I'll come over sometime later."

"I'm glad you're coming and I'm glad you came to see me tonight." I reached for the door handle, stopping when Reagan said my name. "Yeah?" I glanced over my shoulder at him.

"I'm glad I showed up tonight, too. I can't wait to see you play again."

I stepped out of the car and leaned in to grab my bag. "I'll see you tomorrow."

I waited until Reagan pulled away from the curb to turn and go inside. The fact that a light was on in the living room meant someone was waiting up with twenty questions. I stopped at the door, not sure I felt like dealing with it all. My hand froze on the knob, knowing there was nothing I could do to stop the train after it already left the station. The person waiting for me wanted answers. And since there were only two people who knew about Reagan, the choice for who might be sitting inside was up in the air.

With a sigh, I turned the handle and pushed the door open.

"About time," Mari said.

There to my left sat Mari and Heath. *Fuck.* That combo was the last thing I needed. Like a shark who smelled blood in the water. I dropped my bag by the door, knowing there was no way I'd get down the hall to my room anytime soon.

Mari sat forward on the couch, her hands practically folded in her lap like a schoolgirl. The shrewd set of her features said she was anything but that.

"So how'd it go?"

If only she planned to leave it at that.

"Fine. We caught up."

A small growl left Mari's throat and Heath laughed at the sound. I knew better. She was pissed that I'd been intentionally coy. I had no doubt about what she really wanted to ask, except I had no intention of telling her. Not that she'd approve of my answer to the question.

"What did you talk about?"

I shrugged. "The band. Him becoming a lawyer. College."

She lifted her hand and pointed a finger at me. A clear sign that I was getting closer to pushing her over the edge into a freak-out. I had two choices. Tread carefully and give her the information she really wanted or continue to be very literal about her questions. Technically, I had. Reagan and I never actually talked about me being gay.

"Sawyer Alason, don't you dare play dumb with me," she snapped.

"Come on, man. You know very well what we both want to know. Spill it."

I dropped into the chair next to me, resting my head along the back. "You don't want to know the truth."

Mari leapt from the seat like her ass was on fire and stormed over to stand in front of me. "You didn't tell him?"

The way she shouted, I couldn't tell whether it had been a statement or a question. Either way, I could see the flush as it crawled up her neck. I ran a hand down my face at the angry angel standing above me.

"No, I didn't tell him."

She threw her hands up in the air and spun on her heel to face Heath. "Do you believe this shit? He really didn't tell him anything." Faster than I could blink, she was back to facing me, hands on her hips, nostrils flaring. "Why wouldn't you tell him?"

I glanced up at her. "How about you sit down and we'll talk about this?"

The hands at her sides moved up to cross over her chest. "I don't want to sit down."

I peered at Heath around Mari's side, silently asking him for help. Apparently, he got the message. He wrapped his arms around her waist and hauled her back to the couch. She flailed, fighting him the whole way.

"Dude." He shook his head at her. "I have a whole new respect for Cole."

"Oh, really?"

He didn't say anything, simply lifting his brows in challenge. "*Oompf.*" He let her go and wrapped his arms around his middle. Mari had elbowed him in the stomach.

She waved her hand at me to continue. Thankfully, she hadn't gotten out of her seat. "You wanted me to sit. I'm seated. Now talk."

I cleared my throat, trying to figure out a way to explain this without getting her all fired up again. I knew she was only looking out for my best interests. She wanted me to be happy. The problem was I knew there wouldn't be a happily ever after in this situation. I would always be gay and Reagan would always be straight. Not a whole lot could change that. What did either of us gain by trying to force him in a box he didn't belong in?

"You're right. I didn't tell him."

She opened her mouth to start listing all the reasons I should have told him, but I put up a hand to stop her. Surprisingly enough, it worked.

"There's no point in telling him. Neither of us gets a damn thing out of it."

"Maybe the two of you—"

"No," I said adamantly. "This is not a situation where things will work themselves out. Me telling Reagan only leads him to finding out he's the reason I left in the first place and destroys whatever friendship we can salvage from here. I don't need him to feel any pity for me, like I know he would. And I sure as shit don't need to live with the guilt of ruining our friendship again. After tonight I know I still want him and could probably fall in love with him again. The only thing that's going to fix it is finding the guy who's meant for me."

"Damn," Heath breathed. "I'm sorry, man. That really does suck."

"Explains a lot about why I left and why I've avoided this moment for so long."

Mari sat still on the couch, not even a peep leaving her lips. It wasn't often I couldn't tell what

Mari was thinking, except right now was one of those times. Heath and I both watched her until she eventually stood and walked over to me. Like always, she sat on my lap, her eyes focused in on mine.

"I've been sitting there trying to figure out a way to fix this for you. Then I realized it's not something I can fix. You may not agree with it, but you need to tell him."

I started to shake my head and this time it was her turn to stop me with a hand.

"I let you talk, now let me finish before you go arguing all my points."

I dipped my head in her direction.

"No one is saying you have to tell him you were in love with him and that's why you left. The only way he figures that out is if you tell him. Neither of us is going to be the one to give him that information. Now, give me the real reason."

She always knew how to see right through some of my shit. I looked over her shoulder at a photo on the wall, not wanting her to see the sadness in my eyes when I said it.

"I don't want him to hate who I am and walk away. I think it might break me this time."

Mari wrapped her arms around my neck and hugged me close. "The guy I met earlier, the one who waited for you, is not the type of man to stick around to talk to you then run at the smallest bump in the road. I think you need to give him more credit than you are."

"I wish it were that simple," I whispered.

"I have to say, I agree with Mari," Heath said from the other side of the room. "You need to tell him before someone else finds out and exposes your ass. Then, I believe he'd walk away from you. Not for being gay, but for hiding it from him for all these years."

I let out a breath. "I'm just not ready to go down that road. Not until I know for sure what his reaction will be."

Mari scrunched up her nose at that idea. "And how do you plan to figure that out?"

"I've known him since I was seven years old. I'll figure it out."

Mari sighed and stood from my lap. She pressed a hand to my cheek. "You deserve to find someone to love and who will love you in return. I get that's not Reagan, but if you want a true friendship with him, you need to be honest. It's bad enough Jackson and Monty are still in the dark. Reagan needs to know."

I lifted my hand and held hers against my cheek. "I know. Just not today."

She leaned down and pressed a kiss to the top of my head. "I promise, I'll find a way to convince you I'm right. Now go get some sleep. You've been running yourself ragged for weeks."

"I'll try."

She stood and turned to face Heath. "No more song writing for him." She grabbed her keys on the way to the door. "I know he's going to try. Kick his ass to bed if you have to."

Heath nodded then glanced over at me with one brow lifted. "He's going right to bed after you leave."

She scoffed. "Bullshit. I know you plan on talking more when I leave. Not too long, though. I doubt Sawyer has had more than ten hours of sleep this whole week."

"I won't work," I promised. It actually had nothing to do with Mari telling me to go to bed. I had a lot to think about and finishing the song was nowhere near the front of my mind.

She eyed me for a moment before nodding and opening the door. "I'll see you guys at the studio tomorrow."

"Tell Cole we said hi," Heath called out to her.

"I will. Night."

The door shut behind her and Heath immediately stood. I followed him to the kitchen where he was searching through the cabinets and I had a feeling I knew for what. When he popped out of one of the bottom ones near the floor, I saw my guess was right. He held up his hand triumphantly, shaking the bottle at me.

"Yeah, I'll have some," I answered his unspoken question and sat down at the table to the side of the kitchen.

He poured the rum into two glasses, filling the rest of the glass with soda. After sliding one over to me, he continued to watch me with a hawk's eye. *Where the hell was this conversation going?*

After two large gulps of the liquid, he set the tumbler on the table. "Drink up," he said.

I took the glass in my hand and held it up to my lips, letting the cool liquid slide down my throat as I wondered what else Heath would want to say. He rolled the glass around in his hands, almost like he didn't know how to put his thoughts into words. That or he wasn't sure I wanted to hear what he had to say.

"Okay, spit it out. I know you have something to say, so just say it."

"Mari has a point."

"I already said I wasn't ready to tell him. I don't—"

Heath shook his head. “I don’t mean him.”

“Then what are you talking about? All she bitched about was me not telling Reagan.”

He drained his glass and dropped it in the sink. “Mostly. But she also mentioned Jackson and Monty.”

I set the glass down, taking a step back. For some reason, I thought I’d be able to exit a conversation like that by simply stepping away from it. “I don’t want to deal with any of this.”

“Well, you’re gonna have to. Look, I wish we lived in a world where no one else worried about where anyone else might stick their dick, but we do.” He lifted his hands, palms up. “It sucks that you have to worry about what someone else might think about who you choose to sleep with.” I opened my mouth to argue with him, but Heath wasn’t done. “I know you’re going to say it’s not fair. And you’re right. It’s not. But Jackson and Monty don’t deserve to be blindsided when all of this comes to light.”

Heath hit the nail on the head. It wasn’t fair. I shouldn’t have to defend myself to anyone, yet so many times I stopped myself from doing certain things to avoid the judgment. To avoid the looks and slurs. And at the same time he was right about leaving them in the dark. One part of that equation he had yet to consider.

“How will they be blindsided when there’s no reason for the information to come to light?”

He lifted both brows in a disbelief. “You’re telling me you’re planning on keeping your pants zipped?”

“That’s exactly what I’m saying. There’s a goddamn deadbolt on the zipper.”

“Don’t be ridiculous. Not one of us is fucking celibate. You’re just used to hiding it and that’s not going to work forever. Eventually, someone is going to figure that shit out and out your ass whether you're ready or not. I get it, you don't want to tell everyone and I'm not asking you. I'm asking you to tell the two people who hopefully you'll have a very long career with, but at the same time, ones who may not forgive you for keeping them in the dark."

His words hit me right in the gut. He was right, it wasn't fair to Jackson or Monty. They didn't deserve to be caught up in the wave of my life.

"You're right. And if things ever change and I put myself in a situation where I might get outed by someone, they will be the first two people I tell. Until then, can you respect that I want to keep it my business, since right now it doesn't affect anyone else?"

"I wish you'd tell them sooner rather than later, but I can live with that. Keep in mind, if I see that situation and you still haven't told them, I will. And I can guarantee things most likely won't go well then."

"Fair enough." I reached a hand out to shake like we were settling some massive business deal.

He took my hand, shook it quickly, then ran his thumb over my knuckles, pressing down and rubbing back and forth. I hated when he did that.

"Dickhead." I snatched my hand away.

The corner of his mouth pulled up in the sideway grin he had. "Working tonight?" The shit-eating grin on his face made it clear he expected a certain answer.

"Nope."

His eyes went wide. "What did you say?"

"No, I'm not working tonight."

When he was able to speak, he reached up to touch my forehead. "You feeling okay?"

I smacked his hand away. “Yeah, smartass. I’m not in the mood to write. I have enough shit banging around my head.”

Heath grabbed his belly as he pretended to double over in laughter.

Dick.

“I guess you will have to listen to Mari about something.”

“Funny. You can lay your ass right here and laugh all you want. I, on the other hand, am going to bed.”

I followed him out to the living room, where he flopped down on the couch and grabbed the remote.

“Sweet dreams, lover boy.”

I flipped him off and proceeded to march down the hall. I had a feeling Heath was right on the money. Most of my dreams tonight would revolve around Reagan and there was no stopping it. The train had been set into motion and there was no stopping it as it bulldozed through every wall I’d erected over the years to keep Reagan out.

Reagan

I drove into the lot, handing the badge Sawyer had given me to the attendant. Never in my life had I imagined a time when I'd not only be backstage during a concert, but also not have to enter with the rest of the audience. The overhead lights highlighted the few cars already parked in the lot. It seemed surreal to be going backstage at a venue where I'd never even sat in the front row. Seats were way too expensive. Now, I stood ringing a bell at a back entrance, my stomach fluttering. Once I realized Sawyer was the drummer for Jaded Ivory, I'd made sure to download every one of their songs. He didn't need to know I followed their success online. Even though Sawyer had cut me out of his life for reasons I still didn't know, deep down I wanted him to succeed.

It was exciting to watch from afar as their fame increased, but to get to see it up close was something entirely different. Tonight, I got to see Sawyer live in his element. Call me a little starstruck, but after watching them online, I might have been a little awestruck to meet them. My heart beat a little faster than normal as the door opened and a man about my height with arms the size of my thighs stood before me. And that was saying something. Just because I stopped playing football in college didn't mean I gave up the workout regimen. Being healthy was worth trying to squeeze in gym time between hours at the firm. Then again, there I was ditching the ten or more files on my desk for the night to see Sawyer's show.

Without a word, the guy held out his hand. I lifted the lanyard from my neck and handed him the small card attached. He scanned it and a moment later let me in, directing me down a long hall to the last door on the left. The door was unlocked. After pushing it open, I came face-to-face with tables full of food and drinks. More choices that I could have imagined.

Too worked up to sit down, I paced the room, unsure of why they sent me there in the first place. Voices reached my ears, growing louder as they got closer to the door. It flew open and I stopped in my tracks, spinning around to see who was there. In walked a man with long, dark hair. I thought he might have been the keyboard player for the band. He laughed, looking over his shoulder at someone behind him. Another guy stepped through the doorway. This one had short, light blond hair standing up in every direction. He rolled his eyes at the first one. The keyboard player stopped in his tracks, his gaze focused on me.

"Can I help you?" he asked warily.

The rest of the group's attention was drawn to me. Out of the corner of my eye, I noticed Sawyer come through the door. His eyes sparkled, and a smile pulled at the corner of his lips. My heart picked up pace and suddenly I was tongue tied.

"I'm—" I started.

"Reagan!" Sawyer walked over and clasped me on the shoulder. My arm broke out in goosebumps and I shivered before he let me go and turned to the other three people in the room. Strange, what was that about? Nothing like that had ever happened when I'd been around Sawyer. "This is my friend from home, Reagan, the one I've been telling you about."

Their whole demeanor changed. Shoulders relaxed and smiles formed. The one with the light blond hair came forward with his hand extended. "Monty. It's nice to meet you."

I took hold of it and shook, watching as the rest of the guys moved closer to wait for their own introduction.

Slowly the other members were introduced and I just hoped to God I could remember them since I sucked with names. Monty grabbed a bottle of water from the table and dropped into a seat on one of the couches. Sawyer pointed to the tables next to him.

"Impressive, right?" He lifted a brow, a smirk on his lips.

As much as I wanted to smack him in the back of his head for the smartass behavior, I didn't want to draw more attention to myself when it felt like each time I wasn't looking Heath looked at me. Every time I glanced over my shoulder to where he was seated, his eyes would move away.

"It is." I nodded.

"Want something?" Sawyer grabbed a bottle of green tea and waited for my answer.

"Water's fine."

He chuckled. "You don't have to play tonight. Have a beer. Trust me, we'll have plenty of those after the show, but it's better to play sober."

"Tell me about it," Monty said, laughter peeling from his lips.

Jackson flipped him off. It didn't stop Monty from grabbing his stomach and slinking farther into the couch.

I turned back to Sawyer. "Um..."

He waved a dismissive hand. "Ignore them. Jackson had a few beers before a gig one night."

"It was more than a few," Heath chimed in.

"Okay, okay, it was closer to a case." Sawyer glanced over his shoulder. "I was trying to be nice."

Heath shook his head. "Being nice does not explain the story."

"Fine." He looked back at me. "Anyway." He emphasized the word. "Jackson forgot the set list in the middle of the show."

Jackson tucked himself farther into the couch, like he could disappear from the scrutiny. "You guys are such dickheads."

"I thought he might play the wrong first song." Monty apparently got over his mirth from earlier.

"Oh, damn."

"Oh, damn is right." It was Sawyer's turn to laugh. "I'm not even sure he played a song from our set list."

Jackson groaned, covering his face with his hands.

Sawyer held up a bottle of water, shaking it back and forth. "Jackson, want a drink?"

"Fuck off." He rolled his eyes.

The room erupted and I couldn't help the small spark of jealously that rose up in my gut. The relationship between Sawyer and me used to be that way. We had more crazy stories than I could count. We still had those stories, but we'd lost the closeness we once shared in each and every one of them. The laughter slowly died down and after chucking the bottle of water at Jackson, Sawyer plopped down on the empty couch and gestured for me to join him. I sat down and looked around the room, not sure what to say to any of them. Thoughts of all the things I saw them do on social media ran through my mind, but I didn't want them to know how badly I'd stalked them.

So I focused on the food. Something easy. "I don't think I've ever seen so much food."

Sawyer laughed. "You should have seen our reactions the first time they set us up in this green room." He pointed to the table. "Did you eat?"

"No. I was trying to figure out why they'd put me in here to wait."

"I knew you had a late meeting tonight and were coming right here. I wanted to give you a chance to get food before the show started."

Now that my nerves were starting to settle I heard my stomach growl. A clear indication I hadn't eaten since that morning. Sawyer glanced at my stomach then back at me.

"Fine. Eating does sound good right about now." I stood and grabbed a plate from the end of the table. There were so many options, but I ended up with a couple of wrap sandwiches and a bag of chips. I took my seat and tucked into the food on my plate. Heath stood and grabbed a plate of his own.

"What's taking Mari so long?" Jackson said, perusing the table himself.

Sawyer scoffed. "Cole has an away game this weekend. She's talking to him before we go on."

"At least they're not fucking in her dressing room this time." Heath fake shivered.

Interesting. I had a whole new appreciation for the lead singer. If I had the kind of chemistry with someone that I could drop my pants and have sex anywhere, you bet your ass I'd be doing just that.

Sawyer was the last to stand and fill a plate. All of them piled high.

Heath swallowed and looked at me. "Sawyer said you went to Hayward. What did you study?"

"Law. I finished my undergrad at Summerfield but decided it wasn't the best place to earn a law degree if I wanted any of the big firms to look in my direction. And I'd been right. After graduation I got hired at Braddock & Minetti."

"Impressive," Monty said around a mouthful of his sandwich. "How many hours do you put in a week?"

"More than I can count. Now that I've been with the firm more than a year, the hours aren't as bad."

Monty took a swig of his water. "Fuck. That sounds like a lot of work."

"It is. I should be going over notes for a case tonight, but I'd rather see Sawyer on stage."

Heath glanced at Sawyer then back at me. The move was so quick, I wasn't sure what to think about it. I tried to push it out of my head and focused on something else they mentioned.

"You said Mari was talking to someone about an away game?"

Jackson nodded. "Yeah. Mari's boyfriend, Cole, is the offensive coordinator for Hayward."

I lifted the bottle to my lips and dropped it down before taking a sip. "Shit, you mean Cole Wallace?"

I probably should have known that considering I'd been watching the band on social media. In reality, I only paid attention to Sawyer.

Sawyer looked over at me. "Yeah, that's him."

I put the cap on the bottle and set it on the table next to me before running a hand through my hair. "Fuck, I remember him when he played in high school. Every guy I played with wanted to be him. Most of us could have only dreamed about a Division I full ride scholarship."

Sawyer punched me in the arm. "Don't act like you weren't on your own scholarship to a Division I school."

"I did, but I never would have had a shot at playing in the NFL. Cole was probably one of the best wide receivers in the country."

"That he was," a sultry female voice said from the direction of the door.

I looked over to see Mari standing there, watching all of us. Damn, pictures did not do justice to her beauty. The woman was fucking gorgeous. There was a confidence in her walk that Sawyer seemed to lack last night. She dropped down between the two of us, her gaze immediately drawn to me.

"You must be Reagan."

I nodded. "That's me."

"Well, well, well. I've heard an awful lot about you."

"Good things, I hope." It sounded cliché, but not many people wanted to be known for the bad stuff.

"All good." She smiled. And just like Heath, she glanced over her shoulder at Sawyer, lifting a brow.

"Knock it off," he snapped under his breath, still loud enough for me to hear it.

I noticed Mari drop her gaze from me and focused on Sawyer. A brow lifted over one of those blue eyes that seemed to be filled with heat.

"I will not. This is your own fault." She turned back to me. "He's just being a bit touchy."

I had no idea what was going on, but something in me hoped she'd get up and sit somewhere else. Years had passed since Sawyer and I had this kind of chance to hang out and even though we were surrounded by his bandmates, it felt like I had him all to myself when we were alone on the couch. She rested her hand on my thigh, drawing small circles as her fingers slowly moved up my leg. She didn't stop there. After scooting closer until her one thigh practically sat on top of mine, she gripped my bicep, rubbing the muscles under her soft skin.

"Tell me about yourself."

"Mari," Sawyer warned.

She threw her hands up in the air and stood, heading over to the table to grab a drink. Sawyer took the opportunity to slide closer to me, leaving the open space on the other side of him. Not that I minded. Mari was hot, but having a boyfriend happened to be a big, red flag to stay away for me. I didn't want to get involved in the whole cheating thing. More than that, for some reason I felt uncomfortable with the way she was flirting with me in front of Sawyer. I'd come to hang out and watch him play, not pick someone up.

She turned to sit back down and noticed Sawyer had moved. Without a word she took the seat next to him. She called my name. "You still haven't told me anything about yourself."

The flirtation seemed to be over. I didn't know what had stopped it, but I was more than happy for it to end. Instead of giving her a chance to start again, I answered her question. The whole time I talked I noticed Sawyer watching me out of the corner of his eye.

Eventually, someone knocked on the door and stuck their head in. "About ten minutes."

"Got it." Jackson stood, reaching his arms up in a stretch.

"Ready for your first backstage concert?" Sawyer asked, standing and holding out hands to help up Mari and myself.

By then, Mari had completely backed away from her flirtation and I grew more comfortable around her.

"Lead the way." I gestured to the door with my hands.

Sawyer chuckled and moved toward it. That was when I noticed everyone else had already left the room. The closer we got to the main stage, the louder the chanting got. It switched between calling for Jaded Ivory or for Mari. The sound became deafening when we stepped through the stage door. It was in such contrast to the small gigs Sawyer's high school band used to play. Most of them were for school events. Every once in a while he was allowed to play in a club. That was always harder to find, considering he was only eighteen at the time.

The crowd would get worked up when they started to play, but nothing compared to the sound rattling around my ears. The band waited at the edge of the stage, Mari in the back of them. Sawyer stood next to me, talking close to my ear, since it was the only way I'd be able to hear what he was saying.

"Enjoy the show. We'll have drinks and fun later as long as it isn't too late for you."

I shook my head, not sure if he'd be able to hear me. "No. I have a contract to deal with, but not until Monday. I can finish it this weekend. No go out there and show me what new tricks you've learned in the last few years."

His eyes dropped to my lips and quickly lifted. *What was that all about?* I had to have been seeing things. He wouldn't be looking at my mouth. I'd probably imagined it in all the excitement. Apparently, my lack of sleep was starting to melt my brain cells. He smiled, but for some reason it didn't reach his eyes. Before I could say something, he and the rest of the guys were jogging on stage, waving as the crowd went crazy.

The guys took their spots and Mari moved closer to the edge of the curtain. The chanting started before she even walked out into the audience's view. *Mari. Mari. Mari.* The moment she stepped into the spotlight, everything erupted. I didn't think it was possible, but the crowd went even crazier than before. The spotlight followed her all the way to the mic set up near the front. She put both hands up in the air to quiet the crowd.

"Hey, Pinnacle, I'm Mari and we're Jaded Ivory." Screams and shouts filled the night air. "Now let's make some fucking noise."

Cheers went up and the music started. From my position, I could see everything on stage, but my gaze was drawn to the man behind the drum kit. He still had that smooth grace as he moved the stick from one skin to the other. In the background, the voices of the crowd rose as Mari reached the chorus of the song. To a stranger, Sawyer might look like a man in deep thought about what he was playing. Not to me. At the corner of his eyes, I could see the way they crinkled with the smile that was trying to slip free. He loved every minute of being on stage. I could only imagine what it was like to write a song and have thousands of people love it so much they sang along with you.

Song after song, I stood mesmerized by the sounds filling the arena. It was easy to pick out the songs Sawyer had written. I may not have played anything beyond the piano when my parents made me learn it as a kid, but there wasn't much I didn't know about a drum kit. Sawyer had made sure of that. Especially if I helped him move the kit from place to place to play. I'd better set it up right or he'd torture me for the next two weeks about forgetting. Considering he knew all my stats, the least I could do was learn which drum was which. The cymbals took me the longest until I finally learned the difference in the sound. Sawyer preferred the Ride cymbal in his music. It didn't have that loud crash you hear at the end of a song. If you hit it right, it sounded like a bell.

As Jaded Ivory got closer to the end of their set, I noticed the bustle backstage increase as the stage hands were getting ready to set up for the headliner. Watching Sawyer play tonight and the way the crowd chanted for them, I had no doubt they'd be the headliners before long.

Sawyer's deep voice filled the arena. "Thanks for being here tonight. I'd like to take a moment to introduce the band. On keyboards is Heath Marshall, on bass Monty Vance, our lead guitarist Jackson Hadden, I'm Sawyer, and last but not least...Mari Cosmann on vocals."

This.

This right here was Sawyer's dream. He was living it, breathing it. It had been the only thing he ever talked about when we were growing up. Being a famous musician. He didn't give a shit what it took. He was going to get there. And for the first time since we were eighteen, I got to experience the dream with him.

SAWYER

Throughout the set, I couldn't stop myself from peeking to the side of the stage where Reagan listened to us play. Many nights I watched Cole do the same thing with Mari and for a brief moment, I wished we could have had the same thing. Quickly, I pushed it aside. Reagan was back in my life and that was what mattered most. Things had still been a little awkward when he arrived, but I had a feeling we needed time to get to be around each other again.

What shocked me each time I looked over was that his eyes weren't on Mari where I expected them to be. I may like guys, but it didn't mean I couldn't see. Mari was hot and she knew it. Considering the shit she pulled in the green room, I thought for sure I'd find his gaze on her. Blood roared through my ears when I saw her hand on his knee. She wanted me to lose my shit on her. She knew if I went off, I'd have to explain why, which I wasn't ready to do. Hopefully, she didn't try and pull more of that shit with him.

We waved to the crowd as the lights went down and slowly moved from behind our instruments. The stage hands were already racing past us to change out the equipment for The Black Sails, the headliner tonight. The cool breeze hit me as soon as I stepped past the black curtain meant to hide most of the back from the audience. A small bead of sweat ran down my temple onto my cheek. Normally, I went right for the dressing room and the shower. Not tonight. Tonight, I wanted to see Reagan's reaction to the show.

He walked toward me, powerful strides eating the distance between us. A smile dawned on his face. "You were awesome." He grabbed my hand and pulled me into a hug. "You did it! I'm so fucking proud of you."

My arms squeezed tight, enjoying the touch even if it would only last for a moment. Reagan let go and turned to face the rest of the band. "That was fantastic."

The guys nodded and continued down the hall. Hot and tired like I'd been before getting a hug from Reagan. They wanted a shower as badly as I did. A shower, then drinks. Mari, the little troublemaker, sidled right up to Reagan and smirked at me.

"Thanks," she said, wrapping her arm around his bicep. I clenched my jaw shut. "I'm so glad you could come."

"Me too."

Without letting go, she walked down the hall to her own room. "I hope you're having drinks with us tonight."

"I wouldn't miss it."

I had to swallow the bile that rose up in my throat watching the way she squeezed his bicep with her fingertips. Taking the hand of her free arm, I stopped her movement down the hall.

"What's up?" She turned the most innocent gaze on me, batting her lashes up at me like I had no idea what she was up to.

"Don't you need to change before we go out? Reagan can wait in my room while I change."

Reagan's eyes tracked between the two of us. He was smart enough to know something wasn't right with the whole situation.

"But—"

I tugged on her hand a little tighter. "No buts. We'll meet up with you soon enough."

She snatched her hand from mine and patted the arm she still held. "Oh, okay. I'll see you guys before you know it." She winked at Reagan then made a left down another hall to the dressing room she'd used for the night. As I watched her go, she began walking backward and mouthed *tell him* before facing forward again. She disappeared into the room and I breathed a sigh of relief. The first one since she'd shown up in the green room.

Mari may be the best friend I gained when I lost Reagan, but I couldn't stand much more of her shit. In my head, I knew she wouldn't do anything and was just trying to force me to tell Reagan. The problem was my heart and my cock didn't understand that. They wanted Reagan all to themselves.

If only that were possible.

Taking a deep breath and releasing it, I found the pounding of my heart slowing. "Did you want to head to the green room and grab a beer first?"

He nodded. "That sounds good."

We stopped by the room where food still adorned all the tables and grabbed a few beers. Now that Mari was away from Reagan, my mind kept coming back to the feel of Reagan's hard chest as it touched mine. I knew it made me a dick, but I couldn't stop the fantasies from running through my head of all the things I would have liked to do to that chest if only I'd been allowed. Realizing that my fantasizing wasn't going to get me anywhere, I mentally shook off the thoughts and drained the beer in my hands.

Reagan lifted a brow at me. "Rough performance? Not that I noticed. I thought it was amazing. I can't believe how much you've grown as a performer."

That comment seemed to shake me out of my inappropriate thoughts. I opened another beer and gestured toward the hall to keep us moving. "Not a rough performance. Just celebrating."

"Uh-huh. That's not how you celebrate unless something drastic changed in the last few years."

I smirked. "Maybe not, but tonight I do."

"Fair enough." Out of the corner of my eye, I watched as his Adam's apple bobbed with every swallow he took.

We reached the door to my room for the night. I pushed it open and led Reagan inside. He took a seat on the couch and a picture of me straddling his lap popped into my head. My dick immediately began to fill. I needed a cold shower before things got any worse. I lifted the hem of my shirt to wipe the sweat from my brow.

"Why don't you relax while I jump in the shower really quick?"

"Sure. Where are we going when you're done?"

"Not sure. It's Jackson's turn to pick."

I walked into the small bathroom in the room and shut the door. If I didn't get the blood flowing north soon, things were going to go to shit fast. Every single thing he did had my mind wandering to places it really didn't need to go. Something had to give. I was not into torture of the blue balls kind.

I flipped the shower onto cold. Kill two birds with one stone. Wash off and get my body under control. The water felt colder than I thought it would be. Didn't stop me from climbing in and letting the frozen water race down my skin. Goose bumps broke out along my arms and my balls shriveled up to my body. At least my mind wasn't focused on Reagan any longer.

I raced through the shower, clenching my jaw to keep my teeth from chattering. The longer I stood under the spray, the more pain each drop against my skin caused. I rinsed the soap from my body and turned off the water, sucking in lungfuls of air. Apparently, I'd been holding my breath the entire time.

After drying off, I pulled on a pair of boxers and picked up my phone from the counter. Now that my head was clear, I needed to deal with Mari and the bullshit she pulled in the green room.

Me: What was that shit earlier in the green room?

While I waited for her answer, I pulled on a pair of jeans and T-shirt. A drop of water slid down the side of my face. I rubbed the towel over my head to get rid of the excess water. My phone buzzed.

Mari: What shit? We were hanging out before the show

What shit? She had to be fucking kidding me. My fingers were flying across the keys before I stopped to think about it.

Me: Don't start. Why were you flirting with him?

I held the phone tightly in my grip, waiting to hear her answer. Mari had never been good at hiding things from me. She was definitely up to something.

Mari: I was being friendly

Me: I know you're up to something. Knock that shit off.

Only a few seconds later and my phone buzzed again.

Mari: I'll be on my best behavior

"Bullshit," I said even though there was no way for her to hear me.

I had to find a way to keep my cool. Best guess? Mari was trying to provoke me into losing my shit and spilling to Reagan about being gay. I wouldn't let that happen. A quick glance at the clock and I realized I'd been in the bathroom way too long for a quick shower. I ran my hands through my hair a few times, letting the shaggy mess fall wherever it landed. It never stayed where I put it when styled anyway.

I threw my stuff into my bag and reached for the handle. Before turning it, I stopped and took a deep breath. Mari was out to get me all worked up. I had to keep my focus on ignoring her attempts. She'd promised to find a way to force me to tell Reagan and I needed to make sure that didn't happen. Why she was so hung up on him knowing was beyond me. Did she think it would change anything? No matter what was said, Reagan would still be straight.

I finished pulling on my Chucks and opened the door. Reagan lounged on the couch, playing with his phone. Something so simple, yet it reminded me of many nights we spent after practices or rehearsals watching TV and laughing about the shit we saw online. It hadn't hit me until that moment how much I missed having Reagan in my life. The jokes, the laughter, the arguments about winning teams. I missed it all. It was my fault we were in this awkward place. Somehow I needed to find a way to fix it. I'd find a way to push my desire for him aside and be happy with the parts of him I could have.

"Ready?" I asked when he hadn't noticed me.

He looked up from his phone at me. "Yeah. Who's driving?"

"You are." I smirked. "You have the cleaner car."

Reagan rolled his eyes. "I can only imagine the disaster that is your car. Some things never change." He shoved his phone in his pocket and dangled his keys in my face. "Let's go."

My phone buzzed. I pulled it from my pocket to read the message. "Jackson says we're heading to The Lighthouse. It's down on fourteenth."

"Great. I'm fucking starving." He yanked the door open and held it to make sure I'd followed him out.

If I had the chance, there wasn't anywhere I wouldn't follow him.

SAWYER

We pulled into the lot of The Lighthouse. Jackson's usual pick for a night out. The owner liked our music. We'd go there pretty often when we first moved here, heading there after recording sessions for food and drinks. Once the band grew in popularity and he saw the people crowd around us while we were trying to eat, he blocked off a certain booth in the back of the place for us to eat in peace.

After the shit storm from Mari and Cole's time on TMZ, most of us expected to have people following us everywhere. I think a few of the guys were disappointed when the crowds died down around us. At least most of us. Mari still had a decent following always trying to get pictures of her and Cole together. Sometimes they even tried to get them alone talking to others. The tabloids were sleazy as fuck. But Mari and Cole knew that and avoided them most of the time. Me, on the other hand, preferred to stay out of the limelight. The less the camera focused on me, the less likely it would be for me to slip up.

Not that I didn't have years of practice keeping my mouth shut.

"You guys don't get harassed when you go out all together?" Reagan asked as we got out of the car.

I shut the door and walked around to the front where he was standing. "Not here. The owner loves our music and blocks off a table in the back. He felt bad when we were getting interrupted all the time for autographs."

We made our way across the lot to the front door. "That didn't happen last night."

"Nope. Thankfully, it's Mari who's the recognizable one. When they see her with us, they know who we are, but not usually when we're on our own."

"Well, that sucks," he said, reaching for the handle of the door.

"Not at all. A lot of times people will recognize me, but sometimes they have no idea from where unless I'm with her. Benefits of hiding behind the kit. Wait until she shows up tonight. Things won't be very quiet. And that's without Cole. Luckily he's got an away game this weekend. The two of them together are the paparazzi's wet dream."

He opened the door, letting me lead him to the back and our normal booth. I slid all the way to the back of the circular booth, loving how Reagan sat next to me.

"Think it will be like that forever?" He grabbed a menu from the middle of the table.

"No. Right now I think we're lucky. As our music gets played on more stations and our popularity grows, I'm pretty sure we'll all be in Mari's situation one way or another."

"Sawyer! Great show tonight."

I looked up to see Max, the owner of the bar.

"Thanks, Max."

"Just you tonight?"

"Nah, everyone else is on their way. But we can get drinks before they get here." His eyes darted to Reagan and back. Almost like he was trying to protect me from my own friend. "Sorry, I forgot to introduce you. Max, this is Reagan, one of my closest friends growing up." I turned to Reagan. "Max owns the place and is awesome about giving us peace to eat."

Max reached out to shake Reagan's extended hand.

"It's nice to meet you."

"You too, Reagan. I hope you're ready." Max laughed. "Tonight might be a little more wild than usual. I already know there are a few people from the show at the bar. And a few of the guys know Cole is out of town with the team."

"Shit," I grumbled, my eyes shooting to the bar.

"What's wrong with that?" Reagan asked.

"They think they'll be able to pick Mari up tonight and steal her from Cole. And they are relentless, even when she tells them she's not interested."

Reagan nodded. "I get it. She's fucking gorgeous."

I did my best to keep the grimace off my face. Mari was beautiful, but it didn't mean I wanted him to notice.

"Doesn't mean they have a right to be assholes."

I looked up at Max. "Look, if we're gonna cause too much trouble, we can head somewhere else."

"Fuck that," Max said. "Just 'cause you make music for a living doesn't mean you deserve a meal without all the bullshit any less than someone else. If they can't behave they'll leave."

"Thanks, Max. Just remember my offer stands."

He smiled. "I know it does. Now, what can I get you to drink?"

We ordered our beers and Max left the table to get them. "You know I think it's my turn to call you a cocky bastard."

My eyes snapped to his. "And why would you say that?"

"You don't remember saying a few minutes ago that *when* the band gets more popular. You didn't say *if*."

It was my turn to shrug it off. "Simply stating the truth."

"Fair enough. If I hadn't heard you play, I might have to disagree with you. Keep doing what you're doing and you guys are going to kick serious ass."

"How are you the first one here?" Monty's voice carried across the room.

"Dipshit's gonna put more attention to us yelling like that."

If there was one other band member of Jaded Ivory that commanded attention, it was Monty. The crowd knew him for his ridiculous antics on and off stage. He never backed down from the crazy-ass challenges people suggested on social media. Monty was definitely the class clown of our group. Most people were shocked to learn that he wrote a good number of our songs. The rest of us had a few in the lineup, but the majority were his.

Monty slipped into the booth on my right followed by Jackson. Heath and Mari were still nowhere to be found.

Monty dipped his head at Reagan. "Hey, man, how'd you like the show?"

"You guys were fantastic."

"Thank you," Jackson said at the same time Monty spouted out, "Of course we are."

Reagan glanced at me. "I see you're not the only one who isn't modest."

I laughed. "Monty wouldn't know what that was even if you wrapped it in a bow and hand delivered it."

Monty lifted a shoulder. "What's the point in that? We're great. Why not admit it?"

Jackson lowered his gaze to the table and shook his head before lifting it to look at Reagan. "Ignore him. He also has no manners."

A waiter came back with our beers. Reagan took his and brought it to his mouth. I caught myself staring at the way his lips wrapped around the bottle. So many images instantly popped into my head. It wasn't until I noticed Monty trying to snag my beer out of the corner of my eye that I stopped looking.

I snatched it from his hand. "Order your own."

"What?" he asked innocently. "It's not like you ordered us any even though you knew we were on our way."

"Like you ever drink the same thing. If I ordered you something, you'd only bitch about how it wasn't what you wanted. Last week you were on a tequila kick."

"'Cause that shit tastes amazing."

I noticed Reagan's shoulders shaking and I knew exactly what he was remembering. Tequila and I weren't friends.

"I doubt Sawyer would agree," Reagan said between laughs.

Monty propped his elbow on the table and leaned forward. "Oh, really? Do tell."

Reagan peeked at me out of the corner of his eye. "You didn't tell them about you and tequila?"'

Jackson spoke up. "He hasn't told us much of anything about before college."

For the briefest of moments, I saw a look of hurt pass over Reagan's eyes, but as quickly as it appeared, it disappeared, replaced by a spark. *Shit*. I had a feeling tonight was going to turn into Sawyer's dirty secret night. I guess that was my punishment. Whatever, nothing that bad ever happened. Mostly I didn't talk about the times before college because all my antics included Reagan and I wasn't ready to talk about him.

Reagan set his bottle down and rubbed his hands together. "I guess I'll have to catch you up then."

"Catch us up on what?" Mari sat down, sliding over until her shoulder was touching Reagan's, to make room for Heath.

"On Sawyer's sordid past." Monty let go an evil cackle.

Heath caught my eye and lifted a brow. "Sounds interesting."

I lifted my beer to my lips, trying to hide how uncomfortable I was with the conversation. It had nothing to do with the guys knowing all the stupid shit I did as a kid. It was the reason why they didn't know. The waiter came back and took everyone else's order. I noticed Max at the bar talking with a guy pointing at our table.

"Heads-up." I tilted my chin in the direction of the bar.

Mari glanced over her shoulder. Her eyes practically rolled into the back of her head. "Not this shit again."

"Yeah," I said. "Apparently they know Cole is at an away game."

She dropped her head onto the back of the seat. "They're going to be unbearable tonight."

"Max said he'll keep them away. Besides, we can just ignore them."

She lifted her head, a twinkle in her eye as she turned her attention to Reagan. "You'll help me keep them away, right?" A slight pout to her lips. Devious little... When I got my hands on her. She knew exactly what she was doing. I had to remind myself she was only doing it to get a response out of me and there was no way in hell I was going to let her win.

"Um...sure," Reagan offered.

She slid closer, looking at Reagan from beneath her lashes, like she was some shy little thing. Under the table I dug my fingers into my own thigh, probably leaving bruises, to keep from letting her have it.

"Sawyer says you played football in high school?"

"I did. Nowhere near as good as your boyfriend, Cole."

"I'm sure you did."

Man, was she pushing the advantage she thought she had. At least she had to keep her hands to herself if she didn't want pictures of her and Reagan all over the gossip blogs in the morning.

Reagan gave her a smile that didn't reach his eyes. It wasn't the half smile that always drew my attention. He was uncomfortable with all her flirting, which made ignoring it even easier.

"I doubt that. He's one of the best high school players I've seen. Too bad about his leg."

"Yeah, it sucked. He loves what he's doing now, though."

"That's good. I haven't gotten a chance to see a game since he took over the offensive coaching duties. I hope to change that some time this season."

Now that Mari had stopped trying to get Reagan to flirt with her, I sat back and watched the conversation happen. The two people in the world who meant more to me than anyone. It was rare that I thought about Reagan ever coming back into my life. But him getting along so well with Mari was more than I could have ever asked for.

"Well then. I'll have to talk to Cole about getting you seats on the fifty-yard line."

"Wow...just wow. I'm not really sure what to say."

She leaned up and pressed a light kiss on his cheek. And right there, I was jealous of Mari's lips. I wanted to be the one pressing my lips to some part of Reagan's body. She'd be lucky if no one snapped a shot of that.

Conversations broke out around me after that. My focus solely on the man beside me. One thought after another flashed through my mind. We'd ordered a bunch of appetizers to share and were digging in when suddenly the conversation came back around and Monty wanted his question answered.

"So, what *was* Sawyer like growing up?"

Reagan rubbed his hands together, like the villains in the movies would do. “Crazy outspoken. Loud.”

Monty looked over at me. “Yeah, I never would have guessed that.” The bored tone so convincing, I almost burst out laughing. Monty brought his attention back to Reagan. “No seriously. Tell us about the crazy shit he did.”

Reagan appeared to mull the question over. “Well, there was the first time he drank tequila.”

Everyone at the table burst out laughing. Not surprising. Every one of them had seen my fun with tequila and I used the word fun loosely. Let’s just say tequila and I didn’t really get along.

Reagan

"Yeah, tequila is not my friend." Sawyer's face twisted into a grimace.

Mari scoffed. "This I know."

I couldn't help but draw my attention to Mari, although every time I did it, I felt Sawyer tense beside me. "Yeah? I'd love to hear what dumb things he's done after drinking it."

She sighed. "Unfortunately, nothing story worthy. Mostly, dragging his ass home and someone dragging him inside. He's lovely to deal with the next morning too."

I laughed. "Tell me about it."

Heath set his bottle on the table, brows furrowed. "Now, I'm curious what stories you have about Sawyer and tequila."

I glanced over at Sawyer to see how he'd feel about me telling this story. The pieces of our friendship were still there. Now we needed to mend them back together. If Sawyer didn't want his friends to know the story I wouldn't tell it. It had surprised me earlier when his bandmates said Sawyer hadn't told them much about his life growing up. Mari was suspiciously quiet for the first time all night, and something told me she knew more than everyone else. I also had a feeling she knew exactly why Sawyer disappeared without saying goodbye when we left for college.

Sawyer gave the slightest inclination of his head. For some reason, he wasn't bothered by them knowing now. No matter what Sawyer tried to say, I still had a feeling it had something to do with me. To get my mind off the thoughts running through my head, I gave them what they wanted.

"It was junior year, during a team building camping trip for baseball."

Monty threw both hands up. "Wait, wait, wait." He paused for a second, looking at Sawyer then back at me. "Let me get this straight. Sawyer played baseball?"

That caught me by surprise. My head snapped around to him, my face no doubt relaying the shock bouncing around my head. I could feel my eyes practically ready to bulge out of my head. How could they not know? "You didn't tell them?" I asked Sawyer. "I thought you went to college together."

Sawyer fidgeted in his seat, a light flush creeping up his neck. "We did, but no, I didn't tell them because I gave it up."

"You what?" I practically yelled.

I could feel everyone's eyes on the two of us. This wasn't something I could explain. Hell, I didn't even understand it myself. Thankfully, Mari asked the question I wanted to ask. For the first time, I realized she didn't know everything. Seemed as if

Sawyer had packaged himself in little boxes and only gave a few to each person, so no one would ever know the whole guy. That made me sad. I wanted to believe that once upon a time, I was the one person who did know everything about him. Apparently, once he left, he didn't let anyone else all the way in. He let some in more than others, but no one knew everything.

"What did you give up, Sawyer?"

I watched as he reached for his back pocket. Some things never changed. His signature move when he was nervous. Best guess, he'd been looking for drumsticks to twirl in his fingers. For some reason, it always relaxed him. This time he didn't have that shield and was on his own.

"I...uh." He twisted the bottle in his hands. "I gave up my scholarship."

Heath narrowed his eyes. "Scholarship? I thought you didn't qualify for full ride music scholarship."

"I didn't."

I was at a loss for words. He really hadn't told them much when they met. "Why would you do that?" I couldn't stop the question from leaving my lips.

He grimaced. Whether it was because of my reaction or his bandmates', I couldn't tell. "I didn't want to play anymore."

"Okay, I'm really confused," Jackson chimed in for the first time in a while. I noticed most of the time he sat quietly observing it all.

"Me too," Monty agreed. "He's played drums as long as we've known him."

"That's not what he got a scholarship for."

Sawyer sighed. "I got a full ride to play baseball."

"Holy shit," Monty exclaimed.

Mari's jaw had practically hit the table. She seemed to be as speechless as I was.

"Why would you give up a full ride?" Heath asked. "Not that I'm not grateful for it, but you have to be crazy to pay tuition when you didn't have to."

"I didn't want to play anymore. The scouts came to the game and offered me the money. At the time I felt stupid saying no, but deep down I knew it wasn't what I wanted. I wanted to major in music." Not once did he look up during his confession. "For years I split my time between music and baseball and I didn't want to do it anymore. I wanted to focus on music only and I couldn't do that when I'd have to give up rehearsal weekends for games."

"I thought they told you they'd find a way to work around it?" I specifically remembered the conversation he had with the scout about his previous acceptance letter for music. The guy made it sound like doing both wouldn't be a problem.

"They did, but then I saw both schedules side by side and there was no way they could make something like that happen. Not without constantly missing one or the other. So, I made a choice and I've never looked back."

Those green eyes locked with mine and I could see the turmoil raging in them. Did he think I'd judge him for the decisions he made? We all had to make our own path in life. Just because mine led me to sports didn't mean his had to. I clasped him on the shoulder. "I think you made a good decision."

He smiled, the first genuine one since the conversation started. 'Thanks, that means a lot."

"Hold up," Monty cut in. "I want to know more about you playing baseball. Then we can get to the tequila story."

"There's not much to tell. Junior year, I decided I wanted to play again. I'd played in rec leagues with Reagan growing up, but quit once we went to high school. I'd always spend spring break alone while Reagan was down in Florida with the baseball team." He gave me a quick glance out of the corner of his eye. "When I complained about it sophomore year, he told me to get off my ass and join the team. Then I wouldn't be alone during break. So, I did."

This time it was Jackson's turn to have the frozen, mute look on his face. Somehow he located his voice. "And you made the team after not playing for two years?"

"Yeah. I'm sure I was the last one to make the team."

Anything but the last one to make the team. I rolled my eyes. "Yep, hitting a homerun at tryouts definitely makes you sit the bench." The sarcasm was so obvious in my tone I might as well have hit them over the head with the truth.

"Damn," Monty exclaimed.

Sawyer shrugged. "It's not a big deal."

"Yeah, it is," Mari insisted. "You gave up a full ride for music. That says a whole helluva lot."

"I gotta go with Mari on this one," Heath agreed. "That's impressive as hell."

"Thanks." The slight flush spread from Sawyer's neck to his cheeks. He'd never been great at accepting compliments for things he thought didn't deserve it.

Silence settled over the table. I didn't know much about the others, but I had a feeling they were thinking about how little they truly knew about Sawyer, someone they'd been playing with for years. The tension closed in on us like a vice.

"Can we get back to the tequila story now?" Monty whined and brought the glass to his lips. "All of this talk is too serious for me."

The rest of the table broke out into laughter, the tension draining from the room. "Fair enough. Anyway, we were on the camping trip and a few of us had snuck alcohol into our bags after they'd been checked by the coaches." I held up the bottle in front of me. "Most of us brought a beer or two. Not Sawyer, though. That idiot brought a whole bottle of tequila."

"On a school trip?" Jackson seemed slightly shocked.

"Oh, please." Monty elbowed him. "Like you never brought alcohol anywhere you weren't supposed to."

"Not all of us have your track record of doing crazy shit. Of course I brought it places, but not on a school trip."

"Well, Sawyer wanted to prove he could handle the tequila," I continued. "After the coaches had gone to bed that first night, everyone met up in our tent with whatever they brought. Most of us got drunk off the one or two beers we'd brought. Sawyer kept taking shot after shot of tequila before eventually passing out. A few of the guys almost passed out and we forced them back to their tent."

"Did he puke in the tent?"

"Did he wake up the coaches?"

"Did he sleep in the wrong tent?"

The questions were coming at me so quickly I couldn't tell who was asking what. I tried to answer them all at once. "None of those. I left him alone for maybe a minute while two of us got rid of the evidence. I figured he was asleep, he'd be fine."

The corners of Sawyer's lips twitched as he tried to fight off the smile. The one that always brought one to my own face. It made me feel at home.

"I'd been so fucking wrong. When I got back to the tent he was missing. I woke up a few of the guys who I knew weren't too drunk. To help me find him."

Mari wrapped her hand around my arm and moved in closer. "Where did you find him?"

Sawyer's nostrils flared, but I had no intention of calling him out in front of his friends. Whatever was going on between the two of them, they could deal with it when they were on their own.

"More than three hours later, we found him trying to take a bath in the river. From what we could find of his clothes, he'd strip—"

Sawyer wrapped his hand around my mouth. "Okay, that's enough."

For the briefest of moments, I thought about licking the palm of his hand. Something we did as kids when one of us tried to shut the other up. But something I couldn't explain stopped me. For some reason, it didn't feel right.

Monty shook his head. "Oh, no. I want to hear the whole thing."

Sawyer kept his hand firmly over my mouth and tried to stare down Monty. When that didn't work and Monty simply rested his head in his hand waiting, he threw his hands up in the air. "Fine. Tell them."

Once again, I looked at Sawyer to make sure he really was fine with it. Sawyer and I may have work to do to repair our relationship, but he was still my friend. I'd only met the people at the table a few hours ago. Someday we might become friends, but at the moment Sawyer was my only concern.

When no one was looking, he gave me a quick wink. A strange feeling settled in my gut. Nothing that I had any hope of explaining, but I never wanted to do anything to cause Sawyer pain. None of this pissed him off, he just wanted to give his bandmates a hard time. I rubbed my fingers along my chin, making them wait longer for the story.

Mari bumped her shoulder with mine. "Don't leave us hanging."

"Well, apparently Sawyer had tried to take a nap, by hugging a tree."

Sawyer winced. His hand reached down below the table. Probably trying to make sure everything was all in one piece.

"Oh, fuck," Monty breathed. "Naked against a tree?"

Sawyer said nothing, but he gave him a nod.

"Damn, was there anywhere you didn't have scratches or splinters?"

Sawyer shivered. "I don't want to think about those. I told you tequila wasn't my friend."

"No shit." I chuckled and turned back to the rest of the group. "Apparently, he got in the lake to get rid of the splinters."

We were lucky that no one fell out of the booth. Even Sawyer couldn't stop himself from laughing. It was nice to see the way his face lit up around his friends. For some reason, I had a feeling that keeping everything bottled up hadn't been easy for him. I doubt he let go most of the time, afraid he might slip up. The question was, slip up about what?

I pushed the thought out of my head and just let myself enjoy the moment. There was no way our friendship would be completely salvaged if all I ever worried about were the secrets Sawyer kept. Whatever he left unsaid had to do with him and not me, and I needed to remember that. Eventually, at least I hoped, Sawyer would be ready to talk and I'd be there to listen. For now I planned on getting to know the members of the band. The whole 'any friends of Sawyers and all that' and hope like hell that eventually was sooner rather than later.

Chapter Ten

Reagan

The words on the file in front of me swirled around on the page, not making any sense. The light outside my office faded with the setting sun. I'd been staring at numbers for the case in front of me all day. I'd blame it on being tired, since Friday's backstage concert turned into a whole weekend hanging out with the band, but I knew that wasn't the case. While it had been fun, I couldn't get my mind off hanging out with Sawyer alone. All through college, I missed the days it was just me and him. Besides the night I tracked him down, we'd always been surrounded by others. Tonight that changed. Sawyer would be home alone. I planned to pick up dinner and head over when I got done.

I kept trying to focus on the contract in front of me, but by a little after seven, I'd had enough. After shutting down my computer, I threw the files into my briefcase. I'd deal with the contract at some point. I stepped out of my office and practically ran headlong into Madison.

"Where are you going this early?"

"Early." I laughed. "It's after seven."

She lifted a brow. "That's early for you."

Madison and I had been hired at the same time. I'd met her when we were interviewed and thought she was my competition for the job. And that scared the crap out of me. I could tell within seconds of meeting her she had a no nonsense attitude. I'd been right. Turned out they had planned on hiring two people, and Madison made it clear from day one that she would have gotten the job over me. It took a while to warm up to her, but being assigned to most of the same cases forced us to work together. I realized she had a fantastic sarcastic wit. Over time we became close friends. So it wasn't a shock that she'd give me shit for leaving before her.

"Yeah, but unlike you, I have plans."

She sighed. "Don't I wish. Where are all the decent members of your gender?"

I pulled the bag farther up my shoulder. "Hiding with all the rational members of yours." I winked, then dodged her hand as she went to shove my shoulder. "I'll see you tomorrow."

"Don't do anything I wouldn't do."

"Well, that's a pretty short list, so I should be safe."

"Ass," she muttered, shaking her head and walking down the hall in the opposite direction.

I wasted no time getting to my car and turning onto the street in the direction of Sawyer's place. Since I promised to bring dinner, I stopped and picked up a pizza on the way. It wasn't a secret that I never learned to cook. Sawyer's mom had taught him, but both his and my mom agreed that I was a lost cause after trying for months to help me. Mom told me I'd be better off getting a job that paid well so I could either order out every night or hire a chef.

I parked near the curb and climbed out of the car, annoyed I didn't have a change of clothes with me. Sawyer's text came long after I was already at the office and I didn't want to waste time stopping by my place and having to deal with my roommate, Harrison. The second I knocked, I heard Sawyer yell to come in. With the pizza in one hand, I pushed the door open.

Sawyer was sprawled on the couch with a video game controller in his hand. I couldn't stop myself from wondering if he'd gotten better at video games since we were teens.

"Taking the night off?" I gestured with my chin to where he sat without his guitar.

He briefly glanced over before turning his gaze back to the screen. "Fuck yeah. I finally finished the song this morning and I need a break."

"I don't blame you. You've been working your ass off."

He chuckled. "Now you sound like Mari."

If I was being honest, that comment rubbed me the wrong way. As great as I found Mari, the relationship she shared with Sawyer made my chest tighten. It became obvious after spending time with the two of them that Mari had stepped into my role after Sawyer left. And maybe it was part of the reason I wanted him to myself tonight.

Pushing the green-eyed monster aside, I held up the pizza box. "I got pizza. Sausage and pepperoni."

"My favorite." He ended the game and dropped the controller on the couch.

"I remember."

Sawyer stood and looked me over from head to toe. Something in his gaze felt different, but I couldn't put my finger on it. There was something almost possessive about it. Even though I couldn't explain it, my skin tingled at his gaze. "Did you bring a change of clothes?"

"No. Didn't feel like stopping at my place on the way over."

He rolled his eyes. "Come on. I got shorts and a T-shirt you can put on. Wouldn't want you to mess up the fancy lawyer suit."

"Fuck you."

He laughed all the way down the hall to his room. After he took some clothes from the drawers in his room and left them on the bed, he turned for the door. "I'll grab some beers and meet you in the living room."

It was ironic that I was changing into Sawyer's clothes. Throughout high school, we'd worn each other's clothes more times than I could count. Sometimes it was easier to go back to one of our houses after practice and change there, not that we always remembered to bring something to change into.

I folded my suit and carried it back out to the living room. It felt almost nostalgic seeing him with a pizza on the couch, watching TV. Sawyer looked up as he placed a piece of pizza on the paper plate in front of him.

"I remember the last time we had sausage and pepperoni pizza together, it was—"

"Our last night at The Hollywood before we left for school," I finished for him.

The Hollywood had been our summer job since we were fifteen. We started out bussing tables before we both ended up waiting them. It was a small little hole in the wall place that served pizza, burgers, and milkshakes. That last night we'd gotten a pizza before we left with a few extra bucks in our pocket.

"I miss that place. I compare every bacon cheeseburger to theirs."

"Me too and I haven't found one to live up to it." Their bacon cheeseburger was the thing dreams were made of. I dropped down on the couch next to him and took the bottle he handed me.

"Next time we're home we'll go."

My hand froze in the middle of lifting the pizza box as I imagined what a road trip with Sawyer would be like. Out of the corner of my eye I noticed Sawyer tense, but I was too busy dealing with my own jumbled thoughts to focus on him at the moment. Before he left, I thought we'd have plenty of road trips throughout college. Since that never happened, it was something I'd look forward to with him. Excitement bubbled inside as I thought of the fun we'd have.

"I think that sounds like a great idea."

Sawyer's muscles seemed to relax.

I picked up my own slice and set it on my plate. "So what song does the label plan on releasing next?"

"Truthfully, I have no idea. All they've told us so far is that they want to try something different with this release." He lifted the bottle to his lips, my eyes drawn to the way his Adam's apple moved with each swallow. *Where were all these thoughts coming from?* I shook my head, pushing it from my mind and tried to focus on the conversation.

"How long did it take you guys to gain a following?" I had to wonder if they were a college band or if they met up later. I picked up my pizza and took a bite.

Sawyer set down his beer and leaned back against the couch. "It seems like it took forever. We didn't have any real success until Mari started singing with us."

I stopped with the beer halfway to my lips and looked over at him. "What do you mean when she started to sing with you? I thought she was part of Jaded Ivory from the beginning."

"Nope. Jackson used to be our lead singer. He lost his voice one weekend we had a gig and I begged Mari to fill in for him for one night. She knew all our songs and set list. It seemed like the perfect replacement for one night. We never expected the crowd to go absolutely batshit with her at the lead. When the offers for more shows came in, Jackson willingly stepped aside for her and the rest is history."

"Holy shit." I couldn't imagine Jaded Ivory without Mari singing the lead. "That's a story I never expected."

Sawyer scoffed. "I was lucky to get her on the stage the first time. She had stage fright like I've never seen."

"Thank God she got over it."

"You're telling me."

We finished the pizza and Sawyer lay back on the couch patting his stomach. "That was good freaking pizza."

"It's from Antonio's on eighth."

"I'll keep that in mind the next time you bring me pizza."

I gave him a light punch to the arm and he chuckled. “Next time it’s your turn.”

“Whatever,” he said as I settled back into the cushions. Suddenly, a black controller appeared in my line of sight. “Let’s play like we used to.”

“Oh, so you mean, you pick a game, try your best, and I still kick the shit out of you.” It happened every time he coaxed me into a night of video games. He’d swear he’d gotten better, and usually he had, just not enough to beat me.

“That was then, this is now. I’ve gotten so much better.”

I rolled my eyes. “You say that every time.”

“Okay, how about a little wager?” He dangled the controller in front of my nose.

“And what would that be?”

“If you win I cook you dinner of your choice one night, but if I win you clean out my car.”

I shook my head, laughing. “I might get lost or die trying to escape the disaster that is your car.”

He shook the controller again. “I thought you said it would be an easy win. If that’s true, why are you so scared of my car?”

He had a point. And the thought of Sawyer’s cooking made my mouth water even with a full belly. For as much as I couldn’t cook, he could. He was the star pupil of both of our parents. Even my own parents had given up on my cooking skills and taught Sawyer everything they knew.

I snatched the controller out of his hands. “You’re on and I want your mom’s steak and shrimp this weekend.”

He glanced at me out of the corner of his eye as he set up the game. “Pretty sure of yourself?”

“It’s guaranteed.”

And boy had I been right. Sawyer hadn't gotten good enough to beat me. The cursing started pretty early as he called best two out of three, then three out of five. At one point I reached up and grabbed the controller before he could chuck it across the room. It was a reflex and not the first time I stopped Sawyer from throwing his controller. It happened at least once a night when we were younger, sometimes more than once. That wasn't what shocked me.

Throughout the game, Sawyer's arm would brush against mine, making goose bumps rise across my skin and a shiver to race down my back. For the life of me, I couldn't explain why the simple brush of skin would affect me so much. It wasn't like we hadn't touched each other before. The reality was it probably had to do with missing his company for so long. I did my best to push aside my body's reaction and enjoy the time together. With both of our schedules, we didn't have many days for times like these.

Reagan

The book in front of me slammed closed on my hand.

"What the hell?" I snapped, yanking my hand back.

Madison stared at me across the table, drumming her fingers. When I glanced around at the rest of our team, I noticed that all eyes were on me. Oddly enough I had a feeling it had nothing to do with my outburst.

"Maybe if you were paying attention, I wouldn't have to cause you pain."

I flipped the book open, searching for my page with specific code I needed. "I am paying attention."

"Oh, so you heard me call your name five times before I slammed your book closed?" She lifted a brow, daring me to say I heard her.

Honestly, I didn't. A few weeks ago, I promised myself I wouldn't let whatever Sawyer was keeping under wraps bother me, except since then I found that was all I could think about. It had pissed me off the first night when he refused to tell me whatever it was that destroyed our friendship. His promise that it hadn't been anything I did had gone a long way in pushing back the feelings of anger and frustration. Then at dinner the next night, I realized how much his friends didn't know about his life before college and the questions ran through my head over and over again like a bad movie reel.

The weird part was our friendship had gone back to the way it was before. Over the last few weeks, we'd hung out like the last seven years hadn't happened. A bar, his concerts, the movies, didn't matter what we did. The same laughs and fun filled every night.

Almost.

I still noticed Sawyer keeping pieces to himself. Like he'd built walls around each part of his life, only letting certain people see certain things. He was hiding too much of himself from people and for the life of me I couldn't figure out why. So yeah, I'd zoned out when we should have been working.

"Fine, I wasn't paying attention."

Madison leaned forward, resting her elbows on the table. "What's gotten into you? Ever since you went to that concert a few weeks ago, things haven't been the same."

"It was just a concert. I'm pretty sure we've all been to one before." George rolled his eyes. "Now can we get back to this? I want to get this contract sorted. It's Saturday and I don't want to be here all night."

"It wasn't just any concert. My best friend from high school was playing and we hadn't seen each other since before college."

"Really?" Chloe asked. "What band did you see?"

Madison watched me closely. Out of all the members of our team, she'd been hired at the same time I was. We'd worked together enough and she could read body language like a pro. Their questions didn't make me uncomfortable, but she'd know in a heartbeat there was more to the story than I wanted to give away.

"Jaded Ivory."

Chloe's eyes practically bulged out of her head and her jaw almost hit the floor. "You're telling me, your best friend is part of Jaded Ivory and you never thought to mention it before?"

I sat back in my chair. "Like I said, I hadn't talked to Sawyer since before we left for college. The night of the meet and greet was the first time I saw him in seven years."

"You know Sawyer Alason?" Madison asked slowly.

"I've known him since I was seven."

She threw her pen at me, smacking me in the head.

"Stop throwing shit at me."

"You're the one who didn't tell us you knew a member of one of the hottest up and coming band out there. Not to mention the hottest drummer on the planet."

Hottest drummer? I could see that. His long shaggy hair and crystal green eyes called to people. Not to mention the rocker vibe he put off. Everyone wanted the bad boy. Even if it couldn't be farther from the truth. Sawyer never had a shortage of people chasing him. It wouldn't surprise me if there were women lining up for him in college. I rubbed the spot where the pen hit, hoping there was no ink on my head. "And I haven't seen him since I was eighteen. How do you know who he is?"

Another pen came flying at my head. This time I caught it midair and slammed it to the table. "I said, stop throwing shit at me."

A few of the legal assistants walked by the windows, watching us.

"I follow their pages."

Madison shrugged it off like it was no big deal. She had no idea how big of a deal it was. We'd gotten to hang out without too much interference, and he'd mentioned Mari had the largest following. But it looked like Sawyer had started to get a fan club of his own. For some reason that bugged me a bit. On one hand I wanted him to succeed, on the other I wanted time to myself with him. I wasn't sure what that said about me, so I kept my mouth shut.

"Let's get back to work. We can talk about this later."

Curiosity twinkled in Madison's eye. I'd be willing to bet the first chance she had me alone, she'd be all over me trying to get the answers. Until then, I planned to force all of it out of my head and focus. George was right, I needed to get this contract amended by the end of the day. We'd made it through four of the articles and only had one left to go.

"Does anyone have section three of article five? I can't find my notes for it." George continued to shuffle through his papers searching.

Chloe pulled it out. "I have it. Come on. I'll get copies made." She stood with the papers in her hand.

George rubbed his neck. "I need a cup of coffee." He stood to follow her out.

"We'll be right back," Chloe said, shutting the door behind them.

I glanced at my watch. A little after six. We'd been working since noon and I wanted to leave. Sawyer didn't have anything tonight. It amazed me how quickly we'd fallen back into the routine of hanging out with one another whenever we were both free. Catching up, talking, or just spending time together. Almost like no time had passed.

"Why not?"

Once again Madison's voice drew me from my thoughts.

"Why not what?"

Madison's brows were drawn together. "Why haven't you seen him?"

Wasn't that a good question? "I have no idea. The day before we were both supposed to leave for college, I stopped by his house to pick him up for one last day of freedom since we were headed to different schools and his car was gone. I knocked on the door. His mom answered and told me he'd left the night before. That was all she would tell me. I tried texting him, but I got nothing back. When I saw they were playing at the Pinnacle Arena, I decided to go and finally figure out why he disappeared all those years ago."

"And?"

"And nothing. I still don't know."

Her eyes widened. "He still didn't tell you?"

"Nope. Said it was something he had to work through on his own, but it had nothing to do with me."

"Wow. That's fucked up."

"Thanks for the keen observation, Madison."

"Don't start. You know you're thinking it. It's why you can't concentrate for shit lately. You need to ask him again if it's going to be screwing with you."

I sighed. "I've thought about it. The first night when we talked he told me he wasn't ready to tell me. That someday he would be. I think I need to get my best friend back and worry about all the other shit later."

George and Chloe came back to the table, papers and coffees in hand.

"Good luck with that," Madison said.

Chloe's gaze darted between us. "Good luck with what?"

"Nothing," I said, shaking my head. "Let's get this contract done, so we're not here all night."

George nodded. "That's what I want to hear."

I picked up my pen to make a note in the margin when my phone buzzed on the table. Sawyer. In an effort to avoid distracting everyone in the room again, I sent the call to voice mail and sent him a quick text.

Me: In a meeting. What's up?

I didn't have to wait long for an answer.

Sawyer: Cole got me tickets to tonight's game. 50 yard line. You in?

"How much longer do you think we'll be? About an hour?"

Madison narrowed her eyes. "Why?"

"Sawyer got tickets to tonight's game."

She shook her head. "I still can't wrap my head around you"—she waved her hand up and down at me—"being friends with him."

"Would it make you feel better if I wore ripped jeans and had sleeve tattoos?"

"Okay, point taken. I think an hour is good. You guys?"

I looked over at Chloe and George, who both agreed.

"Awesome."

I started typing when Madison put her hand over the screen. "You better damn well be telling that man to meet you here. You did hear me say the sexiest drummer on the planet, right?"

I couldn't help but laugh as I nodded and she moved her hand.

Me: Yeah. Wanna meet me at my office in an hour?

Sawyer: Sure. I'd love to see where you work.

We went back to dealing with the last article, but I found I had to force myself to concentrate on what we were talking about. Every once in a while I noticed my gaze stray to the door, waiting for Sawyer to step through. Almost completely done with the contract, I reread the last paragraph when the door opened.

"Mr. Setton, there's a Sawyer Alason here to see you. Should I have him wait in your office?"

Madison glared daggers at me. She might actually hurt me if I didn't have him brought in.

"Thanks, Bridget. Can you bring him here?"

"Certainly, Mr. Setton." And even though Bridget was normally as straitlaced as a person could get, I noticed the twinkle in her eyes when she turned to get Sawyer.

Less than a minute later, Sawyer strolled in. Larger than life.

"Hey, we're almost done. Give me another fifteen?"

"Yeah, no problem." Sawyer pulled out the chair next to mine.

A foot connected with my shin. "Fuck," I yelped, reaching down to rub the abused bone.

I looked up to see Madison glaring at me. With a roll of my eyes, I gestured to the rest of my team. "Sawyer, this is Madison, Chloe, and George. They're all associates with the firm."

"Hi, nice to meet you."

"Hi." Chloe practically bounced in her seat. "I love your music."

That half grin appeared. The one full of confidence and self-assuredness. The one I couldn't look away from. "Thanks. I'll have to get you passes backstage one of these days."

Chloe slapped a hand over her mouth to keep from screaming and looking unprofessional to the people seated at the cubicles right outside the conference room window. George chuckled and simply returned Sawyer's hello. The real surprise was Madison, who sat there, mouth agape, simply staring. For the first time since I'd known her, Madison didn't seem to have a single word to say. Maybe it was time for a bit of payback.

I set my elbow on the table, resting my chin on my palm. "Madison, I thought you were a big fan of Sawyer and Jaded Ivory."

Her eyes flared as a light flush crept up her neck and jaw. "I...um..."

Sawyer turned the full power of his smile on her. It took my normally outspoken friend and turned her into a mute. I knew I was in for it later.

"Can we get this last part done, so we can all get out of here?" George said.

"Yes, please," Chloe agreed.

While working through the last part, I found myself hyper aware of Sawyer sitting next to me. Weird. It wasn't the first time we did work together, even if this time Sawyer was only watching. I had a feeling it had more to do with the way Madison continued to peek up at him through her lashes. For some reason it made me want to claim possession of him. He was my friend not hers. I kept my mouth shut, recognizing how ridiculous that sounded. Didn't stop me from thinking it.

By the time we finished, I was more than ready to get out of there. Irrational as it might have been, I wanted to get Sawyer out of there and spend time, just the two of us. I packed up all my stuff and told them I'd have the final draft typed up for Monday. As we walked out of the building, I remembered the one problem with him picking me up.

"I have to warn you that my roommate is a total asshole."

"That bad, huh?"

I followed him to his car. "That bad," I agreed. "He's the type people post about and the shit goes viral."

"Oh, man." He winced and unlocked his car. "Why live with him?"

"Rent isn't cheap, so I advertised for a roommate. Trust me when I tell you he seemed normal until after he moved in."

Sawyer rolled his eyes. "Kick his ass out."

"I'm working on it. I need to save up enough to pay for the condo for a few months while I look for another roommate."

I climbed in and groaned. "Shit, you weren't kidding about your car being a disaster."

It wasn't like there was food or fast food wrappers everywhere, but it seemed as if sheet music and old drumsticks covered almost every surface area of the car.

"Hey, I tried to warn you."

I shoved the shit off my seat and to the floor. "Fair enough. I'm warning *you* that we're taking my car to the game."

Sawyer laughed and the heavy baritone settled the nagging, jealous feeling inside me. I didn't have to share him with the world today. Today he was my best friend. Just the two of us, like it had been when we were kids.

I directed him to my building. He stepped out of the car to come upstairs with me. As we approached the elevator, I silently prayed Harrison wasn't there. He was absolutely infuriating to live with. I couldn't imagine how he'd treat a friend of mine. The elevator doors closed behind us.

The doors whisked open and I stepped out onto my floor. I almost groaned when I saw Harrison's favorite little sign hanging from the doorknob.

Do Not Disturb.

Don't ask me where he got it. Hell, I'd already torn up and thrown away more than a dozen, yet they kept reappearing. I reached for the handle, blatantly ignoring the sign, when Sawyer grabbed my hand and pulled it back.

"Dude, doesn't that mean he's got company?"

I glanced over and rolled my eyes. "If only. This is only one of the ways he's made life difficult so far. It usually means he's watching some foreign film and expects me to stay out of my place for hours while he finishes the movie and writes a complete review of it on his blog."

Sawyer narrowed his eyes. "Who does that?"

"The idiot I live with, unfortunately." I pushed the door open. The only light in the room came from the TV to the right.

"Reagan," Harrison snapped. "What have I told you about the do not disturb sign?"

I flicked on the light. "And I've told you I have the lease on this condo. I'm not staying out of my place for hours for this shit. You want to bring home a chick to fuck, then I'll listen. Until then." I took the sign off the handle and tore it in two. "Stop putting them up. I'm just gonna ignore it."

Harrison hopped up from his seat and ran to the light switch, halting his steps the moment he noticed Sawyer behind me. His lip curled. "And why would you bring this…this thug into my place of sanctuary?"

Sawyer had about five or six inches on Harrison and gazed down at him, amusement lighting his eyes. Afraid of what Sawyer might say, I stepped between them.

"Sawyer is one of my closest friends and is welcome here anytime I bring him. I'm not really concerned about your opinion. Now, if you'd get out of the way and let me change we could already be out of your hair."

Harrison reached for the light.

"Don't even think about it. I'm not stumbling through the place in the dark. I'll turn it off when we leave."

Harrison spun on his heel, grumbling under his breath the entire way back to the couch. I ignored him and went straight for my room. Sawyer's footsteps sounded behind me and I thanked my lucky stars he didn't stay there to engage him for his shitty behavior. The minute my door closed behind us, I turned on my heel to apologize to Sawyer and noticed the crinkles around his eyes.

"That is way more than an asshole. Good thing I don't live with him. I'd need to hire a lawyer."

I let out a sigh. "Tell me about it."

"Is he a lawyer too?"

I gripped the hem of my shirt and tugged it over my head, dropping it into the hamper by the closet. "No, he's an engineer. But I'm surprised he's able to keep his job. He spends most of his time on his blog."

I dug through my drawers, looking for one of the Hayward T-shirts I still owned. I could sense eyes on me when I noticed Sawyer had gone silent. When I turned around to see if he was all right, I realized he was on his phone. Strange. I gave myself a mental shake. Apparently, everything that happened at the office still had me paranoid. Why, I hadn't a clue. If Sawyer had been interested in Madison flirting that was up to him. For the life of me, I couldn't figure out why I suddenly felt possessive over my relationship with Sawyer. It could have been my fear of him disappearing again after I'd gotten him back. Whatever the cause I needed to get a grip.

I yanked the shirt over my head and shoved my wallet and phone in my pocket.

"Ready?"

SAWYER

Ready?

He had to be kidding me. I wanted to bolt out the door the minute he took his shirt off. I pulled out my phone as a distraction, afraid if I didn't do something I'd end up running my fingers along all of his golden skin on display. The muscles in his back were more defined than they'd been in high school. Even more tempting for me. My eyes strayed from my phone. I *knew* I was staring and there wasn't anything I could do to stop. At least until he'd turned. I quickly glanced down at my screen to keep from being caught.

Ready?

My ass needed to get out of there. I could feel the hard-on pulsing in my jeans, begging to get free. One look at his bare back and the blood started to flow from my head to my groin.

I jumped from the chair as if my ass were on fire.

"Yep. Let's go." I practically ripped the door off the hinges in my haste to get it open.

I stalked past Reagan's roommate. Asshole was an understatement for that guy. What a judgmental dick. At least he could be my saving grace if Reagan called me out for my weird behavior. I'd blame it on the guy's shitty attitude when we arrived. Once I made it into the hallway, I reached down and adjusted my dick. I didn't need him to see it and wonder where it came from.

He pressed the button on the elevator. "Where are the seats?"

"Fifty-yard line."

I almost groaned when the doors slid shut behind us. On the ride up, I'd been focused on his roommate and hadn't paid any attention to the scent of sandalwood that surrounded him. Now? Now, it was all I could think about. It wrapped around me, making me dizzy and stealing my breath. Nothing in the world would ever smell as enticing as Reagan. A combination of something distinctly him and sandalwood. Only a few floors. I held my breath, hoping like hell I didn't pass out before we reached the bottom.

Reagan went on and on about the seats. How unless he was playing, he'd never been that close to the field. All the while, I tried to clear my mind and calm my senses. How the hell were we supposed to be friends when my mind constantly strayed to the what-ifs? After weeks of spending time together, I thought it would get easier. I'd managed to do it through most of high school. The difference now was I had more confidence in myself. I understood myself and who I was. I spent most of time in high school trying to figure that out.

Now I knew what I wanted and what I couldn't have.

The doors opened and I sucked in a breath. His scent lingered until we stepped outside. The fresh air cleared my head and I was able to think again.

"Cole got them for me. Pays to be one of the coaches."

"Definitely a perk." He winked and walked around the front of his car, climbing into the driver's seat.

We climbed in and I couldn't help but notice the sideways glances he shot me every once in a while on the drive over. I kept my eyes straight forward, focused on the road ahead, knowing how much my face would give away if I looked at him. We made our way toward the entrance gate and I couldn't help but notice the long, powerful strides Reagan made with each step. Or the way his jeans clung to every curve of his ass. *Get a grip*. I handed Reagan his ticket.

"Did you play all through college?" I asked.

"All four years." We scanned our tickets at the gate. "Which reminds me I keep forgetting to ask. Did you miss not playing baseball?"

Thank fuck. Something to focus on besides Reagan.

"A little, but not enough to give up music."

He chuckled. "I can imagine. Did you guys think you'd ever end up where you are?"

I pulled the baseball cap low. Not that I expected any problems, but better safe than sorry. "Not exactly. No one really noticed us at first. Not until Mari started singing with us."

His step faltered. "You told me Jackson was the lead singer?"

"Yep."

"Did he mind giving it up?"

"I think he did a little, but he knew we'd be more successful with Mari in the lead."

We made our way down to our seats. I'd never been down there before. Honestly, I'd never asked Cole to get me down there before. To Reagan I passed it off as if Cole had just given me the tickets. When in reality, I asked him to get them. I knew Reagan would love seeing a game and I wanted to be the one to take him. Cole had been more than happy to help me out. Once he understood that Mari and I would only ever be friends, our own friendship grew.

"Holy shit," he breathed. The awe on his face told me I'd made the right decision. "These are perfect."

We sat down, waiting for the team to emerge from the tunnel. At least that was what Reagan was doing. I'd taken the seat to his right, which gave me a clear view of his strong jaw and chiseled profile, all under the guise of waiting for the team. His cheekbones had grown more defined over the years. Watching him, I realized how different we truly were. When his roommate called me a thug, while I found it offensive, I understood how a close-minded individual like him would believe that. Gauges in both ears, tattoos running along both arms, in an old T-shirt and ripped jeans. If only he'd known about the nipple piercings under my shirt. Reagan, on the other hand, was the definition of clean-cut sophistication. He always had been. Dark denim that hugged the muscular thighs beneath. Short, styled dark hair. Even in a Hayward T-shirt and jeans, he looked every bit of the lawyer he was.

It just proved how looks truly meant nothing. Reagan and I may look like polar opposites, but our personalities couldn't be more alike. I loved watching sports as much as he did. We had the same taste in music and movies. The perfect match in all ways but one.

The team finally emerged from the tunnel, stealing my ability to watch Reagan unnoticed. The minute Cole hit the fifty-yard line, he caught my gaze and gestured to the seats. I gave a thumbs-up and a smile. I owed him one. Although I had a feeling he'd take a referee when Mari got all fired up about something. Not that it hadn't been a role I'd played in the past.

The game felt more like a roller coaster ride than football, neither team keeping the lead for long periods of time. We yelled and screamed each time Hayward scored, getting frustrated each time the opposing team did. There was thirty seconds left on the clock and Hayward was down by three. The offensive line rotated and we waited. The throw from the quarterback went barreling toward the end zone. I think the entire stadium held a collective breath as we watched to see if the wide receiver would come down with it. His fingers skimmed the ball and by some miracle he was able to get a grip on it and pull it down, landing inside the end zone.

The stadium erupted in cheers and shouts as the buzzer sounded. Backs were slapped, high fives given. Suddenly, I felt myself wrapped up in Reagan's arms. Excitement had overtaken everyone. For years, it hadn't been odd for us to cheer and share a quick hug when our team won. Things were different now. He didn't, but I sure as hell noticed the way his firm body felt against mine. Trying not to show the awkwardness that crept through me, I patted him on the back, keeping my hips away from his. When he finally let go I breathed a sigh of relief.

My dick was hard as steel. There'd be no way to hide that from him if our lower bodies touched. The energy in the place faded slightly as the people began to make their way up the stairs to the exit.

"Damn," Reagan said as we reached the landing. "I'm not sure I can sleep for a while after that game. Wanna grab a beer?"

"I thought you had work to do for Monday?"

He gave my shoulder a quick shove. "I do, but I don't think a couple of beers is going to make me forget everything. Plus, I have all day Sunday, unless you have plans to drag me somewhere else."

"Oh, so I dragged you here. I'll remember that next time Cole has seats to give away."

"You can drag me to a game anytime you want."

If only I could drag him anywhere. "I see you're using me for what you can get out of me."

This time a light punch landed on my arm. "And what would that be?"

So many answers sat there on the tip of my tongue, but I held most of them back. "For how much fun I am."

Reagan rolled his eyes. "You definitely think highly of yourself."

"Maybe a little," I joked, trying to hide everything that was going on in my head.

If there was one thing I learned about Reagan over the last few weeks, it was that he could still read me like a book. I made sure to keep more of my emotions locked up tight.

"How about Solitude?" he asked.

"Sounds good," I said absently, my focus still on keeping my emotions locked up tight.

I didn't really pay attention to where we were going until Reagan pulled into the parking garage.

I'd been so focused on all the things in my head, I hadn't been listening when he suggested this place.

"Solitude? I thought you wanted a beer."

"Nothing wrong with a beer and music." He nodded toward the door.

Music happened to be an understatement. Solitude would be full of gyrating bodies as they danced to whatever band played that night. It reminded me a lot of the places where we started. Not exactly a club, but there definitely would be people dancing. My heart leapt into my throat. *Has he figured it out?* Solitude happened to be known as a place where anyone was welcome. It didn't matter if you wanted to dance with men, women or both. No one discriminated there.

"Why Solitude?" I asked in what I hoped sounded like a conversational tone.

"They have local beers on tap I can't get anywhere else."

I breathed a sigh of relief and my footsteps lightened as I followed him inside. The speakers still played while the band set up their equipment. Hopefully, we'd sit and drink without any trips to the dance floor. I had no desire to play the avoidance game with the women in the bar. After we flagged someone down and ordered, Reagan turned to me.

"Thanks for thinking of me when you got the tickets."

If only he knew I thought about him all the time. "Who else would I go with?"

He lifted the pint glass to his lips. "I'm not the only friend you have." I couldn't help but notice the way he stared at me over the rim of the glass before taking a drink.

“I see those idiots all the time. It’s you I want to hang out with.” And that was closer to the truth than I’d been willing to admit up to this point.

He nodded, but stared at the glass in his hand for a long moment. “Is it just me who feels like nothing has changed?”

“That’s ’cause it hasn’t. I made a dumb decision all those years ago.” Against my better judgment, I rested my hand on his shoulder. “But I have and will always consider you my best friend.”

The muscles in his shoulder tightened. He said nothing but glanced at me over his shoulder, a grin on his lips. We sat that way for a few seconds before I pulled my hand away and we both faced forward once again. The TV above our heads caught my attention. It had a replay of the night’s game.

“I still can’t believe Hayward had to fight that hard for the win.”

With his glass in his hand, he pointed to the screen. “That’s ’cause the defensive line was letting number eighty-seven run all over them.”

“I could see Cole getting frustrated.” I chuckled. “At least if they had lost, he could go home and let Mari cheer him up.”

Reagan laughed. “I’m sure she could.”

From there the conversation turned back to the football game. Reagan had theories about what he would have done different with the defense had he been coaching. All was right in the world. At least until I heard it.

“Wow. That’s a lot of sexy sitting in front of me.”

I almost groaned aloud. Turning, I noticed a petite brunette standing there with her hands on her hips, checking us both out from head to toe. Reagan also turned to face her, and I couldn’t help but notice the way his eyes traveled down her body. So much for it being just the two of us for the night. We were so entrenched in our conversation, I hadn't even heard the band had started playing. Odd. Usually one of the first things I paid attention to. Then again, spending time with Reagan always made everything else around me disappear. If only the same thing happened to him.

"Hey," I said, not wanting to be rude, but not wanting to give her any indication I was interested. I turned back to the bar and my beer.

Reagan didn't follow suit, his eyes still watching her. "Thanks. I could say the same about you."

My stomach rolled. I glanced over my shoulder as she stepped closer and ran her finger down the muscles of his bicep.

"Are you from around here?" She peeked at him from beneath her lashes, making sure to arch her back, pushing her breasts into his side.

"I am. What about you?" Reagan took another sip of his drink.

"I grew up around here." She looked over at me. "What about you?"

"Just moved to town," I answered, my voice slightly clipped.

Reagan brought his attention to me, his gaze focused on mine. I said nothing and lifted my beer to my lips. What was I supposed to say? Look at me, not her? How the hell could I explain why I wanted his attention?

Reagan glanced back at her. "It was nice to meet you."

He tried to turn around when her hand grabbed his arm and stopped him. I gripped my glass so hard, I was afraid it might break in my hand.

Forcing myself to relax my fingers, I pretended to watch the highlights of the game. Not that I could have told you a single word they said. I was hyper-aware of everything going on next to me.

"Dance with me," she said, rubbing her thumb across his bicep.

"Maybe another time. My friend and I—"

"Go dance with her," I interrupted. If he wanted her, who was I to stand in his way?

He shook his head. "No, I'm—"

She beamed and linked her hand with his, her attention on me. "Your friend said he doesn't care, right?"

"Nope, have fun." I brought the beer to my lips, like I didn't have a care in the world. My stomach tightened. I clenched my fingers of my free hand into a fist in my lap, to keep me from reaching for Reagan and holding him there with me.

"Great."

Before Reagan could protest, she had him off the stool, heading to the dance floor. The bartender asked if I wanted another round.

"That and a double of Jack."

If I was going to have to spend the night watching the two of them grope each other I deserved to get buzzed while doing it. One look at the dance floor and my chest tightened. I threw back the shot, hoping to get drunk enough I didn't care what Reagan did.

Except for the realization I'd been trying to ignore for weeks. Somehow, Reagan had managed to slip behind my defenses. And just like before, I was falling head over heels in love with Reagan.

Reagan

What the hell was Sawyer thinking? I had no desire to dance with this chick. She was easy on the eyes, but tonight I wanted to hang out with him. Ever since I'd watched the way Madison and Chloe reacted to him at the library, I wanted him all to myself. Instead, I found myself being dragged through the bar to the crowded dance floor. She wasted no time pushing her body to mine. Not even a sheet of paper could have fit between us.

I hadn't even gotten her name.

Unsure how to get out of the situation, I rested my hands on her hips and waited for the right time to excuse myself. One song. Two songs. By the third song I'd had enough. She ran her hands over every inch of my chest and ass, which did nothing for me. For the first time in my life, I felt like a piece of meat. The moment her lips touched my jaw, trying to get me to look down so she could reach mine, I jumped away from her.

"Thanks, but I'm not interested. I need to get back to my friend."

Her face turned three different shades of red and for one brief moment I felt bad for the way I treated her. At least until she turned and started grinding with the guy behind her. Within seconds, she'd shoved her tongue in his mouth. Dodged a bullet.

I stormed back over to where Sawyer still sat at the bar. I stopped in my tracks. I couldn't help but notice the way his shoulders filled out the tight black T-shirt. What the hell? The last thing I needed to do at the moment was notice anything about the way Sawyer looked. He'd just sent me to dance with some chick even after I said I didn't want to. I was fuming. Two empty shot glasses now sat in front of him. Pissed that he served me up on a silver platter, I shoved his shoulder until he was forced to face me. "What the hell was that all about? Why would you feed me to the wolves like that?"

His eyes were a bit glassy. "I thought you wanted her."

I dropped down onto the stool. "What made you think that? I said I didn't want to dance."

"I saw the way you were looking at her. I didn't want you to miss out because of me." He shrugged.

Something was off in his tone, but I couldn't place it. "She's hot. I can't help looking. But you know her type. She wants to rack up the number of guys she hooks up with tonight. Not what I'm looking for."

His head perked up. "What are you looking for?"

"I want a relationship. I did the whole let's hook up with a different girl every few weeks. I don't want that shit anymore. I want someone who wants to be there for the long haul."

Sawyer watched me for a moment, a small smile curling the corner of his lips. "Sorry, man. I didn't mean to throw you to the wolves."

The smile didn't reach his eyes. I thought about that as I ordered another drink. Silence engulfed the two of us like it had that first night. Something was still off with him, but I couldn't put my finger on it. He lifted the bottle to his lips and I couldn't keep my gaze off them. He had the perfect lips for kissing.

Where the fuck did that come from?

Sawyer's voice sounded like it came through a tunnel until I heard him call my name.

I shook my head to clear it. I had no idea what my problem was, but I forced myself to focus on what he said.

"Huh?"

"I asked what were your stats in college?"

I answered his question, shocked at how quickly I could forgive and forget an argument. And in an instant, things were back to normal.

Or almost normal.

A voice in the back of my head screamed that something was off. Deep down I knew Sawyer had a reason for sending me off. Not to mention my weird ass fantasy for a minute there. I had to hope at some point I'd be able to break down his wall and figure out whatever it was that stood between us at times. Maybe then I could explain what was messing with my head.

Chapter Fourteen

Sawyer

"How many more times are we going to have to go through this song until we get it?" I snapped, my patience at an end with the bullshit, childish crap today. For the third time in a row, Monty had played the wrong transition cord.

My mood was for shit the last few days. I hadn't spoken with Reagan since we'd left the bar two nights ago. I pretended things were fine at the little show on the dance floor, but that wasn't really the case. White hot jealousy had ravaged my entire system as I watched the woman press her lips to Reagan's jaw. Had he not pushed her away, I wasn't sure I would have been able to stay in my seat any longer. Even though we spent the rest of the night talking about stupid shit, I hadn't been able to get his words out of my head.

I want someone for the long haul.

The words ate at me like a virus. Could I handle spending time with him when I knew there was a woman waiting at home to give him everything

I wanted to give him? The thought alone made me want to smash something. It kept my temper just below simmering all day. And the bullshit with the song was about to push it over the edge.

Mari gave me a quick glance over her shoulder, a brow lifted, but I took it as my signal to tap us in. With a new song it was easier to do it that way until we'd fallen in the groove where playing it became second nature. Today that groove seemed miles away. Every time we started the damn song, something stupid happened to stop us in our tracks. We hadn't even gotten to the first chorus yet. There was only a little over an hour before we were supposed to be recording a different song for the album the studio was gearing up for release. This time it happened to be a full album, instead of the teaser set they released almost a year ago for the radio stations. At the rate it was going, this song would never make it onto an album of its own. Monty and Jackson started in on the simple introduction with Mari's voice coming softly in to complete the melody. Just as Heath and I were about to pick up the tempo Mari burst into laughter.

Heath stopped playing and froze, his jaw practically on the floor. "Did you just say fart instead of heart?"

Jackson's wide eyes followed her as she walked over and slumped on the couch trying to catch her breath only to giggle more.

"She totally fucking said it." Monty roared with laughter, falling off the bench.

Heath had finally snapped his jaw shut, trying not to laugh. Under normal circumstances, I would have joined in, but the sleepless nights had taken their toll. Not that Reagan's team at the firm helped. It wasn't as bad when I didn't know two of the three other members were gorgeous women. I wouldn't blame him for looking at either of them a second time. It's not like I would ever have a chance.

"Goddammit!" I threw my sticks across the room. As I stormed out, I noticed everyone staring at me. Not that I gave a shit. I needed a break.

The door slammed behind me and I moved down the hall to a room where they kept drinks and snacks for the artists. I grabbed a bottle of water, chucking the cap onto the table and drinking down half the bottle.

"What the fuck was that all about?" Mari shoved through the door, throwing it into the wall behind.

I slammed the bottle onto the table, water sloshing everywhere. "What the hell are you yelling at me for?" I snapped.

Mari's mouth dropped open. "Are you freaking kidding me? You just threw your shit across the room and you want to know why I'm yelling?"

Heath stepped into the room, pointing at me. "You need to get your shit under control."

"I'm the one who needs to get my shit under control? You guys can't get through one song, but I'm the one with the problem."

Mari narrowed her eyes. "We never get a song right this early and we always have a ton of laughs. The better question is why do you have a stick up your ass?"

"I don't. I want to get this shit done and go home."

She threw her hands in the air. "To do what? Stay up and write more songs? If you said you wanted to get home so you could sleep that would be one thing, but you don't. You stay up until all hours of the night writing music only to be a tired, shitty asshole the next day."

I opened my mouth to let Mari have it when Heath raised both hands at us and sighed. It wasn't often that Mari and I fought, but when we did shit truly hit the fan.

"That's not the problem."

Mari's head snapped in his direction. "What do you mean that's not the problem?"

"The song writing is to get his mind off the real issue."

"Reagan?" she asked, although I knew she really didn't need an answer. She knew Reagan was the only man I'd ever wanted for more than one night.

"We need more songs."

Heath shook his head. "Not at the rate you're writing them. And you haven't let us hear any and I have a feeling what's stopping you."

Mari stepped in front of me, her voice softening from earlier. "What are the songs about?"

I shrugged. "Nothing specific. Same as our other stuff."

She laid her hand on my arm. "Don't lie to me."

I ran a hand through my hair and paced away from them, not ready to see how bad this whole thing was affecting me. "They all have to do with him."

A small hand wrapped around my bicep, pulling me around to face them. "Why are you doing this to yourself?"

"What am I supposed to do? He's been my best friend since we were kids. I can't just walk away from him."

"No." She wrapped her arm around my waist. "But you can tell him the truth."

I leaned my chin down on her head. "What would the point of that be? He's straight."

"Maybe. At least you wouldn't be walking around like you have a hundred pound weight on your shoulders."

"I don't—"

She squeezed tighter. "Yes, you do, and I wish I knew a way to fix it."

"He needs to get laid."

We both looked up at the same time to see Heath, leaning against the table with his arms crossed over his chest, looking bored.

"That's not what I need."

"Yes, you do," he argued. "When was the last time you even hooked up with a guy?"

The answer sat in the front of my head, taunting me like it always did. Not that I had an intention of admitting I'd been counting the number of days I had practically been celibate since Reagan had walked back into my life. "I don't know."

"Bullshit. You haven't been out or brought a guy home since Reagan showed back up."

"No," I disagreed. "I haven't been going out to protect the band."

"Don't start. You've been sneaking away for years, even when we got bigger. Don't act like it was for us when it was just to protect yourself against rejection."

I stepped out of Mari's grip. "And what the hell am I supposed to do about it?"

"Find a club," he said. "I'm sure there are plenty far enough from here, no one will know it's you with a hat in the dark."

"Then what? Find some random guy on the dance floor to make me feel better? Don't you get it? I don't want anyone but him."

Mari walked over and stood with Heath, resting her head on his shoulder. "You're looking at this all wrong. This isn't about finding the perfect man. This is about sex and only sex. You don't need a connection with the guy unless you plan on dating him later."

"I have no plans to do any of this."

Heath glanced over at Mari, then back at me. "You *need* to do this. Otherwise, we're never getting another song recorded if this shit continues. You need to get laid. Hell, we *all* need you to get laid. And it doesn't matter two shits about who the guy is. All that matters is that you get some. If you find someone you have more than a physical attraction to, great. If not, no big deal. That's why they call it a one-night stand."

It had been forever since I'd been with anyone. First, it had to do with putting so much work into the band to notice. Then it became about time, but neither made me completely push dating to the back corner. Now, I constantly looked over my shoulder, hoping Reagan didn't figure out my secret. They were right. I couldn't live the rest of my life pining after my best friend. Some day he was going to find a woman to settle down with and marry. If I kept waiting for that magical day he noticed me, I wouldn't be able to handle when the day arrived that he found someone.

Reagan was never going to be mine and as much as it hurt, it was the reality I needed to accept to get on with my life. There was someone out there for me, and I'd never find him if I didn't try. The question was how did I find that person without giving away who I was?

"Fine. You're right, I need to get out without Reagan." I ran a hand over my face, knowing the truth but hating the reality of it all.

"You need to give other guys a chance," Mari warned.

"And how am I supposed to do that without someone recognizing me? Every day our pictures are plastered in more places. Anyone who has social media and follows us will know who I am."

She shrugged. "Maybe, but I'm sure there are things you can do to downplay that. Like you said, they'd have to follow us."

"If anyone recognizes you, tell them you get mistaken for him a lot. Unless it's different in the straight club scene, people don't go out to figure out who is telling the truth. They want to drink, dance, and fuck at the end of the night if they're lucky," Heath offered.

That made me chuckle and roll my eyes. "I'm pretty sure we all have the same basic needs."

"My point." Heath stood and moved to the door. "Now let's get back in there and get these songs recorded. Sawyer has plans tonight."

Heath stepped out into the hall as Mari came up beside me and looped her arm through mine. "You need a night out. Leave all that shit at home tonight and just go out and have fun."

The first words out of my mouth were almost *I'll try*, then I realized the way her eyes were sparkling up at me, she had hope for things I didn't. Then again, I wouldn't know until I tried. Maybe if I gave someone a chance I'd finally find the guy to get my mind off Reagan.

I pulled the phone from my pocket, opening up the Internet to find the closest gay club. If there was any place I would avoid, it happened to be any establishment in the city. A little over an hour away sat a club that looked like it might work. The reviews online made it look very dark and dim in the place. I'd be able to hide and hopefully find a man to help me forget Reagan. At least for one night. More than one night just happened to be a bonus.

SAWYER

How did I let myself get talked into this?

Heath and Mari had a point. If I didn't get laid soon I was going to get sloppy and give myself away. The more time I spent with Reagan, the harder it became to keep my secret. There were many nights I found myself reaching out to touch him only to pull my hand back mere seconds before my fingers connected with him. So there I was in a bar an hour from home, looking for a quick fuck.

No one will see who you are in a place like that.

Reds, yellows, and blues flashed throughout the room in time with the throbbing music. I could barely make out the faces of the people a few feet in front of me. With the baseball hat pulled low, they were right, I'd never be recognized there. I walked up to the bar and ordered a shot of vodka. Anything to help me forget the man back in his office working late. I dropped the cash onto the bar and tipped my head back, letting the warm liquid slide down my throat.

"Your ass is meant for fucking," a deep voice said as warm breath blew over my ear.

The heat of his body burned through my shirt. I set the glass back onto the bar and turned to face the guy whose interest I'd caught. An inch or so shorter than me, his hair was dark, but I couldn't tell the exact color in the pulsing lights. Heavy muscles were visible beneath the tight white T-shirt covering his chest.

I lifted a brow. "And what if I said I liked to do the fucking?"

A sexy smirk tilted the corner of his lip. "I'd say I have an ass for fucking too."

He turned around slowly, giving me an incredible view of an ass that was most definitely made for fucking. I didn't want to think about the similarities between this guy and Reagan. For one night I wanted to forget it all and have fun.

"Seems you do. Follow me." I took his hand and led him to the dance floor.

When we reached the edge of the gyrating bodies, I turned toward him and moved him close. Our bodies began to move to the pounding beat. The low bass thumped in time with the pulsing of my cock as it hardened with each slide of his body. Warm lips touched my ear.

"Kyle," he whispered.

"Steven."

It was a dick move, but the more anonymity I had the better. He cupped the back of my neck and lowered his lips to mine, our bodies still moving in sync. The moment his tongue touched my lips, I opened to let him in. The metal of his tongue piercing caught my attention immediately. I could only imagine how it would feel against the base of my cock. Needing to feel more, I wrapped my hands around his ass and held him closer, letting our bodies connect from our chest to thighs.

Song after song changed. We danced and kissed. The feel of him against me helped push everything else from my head. I slid my hands up his jean-clad ass, slipping my finger between the fabric and his skin. His hips flexed as my finger slipped into the top of his crack. I needed this more than I realized. My dick pulsed in my jeans.

"I'm pretty sure we both want more than grinding on a dance floor." He reached down and covered my dick with his palm.

"Where to?"

He was right. I wanted to slide my dick into the tight ass beneath my fingers and fuck the guy senseless.

"My roommate is away for the next few days, but it's a drive."

I leaned closer and nipped his earlobe. "Lead the way. It'll give me time to imagine all the things I'm going to do to you once we get there."

"Fuck," he moaned, adjusting himself. "Let's go."

Without another word, I followed Kyle to the parking lot, watching the sexy ass as it swayed in front of me with each step. He hadn't parked far from where I was. Once I saw him get in his car, I turned for mine. Then we were on the road. I followed closely behind to make sure I was heading in the right direction. Reagan kept trying to break into my thoughts, but I pushed them back. Tonight was for me. I'd deal with my feelings for Reagan in the morning. When Kyle turned into the lot for Reagan's apartment complex, I almost shit a brick. I knew Reagan spent his Wednesday nights working late in his office. Most of the members on his team stayed late those nights, too. I'd only been to his place once. His roommate was an absolute dick and Reagan avoided him as much as possible. I prayed he didn't live anywhere near Reagan's apartment.

Eventually, Kyle turned into the parking area and followed the drive down to the last few buildings. I wanted to groan when I realized he'd parked in front of Reagan's building. I glanced at the clock on the dash. One hour. One more hour until the time Reagan normally left. I climbed from my car and couldn't keep myself from glancing around. When I realized we were the only two in the lot, I let my gaze wander back to Kyle. The way his jeans hugged his thighs made my mind go blank to everything but the man in front of me. My dick was hard as a fucking rock and I needed to do something about that besides spending time with my right hand. I stalked him step for step until his back hit the wall of the building. Once again I cupped his ass and dragged his lower body against mine.

"Show me to your place."

He thrust his hips into me and nodded. The door next to him flew open and he pulled me through. We both glanced at the stairs and back at the elevator. With how I felt, there would be plenty of exercise soon enough. The doors slid shut and I didn't bother to wait. I gripped his face in my hands and captured his lips with mine. Strong hands wrapped around my waist and his warm tongue plunged into my mouth. Holy hell we clicked and it was even hotter than it had been at the club. The car ride didn't do shit to calm us down. The doors opened and I moved him out the door without taking my lips from his. I backed him up until his body connected with the wall behind him.

He tore his mouth from mine. "Fuck, that's sexy."

Then he dived in again. Tongues dueling, bodies grinding, it was like we were back in the club without the music. Kyle and I had serious fucking chemistry. It was time to mix the two and create an explosion.

"Motherfucker," a very angry, yet familiar voice shouted.

Both of our heads snapped around. Being gay meant you were always prepared for some homophobic asshole to take exception to what you were doing in your private life. Then again we were still in the hall, but there was no reason we couldn't move to the privacy of his apartment. However, I wasn't prepared at all for what was before me.

Reagan stood in the middle of the hall looking like he wanted to murder something. Hands clenched into fists at his sides, his jaw ticking as he ground his teeth together. I should have had an hour.

What is he doing here?

My instant reaction was to step back and make excuses. This time that wouldn't work. There was no denying I'd just had my tongue down the guy's throat. And before my brain could catch up and figure out something reasonable to say, my mouth opened wide and said the first thing on my mind.

"What are you doing here?"

His eyes blazed. "Are you fucking kidding me? What am I doing here? *I* live here. What the hell are *you* doing here?"

I fumbled for words, but this time nothing came out.

He shook his head. “You know what, I don’t give a shit. Apparently you still have secrets you want to keep.” He stormed down the hall toward his apartment near the end.

“Reagan, wait,” I called out, hoping he’d listen. He kept walking.

Kyle narrowed his eyes at me. “You’re with someone?”

“No. He’s a friend.”

Kyle scoffed. “This looks like way more than friendship.”

“I swear it’s not. He didn’t know I was gay.” I saw Reagan reach for his door. “Goddammit, Reagan, let me explain.”

He stopped moving.

I turned back to Kyle, who was now watching me, curiosity lighting his eyes. “Can you give me ten minutes to talk to him?”

He pulled a key from his pocket and stepped around me to the door next to us. “Don’t worry about me. Looks like you’re going to need more than ten minutes. But that’s okay. You have more baggage than I’m ready to deal with.” He glanced up and down my body. “Too bad. I think we could have had fun. If you ever find yourself alone, you know where to find me, but you need to settle the tension between you two first.” He slipped my phone from my back pocket and I unlocked it. In a daze, I watched as he programmed his number and handed it back to me.

“Thank you and I’m sorry about tonight.”

He put the key into the lock. “Don’t worry about it. Shit happens. Although I gotta say this was a first for me.”

The door shut behind him and I looked up to see Reagan still waiting at the end of the hall. I walked slowly to him, afraid if I moved too fast he'd jump inside and lock the door. When I reached him, his back was straight as an arrow.

"Please talk to me."

"I'm not sure there's much to talk about. You apparently didn't think I was important enough to know the truth."

"It's not that." I glanced around the hall, noticing how exposed we were to anyone coming and going to their apartments. It didn't matter to me I was just making out in the same hall, but for some reason I needed to talk to him face-to-face, not from behind a closed door. "Look, I know you and your roommate don't get along. Heath went out with the guys. He won't be home for a while. Please come back to my place so we can talk about this."

His head snapped around. "Does it really fucking matter at this point?"

I placed my hand on his arm and he snatched it away. Bile burned the back of my throat. I knew I couldn't have Reagan the way I wanted him, but I'd been content to have him in my life as a friend. Now I might have ruined everything.

"Please," I begged.

He brushed past me toward the elevator. "Fine. I'll hear what you have to say, but I doubt there's much that will convince me you aren't a complete asshole."

The doors opened and we climbed inside. The silence engulfing us added even more weight to the hundred pounds it felt like were on my shoulders. He stood in the corner as far as he could get from me, with his arms crossed over his chest and a vein bulging at his temple. The elevator hit the floor and for a second I thought about offering to drive and stopped myself. I needed the car ride to collect my thoughts.

I climbed in the driver's seat and hit the gas. How did things get so screwed up in a matter of minutes? One second I was getting sex for the first time in a while and the next thing I knew everything in my life was falling apart before my eyes.

I pulled into the driveway and climbed from the car, more than aware that Reagan wasn't right behind me. My stomach flipped, tying itself into knots. I went inside to wait. Either he was coming or not and having this conversation on my front lawn didn't sit well with me. It would be uncomfortable enough already. I paced the room until I heard the front door slam into the frame. Reagan stalked forward.

SAWYER

“Is that why you fucking left?”

Reagan stormed forward, his hands landing hard against my chest. I stumbled backward, lucky to catch my footing before I fell on the table.

“Why the hell wouldn’t you tell me?”

Staring at the veins bulging in his neck, the way his eyes narrowed to slits, and his hands clenched into fists, I couldn’t believe he actually needed an answer to that question. I stepped forward and shoved him back a few steps.

“Why didn’t I tell you?” I shook my head. “You’re fucking pissed at me. And you wonder why I kept it to myself.”

“Fuck you. You know I’m not pissed because you’re gay. I’m pissed you didn’t tell me the truth from the beginning.”

Reagan spun on his heel and stormed across the room to the door. “Is that why you ran?”

I raked a hand through my hair. My eyes held his. "Yeah. I ran because *I'm* gay and I wanted something I couldn't have."

Why the hell did I say that? Reagan wasn't dumb. He would know exactly what I meant. I might as well have said *I love you.* I flopped down on the couch. Acid burned the back of my throat. How could I admit so much? Closing my eyes, I leaned my head back, unwilling to watch the disgust take hold of his face. "And I was afraid you'd freak out on me and leave."

Silence filled the space. The same awkward silence that once settled between us when Reagan showed up at the meet and greet that first night. Footsteps sounded as Reagan moved to the door. Opening my eyes, I lifted my head and stood. He laid his hand on the knob.

With a quick glance over his shoulder, he shot one last dagger into my chest. "You're a dick to keep something like this from me. Apparently, I valued our friendship more than you, because I'd never fucking leave you to deal with that shit on your own. And I'd *never* keep secrets from you."

Before I had a chance to respond, he flung the door open, its frame rattling as he slammed it behind him.

For fuck's sake.

Things had gone to shit. I knew the risks when I went looking for a quick fuck. What I hadn't expected was for Reagan, of all people, to find me. Pain radiated up my arm as my knuckles connected with the wall next to me. I grabbed my hand, flexing my fingers and hoping to God I didn't break anything. The last thing I needed at the moment was to lose the only other thing that mattered. Besides the blood covering my hand, everything else seemed to be fine.

The front door opened and for one brief moment I thought Reagan had come back. That I hadn't ruined our friendship once again. Long dark hair came into view. *Heath.* His gaze zeroed in on the way I held my hand.

"What the hell did you do?"

I shrugged. "Punched a wall."

He walked over and took my hand in his, pressing on the edges of my knuckles and fingers. "Looks like only a few cuts. You need to ice it before it swells."

I went to the kitchen, bypassing the fridge. A beer wouldn't do after the shit storm that just happened. The sound of the front door shutting reached my ears. I yanked the liquor cabinet open. The half-filled bottle of tequila was front and center on the shelf. Ironic and very fitting at the same time. I grabbed the bottle.

"Damn it, Sawyer. Forget the liquor and ice your fucking hand. We have to play tomorrow."

He yanked the towel off the counter and filled it with ice. Ignoring him, I pulled the top off the bottle, lifting it to my lips. Heath grabbed my hand, holding the ice over my abraded knuckles, while I took another long sip of the warm liquid. The burn as it slid down my throat helped me calm down enough that I took the towel of ice from Heath and held it. I put the bottle under my arm and went back to the living room. After setting the bottle on the floor, I dropped my ass down onto the couch.

Heath followed me, taking the seat in the recliner opposite me. "Wanna tell me why you're punching walls and drinking tequila? You hate that shit, unless you're trying to get wasted."

I laughed humorlessly and took another swig. “That’s exactly what I’m trying to do.”

“Doesn’t explain why. What happened? I thought you were going out to find a guy to hook up with.”

“Oh, I did.” Another swallow. I set the bottle on my knee. “At least until Reagan caught us.”

Heath’s eyes went wide. “What the hell was he doing an hour outside of town?”

“He wasn’t. The guy I picked up happened to live in the same building as Reagan. He caught us making out against the wall next to his door.”

He glanced at my hand. “So you waited until you drove home to punch a wall.”

“I asked Reagan to come here so we could talk without dealing with his asshole roommate.”

Heath rolled his eyes, as I took another drink. “There are so many things to say about how stupid all of these decisions were, but I know you’re not going to remember any of it tomorrow.” He stood and nodded toward the bottle. “You’ll regret that in the morning.”

“Right now, I don’t give a shit.”

He shook his head and walked down the hall to his room. The door slammed shut. Who the hell was he to judge? The one secret I’d kept from Reagan was finally out in the open and exactly like I feared, he left when the truth came out. I’d known all along Reagan would never be mine. I was completely in love with him. Everything about him called to me. It didn’t matter that he was straight. I couldn’t keep my thoughts off him, even when I knew I couldn’t have him. Hell, it was part of the reason I’d left. But that had never been my biggest fear. I never wanted to see the disgust and anger for me on his face. Leaving seemed like the better choice. Maybe it was, maybe it wasn't. At least I didn't have to wonder and worry about what would happen anymore.

I settled farther into the couch, making sure the ice stayed put, and continued to drink myself into oblivion. The hangover would be worth being free of the pain. At least for a little while.

Reagan

The light in the living room was still on as I stared at the house. Someone was awake. It was the question of who that kept my ass rooted to the seat of my car. I'd been there for over an hour watching.

I'd driven around for a bit, before stopping at my apartment to change. Hitting something sounded perfect. Two hours and a heavy bag later I was able to think clearly since the first moment I saw Sawyer kissing that guy. After I'd calmed down, I realized how badly I'd fucked up when I walked out on Sawyer. My best friend, and I treated him like he was a parasite. I had no idea what it was like to let your friends and family know you're gay. Hell, why it mattered to anyone else who you were sleeping with never made any sense to me. As long as it was in your bedroom, why did someone care?

But, tonight.

Tonight, I did a shitty job showing Sawyer that was how I felt. And it had nothing to do with him being gay. I was pissed at being left out. Not that he'd come out and told me. I saw it with my own eyes. Sawyer hadn't seen me when he walked out of the elevator. I'd left work early, exhausted from the last few late nights hanging out with Sawyer. What I hadn't expected was to see Sawyer with his lips pressed to another guy's.

When it finally registered, I froze in my tracks. Sawyer shoved the guy up against the wall, their mouths pressed together. There was a peek of tongue as their lips moved against each other. I couldn't move. My eyes glued to the men making out against the wall. Sawyer's fingers gripped the other man's bicep in a not so gentle grip. My brain couldn't believe what I was seeing. Sawyer was gay? How did I not know?

I kept my eyes glued to them. It was not a sweet makeout session in the dark. It was rough and passionate. As I wrapped my mind around it all, the more pissed off I got. The way they held each other. Sawyer's sole focus on the man before him. Something I wanted. Not that I could explain why.

Of course we had things away from our time together. I had my job at the law firm. He had Jaded Ivory. But every other moment we spent together. Almost like the last few years had never happened. Something about the way they held each other made me want to drag Sawyer away from him.

Fuck.

I was jealous.

Jealous of a man I never met. A man who was kissing my best friend. Of being left in the dark.

When Sawyer hadn't heard the elevator at first, I froze in my tracks. My tongue was tied in knots. Once I regained control, I couldn't help but lose my shit on him. He'd lied to me. I almost didn't come when he asked me to meet him at his place. The longer I drove and visions of what could have happened between them had I not interrupted ran through my head, my anger grew. By the time I pulled up in front of his house, blood roared through my ears.

I let my anger and jealousy, something I wasn't ready to think about, get the better of me. There were two choices. I could go home knowing this was my choice to walk away or I could get my ass in the house and talk to him. I reached for the keys to turn the engine over and yanked them out instead. There was no question. I wouldn't lose Sawyer over this.

Both of his and Heath's cars were parked out front. Not that Heath being home would stop me. I walked up to the door and knocked, afraid to wake up whoever might be sleeping. It might kill me, but if no one answered, I'd wait until morning.

"'ome in," Sawyer's voice groggily called through the door.

Shit. I hadn't wanted to wake him. I pushed the door open and realized I didn't wake him. Sawyer sat on the couch with an open bottle of tequila on the table next to him. God, I was an asshole. I never thought Sawyer would touch tequila again after that night. Yet, there he sat completely shit-faced.

And it was my fault.

He cracked one eye open. "What are you doing here?"

His words were slurred, but that didn't stop him from picking up the bottle and bringing it back to his lips.

"I came to talk. How much have you had to drink?"

He let the bottle drop back onto the table. "Talk? Talk about what?" He pushed himself off the couch. "How much you hate me?"

Sawyer stepped toward me and stumbled. Before he could hit the ground, I rushed forward and wrapped my arms around his waist, hauling him to standing. I held him there, afraid he might fall again. His eyes connected with mine.

"I could never hate you."

Sawyer's eyes dropped to my lips. His words from earlier replayed in my head. *I wanted something I couldn't have.* I'd been too pissed off to realize what he'd been saying. The words died in my throat as I watched him. Everything was happening in slow motion. I knew what was coming, but I was powerless to stop it. And truthfully, I didn't want to stop it.

Sawyer's lips covered mine. And an electric jolt ran through me. I expected it to feel weird, another man's lips on mine, but this was Sawyer. The man I'd rather spend time with over anyone else. And it didn't. His lips were softer than I expected. But he was drunk. I knew I should stop him. I didn't want him to blame himself in the morning for what happened.

I lifted my hands to his biceps to move him backward. Instead, I pulled him closer to me. His tongue grazed over my bottom lip. My head was spinning. Without a thought, I moved my hand to fist in the back of his hair and opened my mouth, letting him inside. A fog filled my head. There was only me and him. The rough scratch of his scruff made me hold him tighter to me. Our tongues twisted and twirled around each other. I could taste the tequila on his lips.

Suddenly, my back hit the wall. I was so lost, I hadn't even realized he moved me. He lifted his head and cupped my face with his hands. For the briefest of moments, I thought he was going to walk away and disappointment burned through me. Then he tilted his head and came back in. The fire began again. I held him tight, letting my tongue tangle with his once more. His hips thrust forward, his hard cock sliding against mine, and I groaned. My dick was hard too, and oh fuck, it felt good sliding against his. Confusion started to seep in, but I pushed it away. I'd figure out what it all meant later. Right then, I wanted to live in the moment.

When Sawyer pulled back again, we were both panting. His eyes were hooded. I couldn't stop my eyes from dropping to see the outline of his dick behind his pants. He ran a hand over his face, swaying on his feet.

"I'm sorry," he whispered.

I watched him stumble backward, barely making it to the couch. He dropped down and leaned his head back, closing his eyes. And I was frozen to the spot. I didn't know what to do or say. My head was a mess. I forced my feet to move forward. I wouldn't let him feet guilty over what happened. I was the sober one. I could have stopped it.

My hands shook as I walked toward that couch. I had no idea what to say to him, but I had to say something. I stood in front of him. "Sawyer, look at me." When he didn't respond, I shook him, only to watch his head loll to the side.

Fucker had passed out on me.

Rolling my eyes, I bent at the waist and threw him over my shoulder in a fireman's carry. Maybe it was the chicken shit way out, but a part of me was relieved we didn't have to talk about any of this until morning. It gave me a chance to figure out what the hell just happened and why even just carrying him to his room made me think about doing kissing him again. Covers bunched at the bottom of the bed where he'd kicked them off this morning. Some things never changed. The man was still a slob. I laid him on the bed and pulled the covers up over him. There would be one hell of a hangover in the morning.

Afraid he'd puke in the middle of the night, I grabbed the trash can from the other side of his room and set it next to the bed. In his condition, there was no way he was making it to the bathroom. He moved his hand to his chest and for the first time I noticed the swelling around his knuckles. *Shit*. Best guess, he'd hit something. His hands were his life. There were small cuts at the edges. It didn't look broken. At least I hoped like hell it wasn't.

The wall between us just kept getting higher. Was it worth the climb?

With everything taken care of, I stood in the middle of the dark room, wondering what to do with myself. Home wasn't far. I could come back in the morning. A part of me feared if I went home, I'd avoid dealing with it all and only cause Sawyer more pain.

Fuck it.

It wouldn't be the first time I slept next to him. We'd done it a hundred times as kids. I toed off my shoes and lay down on top of the covers. No need to give him the wrong idea when he woke up. Then again, what was the wrong idea? I kissed him back tonight. His tongue was in my mouth and I got hard. Painfully hard. Just thinking about it made me reach down and adjust my growing erection. The craziest part? I wasn't freaking out about it. Not yet, anyway.

What the hell was going on in my head?

I stared into the darkness. The light from the street lamp cast shadows through the blinds. There were frames on the dresser and a drum kit in the corner. I had no doubt if I looked around the floor I'd find at least five or more sets of drumsticks lying around.

Sawyer grunted in his sleep. My attention was immediately drawn back to the man next to me. Not once in my entire life had I noticed another man. But I'd noticed Sawyer over the last few months. Little things here and there I'd brushed off as being happy to spend time with him again. Apparently that wasn't the case.

And never had I had the desire to stick my tongue down a guy's throat. Then again it was Sawyer, and I guaranteed if he were awake, I'd want to do it again. His lean muscles outlined by the white sheet and I thought about the way he boxed me against the wall. No woman would have the size or strength to do that. For some reason, that thought alone made me harder than anything.

I liked kissing a guy.

I liked his hard body against mine.

I liked kissing *Sawyer*.

Maybe all of it had to do with seeing Sawyer with that other guy. Whatever it was, I had to know why. Questions ran through my head over and over throughout the night. Sleep was a pipe dream at that point. With so many thoughts and feelings I didn't understand, I knew the only way I'd figure out an answer was with Sawyer. I had to know the reason. It didn't matter that I needed sleep for my meeting, but at the same rate I doubted I'd be there the next day. I'd deal with that later. For once, work didn't seem all that important.

Every time Sawyer moved or made a noise, my whole body reacted to the sound. I held my hands tightly to my side to keep from reaching over and touching him again. If Sawyer wanted to discover this with me, he needed to have a clear head. The night passed slowly. More light began to filter through the blinds and I waited.

"Shit," Sawyer groaned from the other side of the bed.

Time to figure out what last night meant.

SAWYER

Everything hurt.

Including my eyes, which I kept tightly shut. I knew it was morning by the bright lights reflecting off my lids. What I really wanted was to fall back asleep and back into the dream where Reagan didn't hate me. Where he actually wanted me. I moved my head slightly on the pillow and instantly regretted it. How much did I drink last night? My head pounded and my stomach churned. I froze, no desire to puke up last night's bad decisions.

The bed moved again and I groaned.

"Tequila has never been good to you."

My eyes snapped open. The light burned, but I slowly turned my head to the right.

Reagan was lying in my bed.

In *my* bed.

"Morning." He didn't take his eyes off me.

"What are you—"

Images, most blurry, flooded my head. Lots of tequila. Reagan showing up. More tequila. Almost falling. Me kissing Reagan. I clenched my eyes shut. Not just kissing him. Attacking him as I pinned him up against a wall. *Fucking hell.* Tequila really wasn't good to me.

"Sawyer?" A warm hand landed on my shoulder.

My muscles tightened, heat radiating out from where his skin touched mine. The images replayed themselves again and again. "Please tell me it was a dream."

"Sawyer…"

Something about the gravely tone of his voice made me open my eyes. "Please," I begged.

He shook his head. "Not a dream."

My stomach lurched and I threw my feet over the bed. The trash can was already there waiting for me. I grabbed it and emptied my stomach into the can. It had been bad enough Reagan saw me with Kyle. Kissing him had to be the dumbest thing I'd ever done. I lowered the can to floor to the get the smell out of my face and leaned my elbows on my knees. I wasn't ready to face him yet. The bed shifted.

What the fuck had I been thinking?

That's right, I hadn't. My man Jose did all it for me.

"Feel better?"

I shook my head slightly, bracing myself for the pain that came with it. "Not really. No."

"Can I get you something?"

I scoffed and glanced over my shoulder. "A memory eraser?" I said it hoping he would laugh. We could joke about tequila and bad decisions. We'd salvage our friendship. Then I could do everything in my power to forget what it felt like kissing the only man I had ever loved.

He didn't laugh.

"Don't do that. I don't want to forget last night and neither do you."

I turned to face him. He was lying on his side facing me, his head resting in his hand. "Did I miss something when I was drunk last night? Or did you forget you're straight and I'm gay? Why wouldn't you want to forget last night?"

He lifted a brow. "How much do you remember?"

I groaned. "Besides me forcing myself on you?"

"You don't remember everything then."

I turned away from him again, dropping my head into my hands. "I'm not sure I wanna know more."

The bed next to me dipped and I looked over. He smirked. "You look like hell. You're not ready for the conversation I want to have. Go grab a shower, then we'll talk."

There was no trace of the anger from last night in his voice. It was calm. A calm that belied the slight tremor in his hand. I'd fucked everything up last night. My hand clenched into a fist and I immediately released it, hissing out a breath. A quick glance down and I recalled my fist connecting with the wall downstairs. I lifted it to inspect the damage. The swelling wasn't as bad as I feared. I opened and closed my fingers a few times.

"Will you be able to play tonight?" His brows pulled together.

Concern and calm didn't go at all with the 'fuck off' I braced myself for. Made me wonder what conversation he wanted to have.

"Reagan, I—"

He shook his head. "Go get in the shower. We'll talk when you're done."

He took both hands, placing them on my back, and pushed me up until I was standing. The move wasn't out of the ordinary. When one of us wanted to go somewhere we had no problem forcing the other to get a move on. Everything was different today. Each touch set me on fire. A fire I knew I'd have to find a way to extinguish by the end of the day. I'd had my tongue in his mouth and even though I knew it would never happen, I wanted more. I wanted his hands on me, not only to get me to the shower. I wanted them to wrap around my cock and jerk me to release. I glanced back at him.

"Go," he ordered.

Nothing would get him to tell me what was going through his head. My stomach rocked. I didn't think I had enough strength to listen to him tell me he was done. A small part of me thought maybe I was better off if he did. I was completely aware that our friendship would never be the same. Even if a part of it could be salvaged.

I made my way past Heath's door. He had a hell of a lot of explaining to do. Like why the hell I woke up with Reagan in my bed. He knew I didn't handle tequila well and he let him in anyway. I opened the door and closed it quietly behind me. I didn't need an audience for this. Fucker was fast asleep with no care in the world. I grabbed the deodorant from the dresser and chucked it at him. It hit him right in the back.

"What the fuck?" He flipped over, glaring at me. "What the hell was that for?"

"Really, dickhead? I woke up with Reagan in my bed and you wonder why I threw shit at you?"

He sat up. "He's here?"

"What do you mean 'he's here?' Didn't you let him in?"

He scrubbed a hand over his face. "Nope. I left your drunk ass on the couch and went to bed."

"Then how the hell..."

Heath's eyes traveled from my head down. "Jesus, you look like shit and you smell like a cheap-ass bar. My guess is *you* let him and don't remember it."

I leaned back against the door, closing my eyes. Hammers pounded in my brain. "Apparently, there's a lot about last night I don't remember."

"Told ya to put Jose away. He's never been your friend."

"Yeah, yeah. How was I supposed to know he'd come back? I figured I'd wallow in self-pity for a while and deal with the hangover today. I didn't plan on sticking my tongue down his throat."

Heath's mouth dropped open. "You did what?"

"I fucking kissed him. Of all the stupid ass—"

He held up both hands. "Wait. You're telling me, you kissed him and he still stayed the night?"

My head thumped against the door. "Yep."

"Then what are you doing in my room? Go back there and get what you've always wanted." He looked at me again. "Umm...maybe you better shower first."

I scoffed. "That's where I was headed when I stopped in here. Says he wants me to have a clear head to talk."

"Then go get your ass in the shower and get the fuck back to your room." He pulled the covers up and lay back down.

"Even if by some miracle that was a possibility, I can't..."

Heath cracked one eye open. "Yes, you can. It's why Mari and I sent you out last night."

"Fuck, please don't tell me you were hoping this would happen."

He opened both eyes fully. "No. Reagan finding out is just a bonus."

My hands clenched into fists. Would they really want me to out myself when I wasn't ready? He didn't seem to notice and kept speaking.

"You don't need to keep hiding who you are. Shit, Monty and Jackson don't even know. I've been begging you for years to tell them the truth. There's no way you're ever going to be happy keeping a part of yourself hidden. No matter how much success we get. Even if you don't want the whole world to know, finding someone means you won't have to hide anything from the people who give a shit about you."

I opened my mouth to say something, but he didn't give me a chance.

"Now get your alcohol ridden ass out of my room and in the shower. Find out what he has to say."

He turned on his side and pulled the cover over his head. More confused than ever, I stepped out of Heath's room and glanced down the hall at my own door. I didn't think there was a chance in hell Reagan would want me the way I wanted him. I'd already walked away from him once in my life because of my secrets, I wouldn't do it again. If anyone was going to leave, it was going to have to be him.

I went in the bathroom and turned on the shower. Maybe Heath and Mari were right. Keeping a part of who I was locked away wasn't helping anyone. Even the songs I wrote had taken on an edge. I'd chalked it up to what the fans liked. I told Mari before that I didn't want my personal life to hurt Jaded Ivory. Didn't mean I had to keep Jackson and Monty in the dark. They deserved to know, no matter who I was or wasn't involved with.

The tile was cold on my feet as steam filled the room. I reached for my toothbrush first. God, I needed to stay the hell away from tequila. Nothing good came of it. After popping some ibuprofen, I stepped under the warm spray. The hot water beat down on me, driving away some of the hangover. The ibuprofen helped with the rest. By the time I reached for the towel I felt almost human again. There was a low throb in my head, but that was about it. After some water and greasy food, I would be right as rain.

My hand covered the door handle and froze. I came to the shower empty-handed, which meant I now had to walk back to my room with only a towel around my waist and Reagan waiting. If he didn't already want to run, he would now.

I sighed and pulled the door open. There wasn't a damn thing I could do about it now. I didn't want to wait any longer to hear what conversation he wanted to have. For a brief moment, I thought about hiding in Heath's room again, but he'd only kick my ass out. Time to pull on my big boy pants and face the consequences of my actions. I pushed through my door and found Reagan sitting on the edge of my bed where I'd left him earlier.

His dark hair was tousled like he'd been raking his fingers through it and for a moment I was jealous of those fingers. What I wouldn't give to run my fingers through his thick locks and see just how soft they were. I shut the door behind me, moving directly to my dresser. The least I could do was pull on a pair of boxers before this whole situation got any more awkward.

I opened the drawer, searching for something to wear, when two arms boxed me in. I could feel the heat of his chest against my back.

"What are you—"

Reagan grabbed my shoulder and spun me around. Before I had a second to process what was happening, his mouth was on mine.

Holy shit.

Reagan, the man I'd wanted my most of my adult life, had his mouth pressed to mine. It wasn't a dream. Reagan had his lips pressed to mine.

What was he doing?

He'd lost his mind. Then his tongue moved across my bottom lip and I ceased to think at all. My lips parted, his tongue slipping between them to tangle with mine. I moved my hands up his chest and into his hair. The texture was softer than I imagined. How could I have forgotten what his felt like? Desire pulsed through every nerve ending. My body was on fire. This man, this very straight man, was kissing me.

That thought brought me back to the present. This was a really fucking bad idea. I placed my hands against his chest and shoved him away.

"What are you doing?" I panted, trying to get my body under control. There was no hiding the erection the simple kiss caused with the flimsy bath towel around my hips.

"Kissing you." The words were so simple and yet so foreign my brain had trouble processing them for a moment.

I skirted around him, grabbing a pair of boxers on the way by. With the towel still around my hips, I yanked them up and kept my distance from the temping man in front of me. "And why do you think that's a good idea?"

"You're telling me you don't want my mouth on yours?"

I shook my head. "How much did I have to drink last night?" I couldn't fathom a situation where Reagan was the one trying to seduce me.

He took one step forward and I took one back. "More than you needed, but alcohol has nothing to do with this." He moved his finger between the two of us.

"I think it does. Or did you forget somewhere between last night and this morning you don't like guys?"

"I like *you*."

Oh, fuck. I wasn't strong enough for this. "As a friend."

He took another step forward. I matched him step for step until my back hit the far wall of my bedroom. I glanced around the room, trying to figure out a way to escape. Apparently, I was in the Twilight Zone. That or a really bad horror flick and I was the next poor schmuck to die. "Would you stop trying to get away from me?"

I threw my hands up in an attempt to keep him an arm's length away from me. "I will not let one bad decision ruin our friendship. I did that when I left."

"You won't ruin our friendship."

Reagan

Sawyer clenched his eyes shut. His back planted firmly against the wall. I had the feeling if he could move through it he would. I probably shouldn't have kissed him without talking to him first, but something about his lean muscles drew me to him. The way his arms and shoulders tightened as he tried to keep the towel snug around his waist. I couldn't stop myself. He tasted ten times better this morning.

His hard cock was perfectly outlined in the small towel. My hands itched to drop it to the floor and take him in my palm. Something I'd never experienced and had to understand. "You won't ruin our friendship."

He scoffed and looked at me. "Says the man who left in a rage last night."

Regret filled me. I moved backward and dropped down onto the bed. "We've shared everything with each other from the time we were ten. And then you keep something like this from me. I shouldn't have gotten pissed, but it hurt to think you didn't trust me. I'm sorry I acted like a dick."

He opened his eyes and looked at me. "So it has nothing to do with me being gay?"

"Not a goddamn thing. Do you think I would have kissed you if it did?"

He ran a hand through his wet hair. A bead of water slid down the side of his face and onto his chest. "Fine, you have a point."

"Good. Now come over here." I moved over, making room for him next to me on the bed.

He put his hands up. "I don't think so. Let me get dressed and we'll go have breakfast."

"No. I want you to come over here."

He shook his head. "Not happening."

I spread my legs a little wider, adjusting my still hard cock. I couldn't help notice the way his eyes zeroed in on my hand. The irony wasn't lost on me that it was the straight guy trying to seduce the gay guy. Okay, maybe not so straight. But until Sawyer got his ass over here, I'd never get an answer to that question. "Why not?"

"'Cause it's just not gonna happen." Sawyer pushed away from the wall, walking toward his dresser.

"I want to understand."

"Understand what?" He made a big show of pulling clothes from the drawers.

"You sure as shit know what I mean. I want to know why my dick is as hard as steel right now."

He turned to face me and sighed. "I can't be your experiment. I won't be."

I narrowed my eyes. "Who says you'll just be an experiment?"

"You've never been with a man and I'm supposed to assume you suddenly want to be with me?" He turned his back toward me, tugging on a pair of basketball shorts.

I could have argued with him, but I knew when Sawyer got like this, words wouldn't be enough. I had to show him I meant it. I stood and walked up behind him, placing my hands on his shoulders. "Last night *you* kissed me and I've thought of nothing else since. There has to be a reason and I want to understand." Tightening my grip, I spun him around to face me. "You also said you left because you couldn't have what you wanted. Here I am, waiting for you."

He laughed, but I could hear the tension lacing the sound. "Think pretty highly of yourself?"

I took a step closer until our bodies were aligned with one another. "Not really. Just stating facts. I know you want me."

My eyes never left his, and for the briefest of moments, I thought he'd push me away. My fingers itched to grab him and pull him to me. The green of his eyes seemed to grow darker. His breathing sped up. A vein pulsed at the base of his neck. The silence closed in on us.

"Fuck it," he whispered, slipping his fingers into my hair and dragging my mouth to his.

This time I didn't wait, parting my lips and letting his tongue slide inside to tangle with mine. My heart hammered in my chest. I gripped his biceps, no fear of hurting him. The kiss was unlike any other, each of our mouths fighting for dominance over the other. Sawyer plundered my mouth, making everything else disappear. I hadn't realized he walked us back to the bed, until the back of my knees came in contact with it. I dropped down on top, Sawyer landing on me. The weight was welcome.

He lifted his mouth from mine. “Want me to stop?”

I hesitated for the briefest of seconds. Sawyer was a man, I shouldn’t want him, but for reasons that were unclear to me, I desperately did. I pushed my doubts aside.

“No.” I was shocked to hear the rough timbre to my voice.

Sawyer punched his hips forward, his hard cock rubbing against my own. A tortured groan escaped my lips.

“No?” he asked again, a light to his eyes I hadn’t seen in weeks. The smug bastard knew what he was doing.

“Now who’s cocky?” He did it again and my hips thrust up to meet his. “Fuck, no.”

Sawyer ran his hand down my T-shirt to the hem, fingering the fabric. “Can I touch you?”

His fingers were so close to my aching shaft, I wanted to grab his hand and cover my dick with it. “Yes,” I hissed out.

Sawyer, the damn tease, ran his fingers along the edge of the shirt, skimming the skin right over the waistband of my jeans. Tired of his games, I reached behind me, drawing the shirt over my head. I tossed it to the floor and skimmed my hands down the smooth skin of his back. “Touch me, you damn tease.”

He smirked and lowered his head to my nipple. I sucked in a breath when his lips closed around it. An inferno built inside me from each simple touch. I never imagined something so simple being so erotic. “I want to touch you everywhere.”

"Fuck, if it feels that good, you can touch me anywhere."

He lowered his hand to the button of my jeans and in the blink of an eye, he had them unfastened and was reaching past my boxer briefs to free my cock. The head bounced off my stomach, pre-cum leaking from the tip. He took hold of my cock, rubbing his thumb over the head.

"God, you're sexier than I ever imagined."

When he bent his head and ran his tongue over my crown I thought I saw stars. Nothing had ever felt as good as what Sawyer did to me. He had me tied in knots. He stroked once, then twice. On the third time, I couldn't hold in the moan of desire anymore. Every nerve ending was electrically charged, waiting for the explosion.

"I need to come," I begged.

"Your wish is my command."

He bent his head over my crown and sucked my entire dick into his mouth. I felt myself hit the back of his throat. My eyes rolled into the back of my head. For a moment, I forgot to breathe. Nothing compared to a hot, wet mouth wrapped around your dick, but this was much more. Sawyer knew the exact pressure to drive me out of my mind. A groan left his lips, the vibrations doing even more damage to my tenuous control. The sheet bunched between my fingers of one hand, while I slipped the other into his hair, gripping tightly to the soft strands. At that point, I was along for whatever ride Sawyer wanted to take me on.

He worked my aching shaft like a master, taking deep, greedy pulls and playing with my balls at the same time. When he let my dick fall from his mouth, I almost groaned in response. He lowered his head and sucked one of my balls into his mouth. My hips thrust up, trying to get more friction on my dick.

"Impatient, aren't we?"

Impatient? The guy was driving me out of my fucking mind. "Make me come," I ordered.

"Bossy, I like it."

He lowered his head again, taking my aching shaft back into his mouth and using his hand to jerk me off in this magical flick of his wrist that had my knuckles turning white as I clenched my fist in his hair. My balls pulled tight to my body, the suction increasing until I couldn't hold back anymore.

"Shit, I'm gonna come."

I expected Sawyer to pull his mouth and jerk me through my release. What I didn't expect was for him to lower his mouth to the root of my shaft and suck even harder. The climax sizzled up my balls before I had the chance to stop it. Jet after jet of hot come shot into his mouth. Lifting his eyes to mine, I watched as he swallowed down each and every drop of it.

My breath came harder like I'd just run a fucking marathon as he pulled his mouth off me. I dropped a hand over my eyes, trying to get myself under control. I lay there panting. Not a chance in hell would I be able to move anytime in the future. As my breathing settled, I noticed the room was awfully quiet. If I hadn't known better, I would have thought I was alone.

Moving my hand, I saw Sawyer sitting on the edge of the bed, his back to me. Not willing to let him put distance between us, especially not after what just happened, I moved to my knees and laid my hands on his shoulders. Was it the right thing to do? I had no freaking clue, but it was the best I could come up with. The moment my fingers touched his skin he flinched.

Something still had him freaked the hell out. A voice in the back of my head yelled that I should be freaked out, but I wasn't. Even if I was, I'd deal with it later.

When he continued to keep his back to me, I let go and moved to sit next to him. His eyes were focused on something across the room. Wrapping my hand around his bicep, I tugged on his arm, forcing him to face me. He tried to keep his gaze over my shoulder, but I wasn't letting that happen. "Dammit, Sawyer. Look at me."

His eyes slowly moved to mine. "I shouldn't have done that."

"Why the hell not?" I couldn't believe what I was hearing. I'd just had the best orgasm of my life and *he* was the one regretting the decision?

"Because it was a bad idea. I knew it, yet I did it anyway."

He ran a hand through his hair and tried to turn away again. I cupped his cheek with my hand and brought his face back to mine, pressing our lips together. For a moment, he sat frozen, his lips unmoving against mine. The second his mouth parted, I slipped my tongue inside, only for him to jerk backward out of my reach. I would have thought his ass was on fire with how quickly he jumped from the bed.

"Stop," he said, backing away from me. "This is wrong."

"Why is it wrong?"

"This is gonna fuck everything up for us again. I'm not sure I can handle it a second time."

I stood up and moved slowly toward him again. I reached out to take his hand and lead him back to the bed, but at the last second pulled back. Instead, I gestured toward the bed. "Would you please come sit down and talk to me?"

He shook his head. "That might be an even worse idea."

I scoffed. "You talk about ruining our friendship, but you can't even sit and talk to me. I'd say that alone isn't a good sign."

He rolled his eyes. It was good to see Sawyer coming back to himself. "I can talk to you, just not in my bedroom."

"Bullshit. We've talked plenty of times hanging out in one of our bedrooms, sitting on the bed."

"That was different."

"Why was it different?"

"Because..."

Chapter Twenty

Sawyer

Because... What the fuck was I supposed to say? Because I'm scared? Because I love you and want us to be together more than my next breath, except you're only dipping your toes into the gay pool not even sure if you want to get all the way wet?

Warm fingers wrapped around mine. I flinched but didn't stop him as he walked us over to the bed.

"You're scared. I get it. I honestly can't explain any of this. I've never come so hard in my life and the fact it was because of a guy terrifies me."

I tried to stand up and move away from him once more. All the words that left his lips were exactly what I feared.

"Wait." He used his grip on my hand to keep me there. "I wasn't done."

I moved my eyes to the other side of the room, unwilling to let him see the pain his words caused. Each and every one of them was like a punch to the gut. Many more and I wouldn't be able to stand.

"I think you've said enough."

He yanked me down onto the bed, rolling me until his body covered mine. I squirmed to free myself, but when our cocks rubbed against one another, it was all I could do to keep the groan from leaving my lips. Fuck, he wasn't lying. It couldn't be possible. He'd just come in my mouth. His dick was as hard as mine.

"Would you stop jumping to conclusions and reading things into what I'm saying. I'm not freaking out because it's you. You've been my best friend for my entire life. I'm not going to suddenly push you away."

Another shot. That one I more than deserved.

"What do you want from me?" I would be surprised if he couldn't hear my heart pounding in my chest while I waited for his answer. Having Reagan once would never be enough. It was one thing to wonder what it would be like, it was something else entirely to know and then walk away.

"I want you to explore this with me."

"Am I supposed to believe you suddenly want to be with a guy after finding out last night that I'm gay?"

He lowered down to his elbows on either side of my face. "I have no idea what I'd label myself. All I know is that I've been hard since last night when you kissed me. This morning wasn't enough. I don't know what any of it means or why I'm suddenly interested in a man. The only part that makes sense right now is that it's you."

His eyes held mine captive. This was the chance I'd been waiting for, so why did the small voice in the back of my head scream bad idea over and over again. Reagan talked about lust not love, and yet there I sat ready to jump in with both feet. What if he could fall in love with me? What if this was my one chance?

I wanted to take the risk, to tell him yes, I'd do anything for him. The fear of what might happen held me immobile. The silence stretched on, his eyes never wavering from mine, and he moved them to my lips. I knew what was coming and still stayed frozen. He lowered his head and before I could stop him, his lips were pressed to mine. His hands cradled my cheeks as his tongue traced a path across my lips. The blood raced from my head, heat coursing through me.

Our tongues tangled together, our bodies molded from our thighs to our heads. In that moment, I knew, even with the risk of fucking disaster written all over it, I'd give this man anything he wanted. For some reason, I enjoyed finding ways to make my life harder. He'd been my first and only love. No matter how many times I tried to build a wall around myself and bury my feelings for Reagan nothing worked. Even without him knowing it, he'd buried himself deep in my heart.

He lifted his head to look at me and I was lost. Nothing in this world meant anything without Reagan in it.

"Don't screw with me," I whispered.

"I won't."

He dropped his head again, tilting it to gain better access to my mouth. This time I let myself enjoy it. This was everything I'd ever wanted and if Reagan might only be here for the experiment, it would kill me, but I would enjoy every second while it lasted. His body ground down into mine and my eyes rolled into the back of my head. Even through his jeans, I could feel the way his dick slid against mine. What I really wanted was to feel it without any clothes on, but I had no idea if he was ready for something like that and I wouldn't push him. Everything was so much more with him. All the pent-up desire for the man rushed to the surface.

I planted my feet on the mattress and shoved my hips up to meet his. This time the groan left Reagan's lips. I slipped my fingers down to the waist of the jeans he still wore, working my hand between the fabric to touch the smooth skin of his hips. Not like I hadn't already had his dick in my mouth, but I didn't want to push too far too fast. The muscles in his stomach flexed under my touch. The strong, defined muscles of his chest begged me to run my fingers along them. I used my other hand to caress the hard wall of chest above me. Each time my thumbs grazed his nipples, his hips shot forward. It seemed as if we both wanted more than kissing and simple petting. Bracing myself for him to stop us, I moved my hand to the opening of his jeans, pushing it aside with a quick flick of my hands. He broke the connection of our lips and I mentally cursed as it seemed Reagan had finally come to his senses.

"You're right, too much fabric."

He batted my hands away and grabbed the waistband of my shorts, yanking both them and my boxer briefs to my ankles. Could this really be happening? I had to be dreaming. To make sure I wasn't I leaned up on my elbows and gave my side a quick pinch.

Ow.

Nope, not dreaming.

Heaven.

I was in fucking heaven. That could be the only explanation for why I lay there watching as Reagan slid the waistband of his jeans down and dropped his pants to the floor. His boxers quickly followed behind. My tongue darted out to wet my lips as I thought about the way his gorgeous thick dick tasted on my tongue. Someday I wanted to have it in my ass or my cock in his. For today, I'd be happy with touching it again.

Reagan climbed back onto the bed, crawling up my body. He lowered his head and captured my lips again, sucking my tongue into his mouth. Groaning, I reached between our bodies to wrap a hand around my cock. If I didn't get some friction and soon, I might self-combust right there. Every nerve ending and muscle in my body was wound tightly, ready to explode.

The back of my hand grazed along his shaft, making him shudder. "Touch me again," he begged against my lips.

My fucking pleasure.

I held his gaze with mine. "Do you trust me?"

"Always," he whispered. He had no idea how much that one simple word meant to me. If I could record him saying it, I'd replay it at least ten times a day.

"Sit up and straddle my thighs."

He quirked a brow but did as I asked. I took him in my hand. When I realized he wasn't close enough, I grabbed his ass, bringing him closer to me. Our dicks sat, leaking and perfectly aligned. I wrapped my hand around both of us and pulled off a single stroke, the pre-cum helping to smooth my way up and down.

"Oh, fuck. Oh, fuck. Oh, fuck. That feels good," he moaned.

He didn't have to tell me twice. His heat seeped into my skin, setting my blood on fire. "Give me your hand."

He reached out and I guided his hand to join mine around our cocks. Together, we started stroking up and down. Fast then a little slow before picking up the pace again. Every part of me ached with the need to come. Not yet. This time I planned on waiting for us to come together. Reagan's mouth got filthier and filthier as his hip slammed forward, fucking our hands. His eyes were squeezed shut. The muscles in his thighs tensed as he came closer to the edge. I couldn't help but pick up the pace.

"Come on, baby," I whispered. "I wanna see you fall apart for me."

"Fuck," he yelled as spurts of hot fluid hit my chest, making the glide of our hands easier as I continued stroking.

The orgasm hit, stealing my breath as I came all over both of our hands. Reagan dropped down, covering my body with his. Mixing the mess between us. I was sweaty and sticky, being crushed under Reagan's full weight, and I never wanted to move again.

I'd been right earlier. This was fucking heaven.

Time passed and both of our breathing slowed to a normal level. I didn't want to, but I knew if I didn't move, eventually I wouldn't be able to breathe at all. I rolled us to our sides, our faces at the same level. My chest tightened as a million questions ran through my mind. All with answers I wasn't sure I would like. That didn't stop me from asking the most important one.

"What do we do now?" I asked, terrified of what he'd say.

"Give me thirty minutes and I can totally go again."

I shoved his shoulder. Reagan had a habit of deflecting tough conversations with jokes, which made my palms sweat.

"Be serious."

He locked gazes with me. "Sorry. I'm being serious. Honestly, I don't know. I can tell you right now, I've never come so hard in my life. And while I don't have any explanation why, I know it's crazy, but I'm not ready to walk away from whatever this is until I understand." He ran his thumb along my bottom lip. "Let's see where this goes. I wasn't kidding earlier when I said I wanted to explore this with you. Jump in with me and see where it leads us."

Reagan had handed me exactly what I wanted on a silver platter. I could tell him no and wonder for the rest of my life if I made the right call or I could give in and I hope I wasn't wrong.

Even with the danger of drowning exceptionally high, I threw off the life vest and jumped in with both feet.

Hopefully Reagan would catch me.

Reagan

My hands shook as I walked into the recording studio after court. I knew I'd done all I could to get my client the best judgment possible. That wasn't the problem. This would be the first time I spent time with the rest of the band since Sawyer and I had become more than friends. A decision I'd never regret. My life had already been completely entwined with his. I was actually surprised I hadn't felt the connection before. I guess it had to do with always seeing Sawyer as being straight. Either way, I still had to spend a few hours with the band and somehow pretend I hadn't crawled out of Sawyer's bed earlier that morning. I'd probably have to shove my hands in my pockets to keep them to myself.

Since we'd gotten together, we spent most of our time at Sawyer's since Heath already knew. It was easier than trying to deal with Harrison at my place. It was frustrating having to hide, but I knew there was no way around it. Not if we both wanted to keep our jobs. The partners at my firm were definitely not going to be supportive.

When we went to the movies or the bar, we made sure to keep a safe distance from one another. Didn't mean I liked it at all. By the time we got home, all I wanted to do was rip his clothes off.

When we were alone we had a hard time keeping our hands to ourselves. Each time, I felt a little braver, a little more daring to try something new. I hadn't worked up the courage to fuck him yet or for him to fuck me. I figured it was only a matter of time before that happened. Not once in my life had I imagined finding a man's body attractive. All the smooth lines and hard planes called to me. Begged me to touch his golden skin.

In the back of my head I wondered how I would keep my hands off him today. Last night he asked if I'd come watch him record the songs he finished. Being the inspiration for one of those songs, there was no way I could miss them recording it.

After I parked in the garage, I sent a text to Sawyer. Getting backstage of the arena had been easier than getting past the gates of this fortress. He'd already warned me I'd have to go through at least two security checks and that was with him escorting me back to the room.

I stepped out and leaned against the hood of my car to wait. The elevator sat directly across from the space I'd parked in. What I really wanted was to see him emerge from this elevator on his way toward me. The way his jeans would hug the lean muscles of his thighs with each step, and the sexy smirk would pull up the right corner of his lips. And if I was being honest, I wanted a chance to get my lips on his before we went inside for a few hours and had to follow a hands off policy.

The ding of the elevator caught my attention and I looked up right in time to see the door slide apart to reveal Sawyer lounging against the back rail as if he didn't have a care in the world. He looked around until his gaze connected with mine. There was that smirk. He'd always had a warm smile, but this one was different. It was full of lust and desire. From the first moment he turned it on me, I couldn't stop the blood from rushing south.

"Fuck, you're sexy," he said the moment he reached my side.

"I could say the same thing about you."

He nodded toward my car. "Let's sit and *talk* for a second before we go inside."

With the garage full of cameras, I couldn't blame him for wanting to make us kissing less obvious to anyone who might be watching. I sat back in the driver's seat and watched him move around the front to the passenger seat. I didn't give him more than a second after the door closed. I fisted my hands into the front of his shirt, yanking him forward and capturing his lips with mine.

I pushed my tongue past his lips and swallowed down his groan. The taste of cinnamon invaded my senses, making me dizzy. Or that might have been the fact there was no blood left in my head. Sawyer slipped his hand up my chest and around the back of my neck to tighten his fingers in my hair, holding my mouth to his. Eventually, breathing became a necessity and I moved back. His chest heaved with each panting breath and I suddenly had the desire to strip him naked in the backseat and have my way with him.

Luckily, the rational part of my brain still had enough control to rein me in. Fucking around in the backseat of my car in the garage of his music studio was sure to get us both caught. On top of all that, I still hadn't talked to him about telling the rest of the band about us. Mari and Heath knew, and if I was ready to tell my parents, he needed to be ready to tell his friends.

I couldn't stop my eyes from following his hand as he reached down and adjusted himself in his pants. "The things you do to me," he whispered.

"I could say the same thing about you." My eyes were still fixated on the hard-on in his jeans. "Now let's go inside before I forget where we are and maul you in the middle of the parking garage."

"Give me a minute to calm down."

I chuckled. "You and I both know there's no way either of us are calming down while sitting in this car. Now get out and let the fresh air clear your head before the rest of the band comes looking for you."

That seemed to sober him up pretty quickly. It made me a little sad that he still wanted to keep us hidden from everyone. One of these days, we were going to sit down and talk about that.

By the time we made it to the floor where the band was recording they were restless. Sawyer hadn't been kidding about the security. I was surprised they hadn't asked for my first born child to get inside. The upside was now that I'd passed security, as long as my name stayed on their list I wouldn't have to deal with as much the next time.

"Where have you been?" Monty whined when we stepped through the doorway. "If we don't get this song done soon, my stomach might eat itself to keep from starving to death."

"Please. You just shoved a pack of Twinkies down your throat. You should be good for at least an hour," Heath said, getting to his feet. "Reagan, good to see you again."

He glanced over and Sawyer gave a brief, yet subtle shake of his head. The second the smile hit his face, I knew he'd forced it. Whatever might be bothering him, I'd have to wait until dinner to find out.

I dragged my attention away from Sawyer. "Glad I could get a chance to see you guys record. I've always been curious about the process."

Mari practically jumped in my hands, wrapping her arms around my neck for a hug. "I'm super excited you're here."

After almost squeezing all the air from my lungs, she stood back and gave me a wink. Mari had known about us from day one.

Sawyer and I had only crawled out of bed long enough to order a pizza. We were enjoying each other's naked company when a knock sounded on the door. Thinking it was the pizza, I tugged on my basketball shorts and went to open the door. What I didn't expect was to find Mari on the other side.

"Reagan, what are you doing here?"

"I was hanging out—"

"He's hanging out with me."

Mari glanced over my shoulder and after taking in both of our states of undress, it was pretty obvious what we'd been doing.

Mari screamed and bolted for Sawyer. She jumped into his arms, planting kisses all over his face. I had to admit I was a little jealous.

"I'm so happy for you."

He set her down and suddenly she was in my arms. "I'm so glad you gave him a chance."

The green-eyed monster faded away. Mari was happy we were together. She glanced over her shoulder. "Why did you decide to tell him?"

"Well, that's a little more complicated."

In the end she forced us to give her the story. Afterward, she told Sawyer I told you so and made me promise not to hurt him.

Jackson smirked. "Sawyer says you work in contract and business law. Who knows, maybe someday you be here all the time dealing with our shit."

"Yeah, and hopefully it's not bailing me out of jail." Monty practically doubled over at his own joke.

Not everyone had the same reaction, at least not immediately. From what I gathered, Monty was a bit of a daredevil. More than willing to jump in any situation, consequences be damned. I couldn't blame them for taking something like that seriously. One by one, they realized he'd been joking and laughed along with him.

I lifted my hands up. "Not my area of expertise, but I'm sure a few of my friends might be able to help you out."

Heath walked over and clasped him on the shoulder. "How about we keep our shit together and never have to find out who can and can't help? Besides, I thought you wanted to play so you could eat."

Suddenly, Monty forgot his joke but kept holding his stomach, whining about hunger pains.

"For fuck's sake, Monty. Pull yourself together." Sawyer took hold of his shoulders and marched him back over to where his guitar sat on its stand. "You wanna play? We'll play."

Sawyer reached behind him to pull the drumsticks from his back pocket. Maybe I shouldn't have stared, but I couldn't keep my eyes from the way the muscles of his arms flexed with the movement. Slowly, everyone moved into position and I found myself sitting on the small couch in the room, getting my own private concert. I watched the way Sawyer's whole body moved with grace as he switched from skin to skin while he played.

Every once in a while, I'd catch his eyes on me. Unlike the other times I watched him play, he was close enough for me to see the raw heat and desire in his eyes. What I really wanted was to stand behind and run my hands over his sweat-slicked skin. Before, I never would have imagined those thoughts. Now I knew exactly how smooth each inch of him was. The way his skin tasted on my tongue.

I shifted in my seat, hoping to hide my growing erection. Pushing away thoughts of Sawyer's body, I tried to focus on the song they were playing. The words jolted me out of my fantasies.

We're on a collision course
Reaching for each other
Time and circumstances keep us apart
A love I know is there
A love we may never share

They were like an electric shock to the system. My eyes snapped to Sawyer's and I knew by the light flush on his neck and the way he avoided my gaze, that song was about me. When the music ended, I dipped my head slightly, letting him know I heard his words. Words that were no longer true and held no meaning between the two of us.

For the hour, I sat and listened to song after song before it was their turn in the recording booth. Sawyer convinced their musical director to let me sit in the booth while they recorded two songs. By the time they finished, Monty was having a full-blown meltdown about food and I was more than eager to get Sawyer alone and ask about that song.

They finished packing up their equipment, when I heard a voice next to my ear. "He needs to tell them." I looked around to see Mari standing next to me, her hands linked behind her back.

I checked to see where everyone else was. When I realized we were alone in the booth, I said, "It's not my news to tell. You need to convince him."

She sighed. "Heath and I've been trying." She laid her hand on my arm. "But I'll be honest, with the way you two were looking at each other, you won't be able to keep the secret for long. Monty and Jackson didn't know what they should be looking for, but eventually they're going to figure it out and things aren't going to go well when they do."

I closed my eyes. "I know. I'll talk to him tonight."

She leaned up on her toes and pressed a kiss to my cheek. "You'll have better luck than we did."

"I hope so."

She went to leave the room and stopped. "Don't hurt him, okay?"

There was a slight tremble to her voice, that I knew it happened to be fear for her friend. "I promise I won't."

She nodded and left the room. Sawyer stepped in a few minutes later.

"What did Mari want?"

For the briefest of moments, I wanted to lean forward and press my lips to his. With more willpower than I knew I possessed, I kept my feet firmly rooted to the ground

"Let's talk about it over dinner."

He narrowed his eyes at me and I waited to hear what argument he'd make to get me to tell him now. This time he didn't push.

"Give me five and we'll head out."

I left it up to Sawyer to explain why we weren't going out with everyone else. The restaurant wasn't far from the studio.

Chapter Twenty Two

Reagan

I noticed Sawyer's eyes darting around the room, as the hostess led us to a table in the back. She handed us the menus and was on her way. Sawyer was quick to open his menu and practically cover his face with it while he pretended to decide on dinner.

"You can stop hiding now," I said, leaning back in my seat, crossing my arms over my chest.

He lowered his menu by a fraction of an inch. "I'm not hiding."

I hooked my finger in the top of the menu and pulled it back down to the table. "Yes, you are. What are you afraid of?"

"I told you this was a bad idea. Someone's going to figure it out."

"What, 'cause two guys are having dinner together? Do you automatically assume every time you see two guys in a restaurant together that they're gay?"

"Well, no..."

"Exactly. No, because that's fucking ridiculous. No one knows what's going on here, besides the fact we're fighting."

His brows drew together. "And how would they know that?"

"They can see it in our body language. Now, if I really wanted people to know, I could climb in your lap and cover your lips with mine. That I'm sure would be a dead giveaway."

His eyes widened. "You wouldn't."

I let the question linger in the air for a moment. "You're right, I wouldn't, but only because I respect your reason for keeping all of this quiet for now."

"Thank—"

I held up a hand. "Don't thank me yet."

He opened his mouth to ask why when the waiter interrupted our conversation to take our order. Once he'd walked away, Sawyer looked at me expectantly. "Why not?"

"Because you're going to give me one good reason why we should keep our relationship hidden from the rest of the band. Mari and Heath know, but I still don't understand why you never told Jackson or Monty."

He closed his eyes and sighed. "I doubt you'll understand."

My skin prickled. I'd forgiven him for keeping the secret from me for so many years. With all the pieces in place, I may not have liked what he'd done, but I understood it. With Jackson and Monty, there was no reason I could think of not to tell them. He didn't want either of them in a romantic sense. Which left me trying to figure out why he kept them in the dark.

"Then explain it to me," I snapped.

He grumbled and leaned his elbows on the table. "My entire life, besides you, music has been the one constant. The one thing I could turn to no matter what might be going on with the rest of my life. When I came to college, I made the decision that I'd let music take me wherever it might lead. Never in my wildest dreams did I imagine where it would lead me, even though I hoped."

"I know this. Even though you didn't always say it out loud, I knew you wanted to spend your life making music. That still doesn't explain why Monty and Jackson don't know."

He dropped his head for a moment before looking back up at me, his gaze intent. "You're right. Deep down I wanted to be a rock star, but I never wanted to be labeled the gay rock star." His voice lowered on the last part. "I wanted people to respect me for my music, not who I did or didn't sleep with. I was afraid Jackson and Monty would never see me in the same light again. That if I was out and proud and we failed, would it be my fault?"

I watched the haunted look take over his features and I wished more than anything that I could offer him comfort. Since we were in public, the only thing I had to give him were reassurances.

"You have no idea how much I wish I could reach over and hold your hand right now. To show you I'll be there for you no matter what anyone else thinks, but I can't. I understand why you wouldn't want the whole world to know, hell, I doubt very much the partners at the firm would understand, but the band isn't the whole world. What I can tell you is that your friends would never see you in that light. Not the people I met at the concert that first night. They'd respect your decisions. And you should know that based on Mari's and Heath's reactions when you told them."

He shook his head. "You can't guarantee they won't care."

"You're right," I agree. "There are no guarantees in life. Doesn't mean you can hide from it forever."

He grimaced. "I can try."

"And what happens when they figure it out, or someone else does and tells them? What then? Do you deny everything about us to save your own skin?"

"I would never deny what you mean to me."

"How do you think Monty and Jackson will feel when they find out from someone else?"

He rested his arms on the table. "I think they'd be pissed."

"Then you need to tell them. Be honest with yourself. We can hide this from the rest of the world, no problem. But we won't be able to hide it from them. Not if you expect me to be around them with you."

I let that statement linger there for a second. He tilted his head back and forth like he was weighing his options. "You need to tell them."

He blew out a breath, his eyes focused on the table in front of us. "You're right. Deep down, I know you're right. Doesn't make it any less scary."

"Don't be scared. We'll figure it out together."

"Goddamn, I wanna reach across this table and touch you. And since I can't, you better be prepared later. I'm not letting either of us out of bed, until we're too exhausted to move."

I hummed in the back of my throat. Many different images paraded across my mind and I had to suppress a shiver at the thought. "I'm totally on board with that."

"Good, but right now I wanna know what you mean about the partners at your firm not being happy about you being in a relationship with a guy?"

I set my fork down slightly disgusted with their behavior.

"Last week, we had a couple come into the office to hire us to help complete all the legal paperwork for their newest business. Everything was going well, until one of the men reached over and held the other's hand. One of the partners, with fake politeness, had them leave the office. Told us his firm wouldn't represent a faggot."

"That's fucked up."

"Tell me about it. But now you understand why I can't tell them just yet."

The waiter dropped off our drinks and appetizer. Starving didn't begin to describe how I felt. I tucked into my food, inhaling the small portion in no time. Sawyer brought his fork to his lips.

"That song was about me, wasn't it?"

His hand froze and he stared at me for a second, setting his fork on his plate.

"I hoped you didn't notice." He glanced away and I wanted so badly to grip his chin and turn his face back to mine.

"Of course I noticed. Is that how you really felt about me?"

Sawyer was quiet for a long moment, playing with different things on the table before looking up and holding my gaze. "Yes."

"I wish I had known."

"Do you really think it would have changed something back then?"

I thought about that for a moment. He had a point. Would knowing my best friend wanted to be more than friends have changed my mind? I hated to say it, but I doubted it. Shamefully, I probably would have pushed him away. I'd never thought about another guy in my entire life. Then again, maybe it was always there. Sawyer caught me in an unguarded moment the first time he kissed me. I didn't have a chance to think and simply reacted. And I wouldn't change it for the world.

"No, but only because I don't think I was ready to hear it then."

"And now?"

"Now, I thank fuck every day that you kissed me."

A grin appeared on his lips. "Me too."

"I'm sorry I hurt you all those years."

"It wasn't your fault. You didn't know and that's on me." Sawyer picked up his drink and brought the glass to his lips.

"Doesn't make me feel any less bad."

He set the glass down. "I'll tell you what, you can make it up to me someday."

"And how's that?"

He winked. "I'm sure you'll figure out away."

"I can only imagine what you have in mind."

"You have no idea."

He pulled out his phone, typing away. Suddenly, I worried he was looking up all the different ways we could have sex. We hadn't gotten to more than Sawyer giving me blow jobs and rubbing off on one another, but I knew at some point we would move past that. "What are you doing?" I asked suspiciously.

He glanced up, a smirk on his lips.

Oh shit.

"Texting Mari. If *we're* going to talk to the band about our relationship, then we need the big guns."

"Big guns?"

He glanced back down at his phone. "Good. She says she'll help us."

"Help us with what? What do you mean big guns?"

"Food. All big band conversations revolve around food, but Mari is the best cook among us."

I narrowed my eyes. "I know for a fact your parents taught you how to cook when we were growing up."

He laughed and picked his fork back up. "They did, but nothing like the shit Mari can make."

"Better you than me."

"So you never learned how to cook?"

I laughed. "That's an understatement. I gave up after I set a pan on fire in my senior year of college. After that I made sure to order out or eat on campus."

"What were you trying to make?" Sawyer lifted the beer to his lips.

"Ramen."

Sawyer's eyes bulged. For one moment, I thought about holding up my napkin in front of my face in case his beer decided to make a reappearance out of his nose and into my lap. After a moment, he chocked down the liquid and laughed. When our food was delivered, Sawyer jumped in right away, but something had been bugging me. I couldn't stop myself from asking.

"Did you sleep with any of the girls you dated in high school?"

Sawyer stared at me. "Out of all the things you'd want to know, that's what you choose?"

"What? I'm curious. You always had a different girl on your arm. I would have never guessed you were gay based on that alone. So I'm curious, did you sleep with them?"

He lifted one arm in a shrug, his eyes planted firmly on the table. "I slept with some of them. Only hooked up with others. I was still trying to figure it all out myself back then. I figured not being with them would give me away. After so long, I knew there was no way to come out, so I kept up the mirage."

"I'm sorry. That had to suck. Not being able to be yourself."

"It did a little, but honestly, I wasn't even sure who I was then. I knew what I wanted, not that I understood any of it." He started to reach his hand across the table and quickly pulled it back, shaking his head. "Sometimes I forget where I am when I'm with you. Now you know why I had to leave the way I did. I needed a chance to figure out who I was without thinking about you all the time. I know I hurt you. You have no idea how sorry I will always be for it."

"It's okay. We found our way back to each other. Not that I ever imagined ending up together, together. I wouldn't change it for the world."

"God, I'm going to kiss the fuck out of you when we get in the car." He pointed at my plate with his fork. "Hurry up and eat. I have plans for you tonight."

Sawyer always ate fast, but I'd never seen him shovel food in that quickly before. If I hadn't known better, I would have thought he was in one of those food eating contests. In no time, his plate was completely clear. He hurried me along, except I had no plans on eating at warp speed. He started drumming his fingers on the table while he waited for me to finish. By the time I took the last bite, the waitress had shown up to clear our plates. Sawyer didn't even let her finish the question about dessert before he said no. He gave me a wink as the waitress dropped the check and walked away. A quick fight about who would pay ensued. The cash in the billfold and my wallet a little lighter, we stepped into the cool night air.

"You didn't have to pay for dinner," he said as we reached the car.

"No, but I'm counting this as a date, so I paid for dinner."

"Don't you dare compare me to a chick. I don't need to be taken to dinner." I climbed into the seat and watched as Sawyer did the same thing, slamming the door behind him.

"No way I could compare you to a chick." I reached over and cupped him over his pants. "Besides, you're paying next time."

"Fair enough." That seemed to brighten his mood. "Now get us back to my place."

Heat lit Sawyer's eyes. I had no doubt that whatever he had planned, I was guaranteed to come like an explosion. It was how it had been since the first day. I'd expected them to lessen as the newness wore off, but the opposite happened. They seem to grow stronger. All I knew was I couldn't get enough of Sawyer's hands on me. Odd considered I tired of the women in my bed fairly quickly.

I parked the car at the curb, seeing Heath's car missing. I didn't want to be blocked in when he returned home. Hopefully, that was much later in the night.

Sawyer practically ran to the door, but struggled with the lock in his haste to get there. I strolled to the door, letting Sawyer get worked up over my slow pace. He grabbed my hand and yanked me through the front door.

"Now you're all mine."

His lips crashed down over mine and suddenly it didn't matter what he wanted to do to me, I'd love every minute of it. In a tangle of limbs we made it to the bedroom without killing ourselves. Once we hit the bedroom, we began dropping clothes on the way to bed. Naked and twisted around one another, I captured his mouth, pushing my tongue between his lips to taste his.

His kisses seared every part of me. He snaked a hand down to wrap around my dick. I slid my hands down his back until I reached the top of his crack. Unsure of what to do, I kept my hand moving to cup his ass cheek.

Sawyer tore his mouth from mine. "I wanna try something."

My brain was a cloud of lust, but I managed to push a 'yes' past my lips.

He leaned over me, pulling something out of the drawer. But when his lips lowered over my cock, I stopped thinking altogether.

I was a ball of sensation and the only thing that mattered was the hot mouth currently drinking down my cock.

Something cool slid down the crack of my ass and my hips bucked back to get away from it.

Sawyer pulled his mouth off me and rested a hand on my stomach. "Easy."

"Can't say I expected that." No one had ever touched my ass there before.

"Trust me. I'll make you come for days."

"Days?"

"Okay, slight exaggeration, but it'll feel like it lasted for days." He kept his eyes locked on mine. "Trust me?"

I couldn't say no to him. I'd always trusted him with everything and I wouldn't stop now.

"Yes," I panted. "Suck me."

"We're going to have to work on that bossiness."

"Whatever...just make me come."

"As you wish."

He took my cock into his mouth again and I sighed at the pleasure. The man had a wicked tongue. This time, I was ready for the cool finger as it rang along my crease. The muscles in my thighs quivered at the first graze over my hole.

I had no idea something so simple could feel so good. Back and forth, Sawyer continued to circle my hole. My body on fire, my ass bucked against his finger.

"Ready for more?"

"Mmmhmm," I groaned, unable to form a word, and that was before I felt a finger push into me. There was a slight burn.

"Easy," Sawyer said, lowering his head once again. The moment his lips touched my dick I forgot all about it as his finger slipped deeper. He pulled it out and pushed back in quickly, the movement stealing my breath. And that was before he crooked his finger, pressing on a spot that made me see stars.

Unable to stop it, my dick erupted into Sawyer's mouth. It happened so fast I thought I might black out from the sheer pleasure. Sawyer kept sucking me through the longest orgasm of my life. He hadn't been lying.

By the time he pulled off, my body was completely wrung out. "I don't think I can move."

Sawyer leaned up and pressed a kiss to my lips. At first I thought it would be weird to taste myself on his lips, but it wasn't. If I could have gotten hard again, I would have. "Good thing you don't have to."

He curled his body around mine, resting his head on my chest.

"I need to take care of you," I argued, my eyes still closed.

"You can do that in the morning. Get some sleep."

He pressed a kiss to my cheek. It wasn't passion or desire filled. Just a sweet kiss letting me know he was still there. And that was more important to me than anything else.

SAWYER

My palms were sweaty and my stomach rolled. I hadn't even been this nervous when I told my parents. It didn't make any sense that I would be this nervous. Then again, I hadn't only told one of my parents and kept it from the other. Heath and Mari had known my secret for years. Monty and Jackson were in the dark and I had no idea how they might react to the truth. I couldn't keep it from them any longer. I may not want the press to know about mine and Reagan's relationship, but everyone in the band deserved to know the truth.

"Would you stop pacing?" Reagan leaned his shoulder on the doorway between the kitchen and the living room.

My feet stopped moving and I looked up shocked I'd been moving. The last thing I remembered was sitting on the couch trying to figure out what to say. A drumstick was held tightly in my hand. "I didn't realize..."

"You know, out of the two of us, I should be the one freaking out. You've at least done this before."

"This is not the same things. And besides, those were my parents. I knew they wouldn't hate me in the end. Hell, I think they knew before I did."

He pushed off the wall and walked toward me. "What makes you say that?"

I brushed a stray lock of hair from his forehead. "My mom mentioned the way I watched you the night I told her."

The corners of his mouth pulled up. "You watched me?"

"Yes." I wrapped my hand around the nape of his neck. "But you already knew that."

He leaned forward and pressed his lips to mine. "Doesn't mean I don't like hearing it."

"You're an egotistical bastard."

A dark brow lifted and he shrugged. "Yeah, but you knew that before you sucked my dick."

"Woah, way too much information."

Both our heads snapped to the kitchen door to see Mari standing there, hands raised in the air, a wooden spoon in one of them.

"Oh, please." I rolled my eyes. "Like I never had to listen to or watch you with Cole."

"Fair enough." She pointed between the two of us with the spoon. "Now both of you get your asses in the kitchen and help me before I forget I'm doing you a favor and leave you both to your own devices."

"Well, at least I can cook." I threw my thumb over my shoulder at Reagan. "He can make like three things. Hot dogs, grilled cheese, and frozen pizza."

"I can make more than that," Reagan protested.

I stopped in my tracks and spun to face him with my arms crossed over my chest. “Oh yeah, like what?”

“I make an unbelievable bowl of Ramen.”

“Eww.” Mari scrunched her nose up as I burst out laughing. We both knew he burned that shit every time. “That shit’s nasty. You’re not eating it in front of me.” Still grumbling, she disappeared into the kitchen.

“Ramen? Really?” I asked, still laughing.

Reagan took a step forward. “What, you don’t like burnt Ramen? Unless someone wants to cook for me more often.”

“Ha. Nice try.”

He cupped my face in his hands. “Relax. They’re your friends, they’re not going to care. If they do, fuck ’em.”

I rolled my eyes. “Fuck ’em? Is that your answer to everything?”

“When someone doesn’t see things the way I want them to.”

“I’m sure that will go over well with a judge and jury someday.”

Mischief lit his eyes. “Maybe not, but who says it will ever get to a jury?” He took another step forward, pressing our bodies together. “I can be very persuasive.”

I wrapped my hands around his wrists. “This I already know.”

“Get in here,” Mari yelled.

Intense brown eyes focused directly on mine. The heat in them drew most of the blood from my brain and suddenly I wished we were alone in my bedroom instead of cooking for the band. Even through our pants, I could feel his body harden against me. I leaned forward to take his lips with mine.

"Sawyer!"

Reagan jumped at the sound of Mari's voice. He glanced over at the doorway. "She sounds pissed."

That made me laugh. "She's not. That's her way of getting my attention." I nodded to the door. "Let's get in there. Since I can't have the distraction I want, I'll take what I can get."

He gestured forward. "Lead the way."

We walked into the kitchen where Mari was stirring something in a pot on the stove. She looked over her shoulder at the two of us. "The chicken is already in the oven and I'm working on the sauce."

Reagan clasped his hands together. "Sawyer wasn't lying about my cooking skills, but I'll do whatever you tell me."

She pointed farther down the counter where there sat a cutting board and knife. "You're on salad duty."

Reagan lifted his hands and laughed. "Fair enough."

I grabbed a bowl from the cabinet and set it next to the vegetables he pulled from the fridge.

"Oh no, you don't get to make salad and flirt with your boyfriend. You get to make the garlic bread and pasta."

Unfortunately for Mari my brain stopped listening at the word boyfriend. Reagan's eyes met mine and for that moment in time nothing existed but the two of us. We'd never discussed labels or dating or anything more than being together. A relationship with Reagan? Something I wanted more than anything. That didn't mean he would be ready to define whatever this was as a relationship. He had just accepted he was attracted to another man for the first time in his life and I didn't want to push him. A part of me still feared him freaking out about all of this and running. My heart pounded in my chest as I waited for his reaction. I should have known better than to question him.

"You're no fun, Mari. I like flirting with my boyfriend."

He didn't blink or flinch as the words left his lips. And to prove his point, he grabbed a handful of my ass and pulled me closer. He must have noticed the shock on my face because he gave me a wink and turned back to the task at hand. In a daze I walked over to the table, where Mari had already set the bread out, and got to work.

I'd just dumped the pasta into the boiling water when someone called from the front door. "Anyone home?"

Mari dropped the spoon and bolted from the room. I kept my feet firmly planted where I stood.

"Who's here?"

I chuckled. "Cole. Mari only runs if it means getting down and dirty with him."

Cole had been on the road so often lately, Reagan hadn't had the chance to meet him yet. The few times Cole had been around since the season started, Reagan had been at work or home going through a case. Cole came back into the kitchen with Mari's legs wrapped around his waist.

"For fuck's sake, get a room."

Mari scoffed. "I would, but I'm doing your sorry ass a favor. Besides, this is cleaner than what I walked in on earlier."

Cole glanced down at Mari. The way the corners of his mouth curved up watching her made you realize how in love with her he was. Not for the first time I wondered if I had the same smile when I looked at Reagan. I'd be willing to bet I did. The question was did anyone recognize what it meant? Mari and maybe Heath did, but they were the only ones who knew how deep my feelings went for the man on the other side of the kitchen.

Reagan watched the two of them, then his eyes went wide. "Shit, I can't believe I'm meeting Cole Wallace."

Cole wasn't an idiot and looked back and forth between the two of us. He glanced at me with a smirk on his face. "About time you met someone."

"I actually met him a long time ago. Things just finally lined up for the two of us."

He let Mari slide from his grip and turned toward Reagan with his hand extended. "Nice to meet you..."

Reagan dried his hand off on a towel and took his hand. "Reagan Setton."

"It's nice to meet you. I see Mari's put you to work."

"He apparently has the same ability to cook as Jackson," Mari offered

Cole's face scrunched up and I understood the feeling. "That bad?"

"It's pretty bad," Reagan assured him.

I nodded. "It's definitely Jackson level bad."

Cole walked over to me. "Good thing you and Mari are in charge."

Mari plunked her hands on her hips. "Who's this you and Mari? It's just Mari, thank you very much."

"Fine, fine." He pressed a kiss to her cheek. "What do you want me to do?"

Mari watched me out of the corner of her eye as she turned back to stir the sauce. "Get Sawyer a drink before his hands shake so bad he drops part of dinner."

"I'm fi—" When I saw the movements of the colander in my hand, I knew she was right. I thought I'd pushed it all out of my head. Apparently, I'd been pretty wrong. "A drink would be good."

Cole moved to the cabinet where we kept the liquor and scanned the contents. "How about a shot of tequila?"

"No," the three of us practically shouted at the same time.

Cole's head snapped around. "'Kay, no tequila."

"Let's just say Jose and I don't have the best relationship."

Reagan lifted a brow over the dark eyes focused on me. "I don't know. You've had at least one good night with Jose."

"Not sure I'd call that a good night, but I'm happy with what happened the next morning."

Cole moved to the fridge and pulled out four beers, handing one to each of us. "So what's the occasion? Why the big dinner?"

Mari sidled up next to Cole. "Sawyer's finally planning to tell the rest of the band."

Reagan brought the bowl of salad to the table and came to stand by me. Every time I looked at him, I got caught in his gaze. Being surrounded by our friends made no difference. It was like everything else in the room faded away. "I finally have a reason to tell everyone."

"It's time they know." Heath stepped into the room, running a hand through his long black hair.

I sighed. "I know, I know. You both have been trying to convince me of that for years. I probably should have told them earlier, but honestly, I never thought I'd have a reason it would matter to anyone but me."

A timer went off. Mari grabbed the pot holders and pulled the chicken from the oven, setting it on the table to cool. I flicked the water off on the pasta when I heard the front door open.

"We're here," Monty yelled, dragging out the words.

My breath caught in my throat. Was I really ready for this? Mari walked over and cupped my cheek. "Breathe. For crying out loud, breathe. They're not going to care. They might be a little pissed you waited this long to tell them, but they won't care."

"She's right," Heath chimed in. "We'll go keep them occupied and give you a few minutes to calm down."

Mari leaned up on her toes and pressed a light kiss to my cheek. With a small smile, she followed Cole and Heath into the living room. Reagan wrapped his arms around my waist, pulling me flush against his body. "It'll be fine. And I'll be here no matter what happens. Whatever you need."

I rested my head on his shoulder and turned my lips to his neck. "Thank you," I whispered.

We stood there for a few more seconds, when Reagan began to fidget. "I know you want to tell them, so unless you want to let them hear what's going on between us, I think you need to get your lips off my neck and let me calm down for a moment. Otherwise I'm taking you down the hall to your room and let them hear the truth."

The statement was so outrageous it helped settle my nerves enough that I could draw a full breath. I stepped back and ran my eyes over the room, making sure everything was done. Steam rose from the boiling pasta. I pulled if from the stove and after draining it, poured it into the pot of sauce. I moved it to the table and looked over at Reagan.

"Do I tell them now or after dinner?"

Reagan

Sweat beaded all along Sawyer's brow. Before long, he'd be trembling again and I didn't know what to do to help him.

"What do you think?"

He shrugged. "I honestly don't know."

He tried to play it off like this was him asking if they liked the lyrics to the new song he wrote. I knew better. His words and actions didn't line up. I wanted to wrap my arms around him and drag him down the hall to his room. If I could cocoon him away from the pain people might cause him, I would. Not that I had any experience with any of this. This was all new for me and there were so many things I hadn't considered.

For the first time in my life, I saw a man as more than a friend. And that didn't even begin to describe my feelings for Sawyer. The easy camaraderie had been there since we were little kids, but there was a sexual attraction I couldn't explain. Everything about Sawyer made me want to get him naked. It didn't end there, though. This was a man I cared deeply about. We shared so much with each other, I could see those feelings growing into more than either of us was ready for.

I shook those thoughts away. Right then, we needed to deal with Monty and Jackson. I had a feeling Mari and Heath were right. They wouldn't give a shit who Sawyer was sleeping with. They might be pissed at being left in the dark, but that would be about it. At least, I hoped they were right. I didn't want to think about what would happen if they were wrong.

I placed my hands on Sawyer's shoulders and massaged the muscles. "I figure it this way. You either tell them and risk them getting pissed and leaving before we eat, which means more for us."

Sawyer rolled his eyes. "Go on."

"Or you wait until after we eat, which means you won't touch a bite of food until after you talk to them and most likely make yourself sick in the process."

"Why wouldn't I eat?"

"I know you. You'll be too nervous."

He closed his eyes. "You're right." He cracked one eye. "And you know how much I hate admitting that."

"Oh, trust me, I know." I chuckled, which made him laugh. When the laughter died down, I continued. "I think you tell them now. Why wait and give yourself an ulcer in the process? Wouldn't you rather know their reaction sooner, rather than later?"

Sawyer leaned in and pressed a soft kiss to my lips. It wasn't erotic or sexy. It was to remind me we'd take it on together.

He glanced at the door. "Let's get this over with. If they get mad and leave, at least they'll have time to cool off before we play again."

"Tell them. I'll be right here with you."

Focusing on Sawyer's predicament with his friends made me think of my own with my friends and family. How did I explain to them that I suddenly liked men? Not that I could say I liked all men. It all had to do with Sawyer. I hadn't thought about what label I might use to describe myself. The whole label thing made me want to open my own bottle of tequila. Being with Sawyer didn't scare me. It was the consequences of that decision that almost had hives breaking out all over my skin. One of the partners at the law firm turned down a case a few weeks ago because he refused to represent 'faggots.' I had no idea what they'd say about one working for them. *Ugh. This is not what I need to be thinking about right now.* I turned my attention back to Sawyer and saw he was still standing in the kitchen, staring at the door.

His back looked like a rod had replaced his spine. I stepped forward and trailed kisses up his neck. "You can do this."

He nodded. After another moment he lifted his head and rolled his shoulders back. "Let's go before I fucking drink the tequila."

I gave him a light shove to the back. He walked to the door with me following closely behind. We stepped through and found everyone else sitting around like it was any other night.

For them it was.

Sawyer shuffled into the room and Mari's eyes caught mine over his shoulder. I could see the way her brow creased with worry.

"Yo, Reagan. What's up?" Monty reached out to slap hands with me.

"Nothing much, man." I hoped I could give Sawyer a few minutes to get himself together.

"No work tonight?" Jackson asked.

Cole sat on one end of the couch with Mari in his lap. Sawyer had taken the seat next to them. For the briefest of seconds I thought about sitting with him but stopped myself and leaned against the doorway. This was a move Sawyer needed to make on his own. I couldn't nor would I force him into it. He sat with his arms on his thighs, his head bent.

"Nope, but I have a brief due to the court by Monday."

Monty raised his beer. "Better you than me. Best part about a music degree, we never had to write papers."

"Don't I wish."

Sawyer finally lifted his head. "We need to talk."

Silence filled the room, pressing in on my chest, making it hard to breathe as I waited with everyone else to hear what Sawyer would say. Heath sat forward on the chair.

"Dude, you don't look so good," Monty said, watching Sawyer. "Everything okay?"

Sawyer sucked in a breath and moved his gaze to me for a second before looking back at Monty. "Everything's great, but there's something you need to know. Something I should have told you a long time ago."

"What is it?" Jackson asked, his attention completely focused on Sawyer.

His hand trembled as he ran it through his hair. I wanted nothing more than to go over and hold that hand in mine. Sawyer stood from his seat and began pacing the room. He stopped in his tracks and turned in my direction. I nodded at him, hoping to give him the courage to continue. He came over and stood next to me.

"I'm gay." He slid his hand into mine. "And Reagan is more than my friend."

Mari's smile dawned like sunshine. Jackson stared at the two of us like he'd never seen either one of us before. Monty laughed and jumped up from his chair.

"I knew it."

Sawyer's head snapped in his direction. "What do you mean you knew?"

"I'm an observant motherfucker." He pointed between the two of us. "I saw the way you watched him. No guy watches another guy that way unless he wants in his pants."

"Jesus fuck, Monty," Heath scolded, but Sawyer wasn't done.

"You knew and didn't say anything? Why?"

Monty stopped laughing and faced us head-on. "It was your secret to tell. I figured when you were ready, you'd tell us. Until then, it wasn't my business."

"And you're not pissed I didn't mention it before?"

Monty shrugged. "I figured you had your reasons."

"I did. But the more I think about them, the more ridiculous I realize they are."

Monty turned to me. "So, just an old friend from high school?"

I laughed. "Up until a month ago, that's exactly what I was. Things change."

The corners of his mouth turned up. "I'm happy for you two. Maybe now you'll stop writing such brooding songs."

"Maybe, maybe not."

Sawyer's hand squeezed mine. I could see the release of tension from his shoulders. It was as if the weight of the world had been lifted from them. A smile tugged at the corner of his lips. I wanted to press a kiss to those inviting lips. I glanced around the room first wondering how people would react to seeing us kiss. That's when I noticed Jackson still hadn't moved or said a word. In Monty's uproar, I'd forgotten about Jackson. I nudged Sawyer in the ribs. When he focused in on me, I gestured my head to the corner where Jackson sat.

Sawyer let go of my hand and walked around Monty to stand in front of Jackson. "What about you, man? Does me being gay bother you?"

Jackson looked up as if he'd just figured out that Sawyer stood in front of him. "What?"

"I asked if it bothers you."

Without a word, Jackson stood and pushed past Sawyer to walk out the front door.

"Fuck," Sawyer cursed, plunging his hands into his hair and tugging on it.

I couldn't stand by any longer. I pushed off the wall and went to Sawyer. When we were kids, I refused to let the jerks who tried to push Sawyer around 'cause he was in band get away with that shit. Even after he got big enough to take care of himself, it didn't stop me from watching out for him.

He still hadn't turned from the empty seat vacated by Jackson. I took his shoulders in my hands and turned him to face me. The color had drained from his face. Ignoring the reactions of everyone else in the room, I pulled him close and said only loud enough for him to hear, "What can I do?"

His eyes met mine. The sadness and worry reflected in them was devastating. "Nothing." He spun out of my hold and disappeared down the hall, presumably to his room. That was the first time since he kissed me that he'd walked away like that.

"Christ, this is a mess." Heath sighed.

I turned to see him looking down at Mari, who now had tears in her eyes.

"What do we do?" I asked the room, hoping one of them would have an idea of how to bring them back together.

"I need to figure out why Jackson's so pissed off right now." Heath looked at Mari, then over at Monty.

Monty flopped back down into his seat. "If I had to hazard a guess, I'd say he's pissed because everyone knew but him."

"Maybe, but that's not what Sawyer is thinking right now. He's pacing his room worried he single-handedly destroyed the band because Jackson hates him and the fact he's gay," I said.

"Shit," Cole spoke for the first time since the whole shitshow started.

I started toward the hall. "I'm going to get Sawyer to come back out here, but I need someone to get Jackson to listen to him if he does." Heath stood and pointed at me. "Go deal with Sawyer. We'll," he said, gesturing to everyone else in the room, "go and calm Jackson down. He doesn't hate Sawyer. It won't matter that he's gay. I think Monty's right. He'll get over it in a minute."

Jackson wasn't something I could worry about right then. I followed Sawyer's path down the hall and opened the door. True to my word, Sawyer was wearing a hole in the middle of the floor. I shut the door behind me and locked it. Right now, there was no need to have an audience for our conversation. Knowing there were very few things that would calm him down, I stepped into his path and tilted his face up to meet mine. His eyes glistened.

"Everything is going to be fine." I pressed my lips to his.

After a moment, he took a step back. "How can you say that? I just ruined everything we worked so hard for over the last few years."

I took hold of his shoulders and gave him a brief shake. "That's bullshit and you know it. He's pissed because he's the only one who didn't know."

"How can you be sure?"

"I can't be positive, but he has no reason to hate you, and everyone agrees. They're talking to Jackson now." I took his hand and led him to the end of the bed to sit down and relax for a few minutes.

I took his chin between my thumb and forefinger, holding him in front of me. This was not the confident Sawyer I knew staring back at me. A shadow of doubt lingered in his eyes and I wanted to figure out a way to remove it, whether it had to do with me or not. "Talk to me. Do you truly believe you've just destroyed the band? Or is it something else that has you hiding instead of confronting Jackson like I know you normally would."

He tried to pull his face from my grasp, but I wouldn't let him. I needed to look in his eyes as he answered me. Slowly lowering to my knees, I kept the connection of our gazes. A sigh left his lips.

"A little bit of both. I guess a part of me knows they wouldn't care, but I wonder how it will affect our sales if the press gets wind of it. Or what will happen with your job?"

When it was clear he wasn't going to try and pull away from me, I let go of his chin and ran my hands up and down his thighs. "And what if they never find out?" In reality, the idea seemed impossible, except a part of me hoped it wasn't. I knew the partners would be very accepting of our relationship and until I figured out where else to go, I needed the job. How could you hide a relationship from anyone indefinitely? And that left me as the dirty little secret, something I didn't want to really think about then.

"You want to hide this forever?" He gestured between the two of us.

"No, I can't imagine I would, but everything between us is so new, I'm perfectly okay with staying out of the limelight for a while."

He lifted a brow. "Forever."

"Not forever. At some point sneaking around won't be enough for either of us. Today is not that day. And until I find a firm whose opinion on gay associates is higher than my current one, I need it to stay quiet. But someday that won't be a problem."

He closed his eyes and flopped back onto his bed. "Why do I feel like I'm pushing you and you're going to hate me in the end?"

Did he really believe that? After coming back here the night he kissed me to the time we'd spent together over the last few weeks, the weight of his words pressed in on my chest, making it difficult to breathe. I'd do just about anything to see him smile or laugh. My hands continued to run up and down his thighs, trying to offer comfort, except at the same time I was beginning to drive myself crazy. My own cock began to harden as I felt the muscles beneath my fingertips flex and jump with each stroke of my hand.

I wanted to show him how much he wasn't pushing me into anything. The button and zipper of his jeans were just out of reach as my fingers slid higher and higher with each pass. My thumbs lightly grazed over the outline of his cock, feeling it begin to swell and harden. Finally, I reached the top and in seconds had his pants undone and his dick in my hand.

The mushroom head begged to be tasted. Knowing what I liked, I swirled my thumb over the head. It still seemed weird to have a dick that wasn't my own in my palm, yet somehow it felt right. This was more about jerking him off. We'd done that. To prove it was my choice to be there, it needed to be more. So, for the first time in my life, I bent my head and stuck my tongue out to lick across the tip. The salty taste of him hit my tongue. Not once did I let my gaze waver from his. His eyes snapped open, locking with mine.

"What are you doing?"

"Showing you I'm here because I want to be here." I did it again and enjoyed the soft moan that left the back of his throat.

"*Fuck,* everyone is out there and you choose to suck my dick for the first time right now."

With my free hand, I reached up and covered his lips. "Yep. I guess you better be quiet then. Now lie back and I'll do my best to make sure you enjoy it."

I bent my head and wrapped my lips around the head of his cock. Since I had absolutely no idea what I was doing, I figured the best thing to do would be everything I liked. I swirled my tongue around the tip again as his fingers slid into my hair. For a moment, I thought he might hold my head in place. When his grip on my hair tried to pull me back, I swatted his hand away. We both needed this.

"Let me do this for you, even if I'm bad at it." I begged him with my eyes and flicked my tongue, drawing a line up the underside of his cock.

A guttural moan tore past his lips and the hand against the back of my head released its grip, pushing me toward his prick instead. Opening my mouth, I took him back in my mouth and drew him in as far as I could go. He was too big to take to the back of my throat without any practice. That was something I'd have to work on. And I had little doubt Sawyer would mind being my practice dummy.

"Oh fuck," he cursed. "You could never be bad at this. Just the thought of you with your lips around me has me ready to blow my load in seconds."

I lifted my head and wrapped a hand around his shaft, gliding it up and down. "You better not come yet, or I'll stop and this is all you'll get." For emphasis, I moved my hand to the base of his cock and squeezed hard enough to slow him down.

"Shit, don't stop. Don't stop."

With a smirk, I lowered my head again, sucking him down and using my hand to add extra friction along his dick. Each sound and curse that came from Sawyer's lips pushed me even further. He fisted his other hand into the sheets by his side, his knuckles turning white. I used my free hand to take hold of his balls and swirled them around in my palm. Knowing how much I liked the head of my cock played with, I drew my lips back up him and went to work on the tip, sucking and tonguing the slit.

"Fuck... Oh Fuck, I'm gonna come," he called out, once again tugging on my hair.

My first instinct was to pull off and jerk him through his release, but something stopped me. I wanted to take him all the way and if that meant swallowing on my first ever blow job, then that's what I'd do. My dick pulsed in my jeans. I bent my head and increased the suction I had on him. His body jerked and the first jet of hot come hit the back of my throat. Without any other option, I swallowed him down, just in time for a second and third jet to hit me. I didn't pull off until his dick began to soften in my mouth.

His eyes were closed as he panted for air. Damn, I knew how to torture myself. I was so hard, I had no doubt I could pound nails into a two by four. There was no time for relief, so I reached down into the top of my jeans and snaked my way down until I was able to wrap my hand around my prick and squeeze. No way did I want to spend the rest of the night stuck in soggy jeans.

I assumed I'd done an okay job when Sawyer lifted his head and gone was the worry in his eyes. It had been replaced by a deep satisfaction and sense of relief.

"That was incredible. I'm not sure I can move."

SAWYER

My brain had melted into a pile of mush. I was shocked I'd been able to form a coherent sentence.

"Really? It was okay?"

Those dark eyes lifted to meet mine and the vulnerability there blew my mind. He was trying to hide the fact he felt insecure, but I could see it there in his eyes. Something he didn't need to feel with me. I wasn't lying when I told him that his lips around my dick would make me come. What I hadn't expected was how expertly the man played my body. If I didn't know any better I would have thought he'd done it before.

"Okay? I think shooting my brains through my dick says it was more than okay."

The simple words brought the confident smile back to his face. Each one of my muscles no longer felt as if they would crack under the strain. As much as I wanted to stay in my room, in our own little bubble, I knew I needed to talk to Jackson.

There was no avoiding it. Reagan's hand snaked down to grip himself through his jeans. He hadn't come yet. I covered his hand with mine.

"Let me take care of this for you."

He shook his head. "Not right now. That was for you. Right now you need to talk to Jackson."

"But—"

"No buts." He leaned forward and pressed his lips to mine. I could taste myself still on his tongue and my dick twitched. I didn't think I'd be able to get hard again after coming so spectacularly. Boy, was I wrong. My dick hardened even further. Then again, with Reagan, I had no idea what my body might be capable of. He kissed up my jaw line to my ear. "Besides, you can make it up to me later. Now get dressed."

I nodded and stood from the bed to fasten my jeans. "Can't we just stay in here all night?"

He walked over and stood before me, taking my hips in his hands and pulling me closer. "While I would love nothing more, you won't be able to sleep right or focus on all the things I want to do if you're worried about Jackson."

"I'm not sure I can do this," I whispered, looking down at the ground. "I can't have him abandon all of us."

"If he's actually willing to abandon you for being who you truly are, then he wasn't meant to be part of your life anyway." He took my hand and led me to the door. "But I think you'll be quite surprised at what you find out there."

Reagan led us from the bedroom and down the hall, still refusing to take his hand from mine. When we reached the living room, I stopped dead when I came face-to-face with Jackson. I swallowed the lump in my throat and nodded to the kitchen. "Can we talk? Just the two of us?"

He nodded and walked through the door connecting the two rooms. I followed him and braced myself for the tirade I knew was to come. But when the door shut behind me, he said nothing, just crossed his arms over his chest and leaned against the counter, waiting for me.

This was no time to beat around the bush. Better to know what I was up against than to keep myself guessing. I went straight to the point. "Do you have a problem with me being gay?"

Jackson shook his head. "What? Is that what you think?"

I ran a hand through my hair. "I have no idea what the fuck to think. I tell you my biggest secret and you're the only one who storms off, making me think I ruined everything. So I'll ask again, do you have a problem with me being gay?"

Jackson sighed. "No. God no. Sorry. I didn't mean to make you think that. I'm pissed because you kept something that big from me. I've trusted you with plenty of things over the years, and yet you couldn't trust me."

"It had nothing to do with trust. I don't want to be the gay musician."

"You had no problem telling everyone else before now. Fuck, even Cole knew." He began to pace the floor of the small room.

"I didn't tell Monty. The observant little shit that he is figured it all out on his own. And the only reason Cole knows is 'cause Mari begged me to tell him. He thought I wanted her."

"Heath and Mari?"

"They lived with me. I'm not a damn virgin."

He stopped in his tracks. "Oh, and I guess Mari and Heath just happened to be in the right place at the right time?"

I leaned back against the counter. "I'm not sure what you want me to say."

"Put yourself in my shoes for a minute. How would you feel if I kept something this big from you, but come to find out everyone else knew?"

"*Fuck...*" My head fell forward. "I should have told you before now. We've been friends for years. Please tell me I haven't ruined that."

"No, you haven't." I moved my gaze back up to his. Jackson pulled out a chair and took a seat. "But there's something I want to know."

I took the seat across from him. "What's that?"

He drummed his fingers on the wood. "Why now? Why keep something like that from us all these years? You had to know we wouldn't give a shit who you had in your bed."

I leaned farther back into the chair. "You're right. I knew you wouldn't care, but I used it as an excuse."

"An excuse for what?"

It would probably piss him off, but I gave him the truth anyway. "If it weren't for Reagan, I probably would have kept hiding it from everyone."

Jackson narrowed his eyes at me, but I continued before he had a chance to say anything.

"Before him I had no reason to come out. I knew I'd never want another man the way I wanted him, and he was straight, or at least I thought he was. When he showed up at that meet and greet, I still hadn't been ready to tell him. It wasn't until he caught me hooking up with a guy on his floor that he knew."

"You love him." It wasn't a question. It was a statement about the reality I'd yet to deal with when it came to Reagan.

"I've loved him since I was sixteen years old. I spent years in college trying to forget or at least fuck him out of my head. Which is why I told Heath. I didn't want him to walk in on something he wasn't expecting."

Jackson fell silent and sat quietly for so long, I braced myself for the possible explosion. Of the five of us, Jackson was the most level-headed and reasonable in any situation. He had a way of looking for the positives in everything. Most of the time. Deep below the surface lurked a raging temper. One that when pushed to the limit would come out swinging.

He looked at me again and something in his gaze had the weight lifting from my chest. "I can respect that. I can't imagine falling for someone and knowing no matter what you did, they would never fall for you."

"Are we good?" I held my breath. His answer made the difference in not only our friendship, but possibly the future of the band.

"We're good."

I stood, ready to join the others in the living room, and was surprised when Jackson reached out a hand to me, pulling me into a quick bro hug. That one simple act proved beyond a shadow of a doubt that he didn't care about my sexuality. Any guy who did would keep their distance, probably afraid of what that might mean to me. It was honestly one thing I never understood. Straight men were able to keep themselves contained in a room full of beautiful women. Why wouldn't I be able to keep my dick in my pants when surrounded by men? Whatever. Right now, that didn't matter.

"Let's go talk to your man."

I chuckled. "You do realize you already know him, right?"

He stopped at the door. "Yes, but now I have a whole new set of questions, like what he sees in you." He pushed it open and walked into the living room.

"Fucker," I muttered under my breath as I followed him.

"I heard that," he called over his shoulder.

Reagan's eyes met mine the second I emerged from the kitchen. A brow lifted and I nodded, answering his unspoken question, *are you okay?* And really, I was. I took the seat next to Reagan on the smaller couch. My heart thundered in my chest when he reached over and intertwined our fingers. It had been the first time he'd initiated a connection when we were in the presence of others.

Monty clasped his hands together. "Let's talk."

"And what do you want to talk about?"

He threw his hands up in the air. "Umm...maybe the fact you're not only gay but also have a boyfriend."

"And..." I let my sentence linger in the air, trying to figure out where he was going with this.

"And, does that mean we're going to see more of Reagan on the road with us?" He jerked his head to where Mari and Cole sat in the same position I left them. "We see plenty of Cole when he doesn't have games."

"No," Reagan said at the same time I said, "Yes."

My head snapped in his direction. "What do you mean no?"

"What do you mean yes?" he countered. "When you're on the road, the paparazzi is everywhere. There's no way we wouldn't get caught unless you're suddenly ready to come out of the closet to the world."

"Wait," Monty said. "You're not coming out to everyone?"

I brought my attention back to him and shook my head. "No, I'm not."

Heath spoke up. "And how do you expect to keep hiding that? Monty figured it out. You think others won't?"

Jackson held his hands up. "Don't look at me. I didn't have a freaking clue."

I knew Heath had a point. "We'll just have to be careful."

"Which means no 'on the road'," Reagan said.

Cole sat up in his seat, bringing Mari with him. "Why don't you want everyone to know?"

I noticed Jackson and Monty looking at me with the same curiosity in their gazes. It was like they accepted it, so everyone else should. If only life worked that way.

"If people found out, it could affect the band. Places we were supposed to play might cancel. And we don't think Reagan's law firm will be very accepting either."

Monty's lip curled up at the corner. "Okay, a few small-minded bigots cancel. I wouldn't want to play for them anyway. What about all the people who'd start listening to our stuff because of that?"

"Except, I don't want to be the poster boy for gay musicians everywhere."

"Oh please," Monty scoffed. "There are plenty of artists who already claim that title."

"And most of them aren't a rock band. I have no idea how the crowd would react to the news, but it's not something I'm willing to risk."

"It shouldn't have to be a risk," Jackson argued. "You shouldn't have to keep a very large part of you buried in the closet. It's who you are. You get to embrace that as much as we do."

"And I wish life were that simple." I lifted Reagan's hand to my lips. "One day I'll be ready to tell the world. Right now everything is new for us, especially for Reagan. Give us time to wade through being a couple before we have to try and stay afloat in a tsunami."

"Yeah, okay." Monty nodded. "I don't like it, but I can respect that."

Jackson groaned. "I may not like it, but I get neither of you wanting to ruin your careers when they're just starting."

"Thank you. Now who's hungry? Mari made chicken parm."

"Fuck, yes." Monty punched his fist in the air like a five-year-old finished the monkey bars on the playground. He jumped from his seat and practically ran to the kitchen. Mari and Cole were right behind him.

"He'll eat everything if we don't watch him," she called over his shoulder.

"She's got a point," Jackson said on his way back to the kitchen.

Out of the corner of my eye, I noticed Heath hanging back.

"Something you want to tell me?" I asked when the kitchen door closed behind Jackson.

"I just want to make sure you're good."

I glanced over at Reagan, and the smile he gave me set my blood on fire. To anyone else it looked sweet and devoted, but I knew better. The brazen tease who blew my mind and my cock earlier lurked just below the surface. "I'm better than good."

"You better be," Reagan whispered in my ear.

Heath smiled. "When you want to tell people is your choice, but I'm proud of you for coming clean today. That secret was kept entirely too long."

"You're right, it was. Someday the time will be right to tell the world and when it is I'll be ready."

"Good," Heath said, walking into the kitchen, leaving Reagan and me alone.

Cupping my cheek, he brought my face to his. "Are you sure you're okay?"

"More than I have been in a long time."

SAWYER

I never imagined how free I'd feel by just having the band know. Now whenever we spent time with the band, outside of public situations, I could be myself and enjoy holding Reagan's hand, sitting next to him, or placing a kiss on his lips. I never realized how much of myself I held back by keeping the secret. Good thing I managed to thank Reagan for helping me to see the light, multiple times a day. His dick in my mouth, my dick in his, or just a good old-fashioned hand job. There was something different about Reagan's hand wrapped around my cock.

Of course my brain had traveled to places it couldn't go tonight. Reagan had been given his very own case. Well, he still had someone overseeing the job he did, which meant he had to check in with his progress. That way if he was heading in the wrong direction, it could be corrected before the train derailed. It also meant, he was working late tonight, which left me home alone with my guitar. Well, not completely alone. Heath and Monty went to pick up pizza and beer while I worked through the notes on another song.

We'd gotten a call that the label wanted to release another single and with the reception of the last two, they wanted to include a PR tour, along with another possible full album release. We had more than enough songs for one album, but you could never have too many songs. Especially when the music and lyrics were flowing onto the page. Also better to have backups in case they didn't like all the ones we presented to them.

This was the first song I'd written with Reagan as the muse that didn't have depressing undertones. I jotted down the cord, when the door burst open.

I pointed at him with the pencil in my hand. "Jesus, Monty. If you damage the wall you're paying for that shit."

"They're heavy." He barely lifted a case of beer in each hand.

"You're full of shit. You just wanted to make a scene."

He walked to the kitchen and glanced over his shoulder with a wink. "Maybe I did."

Heath walked in the door. "Why the hell is the door—"

Monty stepped in from the kitchen area.

"Never mind. I forgot we had Mr. Attention with us tonight."

Monty flopped on the couch next to me, making my pencil slide across the paper. "And don't you forget it."

"Ass." I erased the extra marks and rewrote the line. Heath dropped the pizza boxes on the table.

"So why are you here anyway?" Monty lifted a bottle to his lips.

"Where else would I be? I live here, you dumbass."

"I know you live here, dickhead. I'm wondering why you're not with Reagan."

I set the guitar down and sat farther back on the couch. "He got assigned a case, so he's working late tonight."

"That sucks. Well, not him getting assigned a case."

"Nah, it's what he's been waiting for."

"I got plates." Heath stepped out of the kitchen holding napkins and paper plates.

"Thank fuck. I'm starving." Heath narrowed his eyes at Monty.

"Your legs look like they work just fine. If you wanted pizza as soon as we got back, you could have gotten your own damn plates." He handed me one, took one for himself, and tossed the rest of the stack at Monty's head.

If the paper plates wouldn't have separated as they flew through the air, I had a feeling Monty would have caught them with how quickly his hand shot up. Instead, he spent the next few minutes grumbling as he picked up all the plates.

I put a pizza on my plate and took the first bite when there was a light knock at the door. "Did you guys call Jackson or Mari?"

Heath shook his head. "Jackson has a date and Cole's home."

"Fair enough, but who the hell is here?" Expecting some door to door salesmen, I stood and yanked the door open, a frown on my face. The reality was so much better than the expectation.

Standing on the porch with a laptop bag on his shoulder was Reagan, his long, muscular legs encased in navy pants. The suit jacket fit perfectly over his shoulders. He'd already managed to ditch the tie and the top button of his shirt. My mouth watered at the sight before me. Reagan in jeans and a T-shirt was hot. Reagan in a three-piece suit exuded quiet intelligence and smooth sophistication.

"What are you doing here? I thought you were staying late at the office." I took his hand, dragging him into the house and shutting the door behind him.

"I was bored being there all alone. You said you were staying in to song write. I figured there was no reason I couldn't work on my laptop in the same room you were working."

Gripping the back of his neck, I pulled his lips to mine. "I think that's the best idea you had in weeks."

He rolled his eyes. "Don't be ridiculous. I've had plenty of good ideas." That was when he seemed to notice we weren't alone in the room. He lifted his hand in a wave. "Hey, guys."

"Evenin', Reagan," Heath said, while Monty mumbled something similar with half a piece of pizza in his mouth.

I leaned closer to Reagan's ear. "As much as I love the way those pants hug your tight ass, do you want to grab a change of clothes from my room?"

"I'd love too."

I turned to Monty and Heath. "Be right back."

For a brief moment, I thought about a quick hookup in my room. I knew we'd be a while and I didn't want Reagan to head to bed before I got to spend any real time together.

"Don't even think about getting it on," Monty warned. "You said we were going to write tonight and that's what we're going to do."

"Like you need my help with that. You write most of the music anyway."

"Yeah, but tonight I want company while doing it. Maybe you can sit in my lap."

"Shut the fuck up and eat your pizza."

I grumbled but led Reagan to my room. After I pulled out a pair of shorts and a T-shirt, I sat down on the bed. If I couldn't get my hands on him right then, I sure as hell planned to watch him change and see all that silky, smooth skin on display for me. Reagan began undoing the buttons on his shirt. One by one they popped free, revealing tan golden skin. I fisted my hand in the comforter to keep from going to him and touching every inch. Once I started touching I didn't think I had enough self-control to stop.

Reagan's heavy lidded gaze lifted from his task to mine. "My dick is hard, just from having you watch me undress."

He ran a hand down the front of his pants to prove the point. Not that I couldn't already see the outline of his cock for myself. I reached down to adjust my own aching shaft. Reagan took a step forward. Almost as if my ass was on fire, I leaped from the bed and backed up toward the door.

"Where are you going?" His voice sounded raspy.

"Unless you want an audience, this will need to wait until later."

Reagan's eyes darted toward the door and understanding dawned on his features. Monty would have no problem busting into the room to hurry us up so we could work on music. Even Reagan knew that by now. But I understood the ability to forget about everything else when he was around. It happened to me more often than not.

"Shit, I forgot they were here."

I winked. "When you're around, I always forget about other people."

Reagan dropped his shirt to the floor. "Then I guess you better get back to work so I have time to play with you later."

I swallowed hard, forcing myself to stay in place. "That's what you say to me right now? I'm ready to storm over there, rip all our clothes off, drop to my knees, and take you in my mouth, and you want to send me back to work."

A sexy side smirk lifted the one corner of his lips. "If it means me getting my hands on you sooner, I'm all for you going back to work." I crossed my arms over my chest, unable to believe my ears. "Then I can suck you until you can't think."

A shiver ran down my spine, making my body shudder. I stepped backward toward the door. "I think...I think it's time for me to get back to work."

"I think you're right."

I told myself not to look down, yet there was nothing to stop me from looking at Reagan, who was now pantless, palming his erection through his boxer briefs. "Fuck them. I need my lips on yours." I walked purposefully toward Reagan. Desire made the brown of his irises darken, his erection clearly outline by the tight boxer briefs. Wrapping my hand around the back of his neck, I sank my fingers into his hair, tightening them a bit and pulling his head back. The second my lips touched his, I parted them with my tongue and sank it inside for a taste.

The same addictive flavor that was unique to Reagan burst across my tongue. I couldn't help but align our bodies from head to toe. Our cocks grazed each other through the fabric. I started to lose myself in the kiss, backing Reagan up toward the bed when a voice rang out.

"You have thirty seconds to come out before I come and get you," Monty called out.

We broke apart and I jumped out of Reagan's reach.

No doubt he would.

Reagan shook his head, laughing. "You better get out there."

I lifted both my hands up. "I'm going."

I took a few more steps back, then turned and walked out of the room. With Monty already fired up, I braced myself for what would come out of his mouth when I reached the end of the hallway. And he didn't disappoint in the least.

"I thought I was going to get to watch my first episode of gay porn."

"For fuck's sake." Heath rubbed his temple with his thumb and forefinger.

I, on the other hand, knew better than to back down or ignore Monty when he was like that. He'd keep going until he got a reaction out of you. I walked over to my vacated seat. "And I'd be willing to bet I'd find you jerking off watching the two of us. We're hot when we're together."

"Jesus, Sawyer." I turned and found Reagan rolling his eyes at the end of the hall. "You guys keep this up and I'll need to go work in the kitchen."

My head lurched forward a bit. I reached for the back of my head where Heath had slapped me, the same as Monty. "What the hell was that for?"

"They'll behave," Heath promised.

Reagan looked skeptical but took his laptop out, along with a stack of folders, and sat on the recliner in the corner of the room. He opened his computer, watching me over the top of it. I was so focused on him I hadn't realized Heath had spoken to me.

He gave a light shove to my shoulder. "Hey, dumbass."

Turning my gaze away from Reagan, I glanced over at Heath. "Huh?"

He gestured with his chin in front of me. "How're you gonna write music without a guitar?"

I wanted to smack myself in the head. There I was acting like a lovesick puppy. Okay, so maybe I was hopelessly in love with Reagan, but there was no reason for him to know that yet. One step at a time.

I picked up my guitar and for the next few hours I helped Monty work out the chords in a song he'd almost finished and started one of my own. The entire time I found my eyes, straying to Reagan and every once in a while I'd find him staring back for a second before looking back down at the work on his screen.

The shutting of a laptop drew my attention. Reagan was done with whatever work he'd brought home and was now watching us work. To say it make it hard to focus happened to be a huge understatement. Even across the room, I could feel the heat in his gaze. When I continued to hit the wrong cords, Monty set down the pencil in his hand.

"I think we've kept you away from your boy long enough." Monty chuckled.

Heath collected the sheet music, while Monty and I packed up the guitars. Reagan was still lounging in the chair watching us. Or at least that's what I thought he was doing at first glance. Not so much. His eyes tracked every movement I made.

Hastily, I put everything away and looked over my shoulder at Reagan, who didn't waste any time getting up and walking down the hall to my room. I hadn't even bothered to say good night to Monty and Heath before I was already only a few steps behind him.

"Night, lover boy," Monty called after me. "Don't be too loud. We'll be listening."

When I turned to look at them, Heath had his head resting against the back of the couch. His eyes closed. Monty, on the other hand, sat on the edge of the couch watching me.

"Hopefully we can give you a good show." I winked and walked down the hall.

And much to my pleasure, I opened the door to find Reagan lying on my bed, not a scrap of clothing in sight.

"I think I could get used to coming home to this."

"I already told you, I wanted to suck you until neither one of us can leave the bed."

After breaking records in undressing, I climbed on the bed between Reagan's legs and rested my body weight there. He leaned up and covered my mouth. Reagan's lips devoured mine. Our cocks aligned, creating the perfect friction to make us both come in an explosion. But tonight? Tonight, I wanted something different.

I wanted Reagan to fuck me.

I'd always been a switch, whether I wanted to top or bottom. But I had a feeling Reagan wouldn't be ready for me to take him. Not yet anyway.

He slid his hand down my shaft and over my balls to reach the bottom curve of my ass. Every muscle in my body tightened almost to the point of pain as his finger played with the top of my crack.

Something in me snapped and I thrust my hips forward even harder than I planned. Reagan groaned and slipped his finger down the crack, rubbing over the sensitive pucker, making me squirm. When he pressed his finger lightly against me, the breath whooshed out of me.

Reagan had only pushed the ass play to this point once before. I loved it, but his fingers never made it to the area again. I gripped his biceps tighter. "Lube is in the drawer next to your head."

His gaze snapped to mine. "What?" he breathed.

I lowered my head, taking his lips in a kiss so raw and passionate his hips continued to thrust against me. I lifted my lips and locked eyes with him.

"Lube is in the drawer. I want you to fuck me."

Reagan

I couldn't have heard him right. My mind was fucking mush. Every glide of his dick against mine sent me closer and closer to a place where the only thing that mattered was coming. Forcing myself to focus, I lifted up onto my elbows, knocking him to the side of me.

"Did you just say you want me to fuck you?"

My balls pulled tight to my body at the thought. I'd wanted to fuck him for weeks, but being new to the whole sex with men game I wasn't exactly sure how that worked. Okay, I knew how it worked. What I didn't know was who got fucked and who did the fucking.

"I did." He reached down and grabbed me, sliding his hand up and down my shaft, making it harder to think. "I want to feel you deep inside me."

"I..." Words were escaping me as my brain melted from the heat right then and there. My eyes rolled into the back of my head.

Sawyer started to move away. I grabbed his arm and tried to pull him back. He shook me off and sat on the edge of the bed. Flashbacks of that first morning together hit me.

"Where are you going?"

He shook his head. "I pushed you too fast. I'm sorry."

This time, I held tight as I gripped his shoulder and tugged him down to the bed. "What the fuck are you talking about?"

He kept his eyes averted. "You're not ready. Who am I kidding? You may never be ready for that."

I straddled his lap and took his chin in my fingers, forcing him to face me. I gave my hips a quick punch forward and almost groaned at the sensation that shot up my spine. Fuck, if I didn't come soon, I might lose my mind. "Does that feel like I'm not ready?"

"No, but why else would you lie there staring at me?"

It was there in his eyes. Nothing had changed in the years we'd been apart. I could still read every emotion that crossed his face. The wide-eyed stare facing me said it all. He was still afraid I'd leave him for a girl. That I didn't want to fuck him because he was a guy. What he didn't realize was that I wanted him more than my next breath.

I bent down and kissed his lips, drawing a path with my tongue up to his ear. "Stop thinking I'm comparing you to screwing a girl. I don't want them. I want you."

"I never—"

I covered his lips with my fingers. "You don't have to say it. It's written all over your face." I ran my hands down his chest, grazing my thumbs over his nipples, and watched as his skin rippled at my touch. "I've wanted to fuck you for weeks."

His eyes flashed. "Then why didn't you say anything?"

"I'm new at this whole thing. I wasn't sure..."

He started to laugh. "You weren't sure who would fuck who."

I gave him a quick pinch to the ass, making him squirm below me. His stomach glistened with the evidence of both our desires. "Don't laugh at me, asshole."

He reached up and cupped my cheeks with his hands. "Right now, I want you to fuck me, but make no mistake that I'm going to want to fuck you too."

I squashed the fear that rose up in me with the thought of the pain I'd feel. Right now, the only thing that mattered was getting my dick inside Sawyer. "That I can do."

Standing, I moved around the end of the bed to the table next to it. Exactly like Sawyer said, there were condoms and lube. A brief spurt of jealousy hit as I wondered who he might have purchased it for. Then I realized it didn't matter because now Sawyer was mine and I had no plans on letting him go. I grabbed them from the drawer and turned to find Sawyer lying in the middle of the bed stroking himself. His eyes were fixed on me.

I crawled across the edge of the bed and batted his hand out of the way. "That's mine."

"Yes," he groaned, thrusting up into my hand.

I captured his lips, sucking his tongue into my mouth. The heat from a moment ago went molten. My skin tingled. I reached down, cupping his balls, loving the feel as he seemed to grow harder in my hand. I kept my hand moving backward, running my finger along his taint and up his crack, until I finally found the small pucker. He was hot there. As if all his heat and passion were centered in that one spot.

"Show me what to do," I begged, our lips only millimeters from each other.

I've had my fair share of sex, but never had to stick my dick in anyone's ass. The only thing I could imagine was the pain. Then again, I knew he wouldn't be begging me to take him if the only thing he would feel was pain. Little noises left his lips the longer I ran my finger down his crack. My own dick begged me to take him, to bury itself in that warm, tight hole. I held back and removed my finger. His eyes snapped to mine.

"Don't stop." A raspy edge had taken control of his voice.

I thrust my cock against his thigh once again, showing him with my body I didn't want to stop.

"Trust me, babe. I don't want to. You have to tell me what to do so I won't hurt you."

The words seemed to register. He stopped fucking my hand. "You've never had anal sex."

It wasn't so much a question as a statement. "No. So tell me."

"Fuck," he moaned. "I do love being your first for things." He picked up the bottle of lube and handed it over. "Coat your fingers and use them to stretch me open."

What am I getting into?

When I kept looking at the bottle in my hand, he covered it with his own and popped the cap. He poured some of the cool liquid, first in his own hand and then in mine. Shutting the lid, he tossed it on the other side of the bed and reached down between his legs. And everything left my head in a rush. Never in a million years would I have believed that a man fingering his own ass would be hot. Shit, had I been wrong.

"Holy hell," I breathed. I clamped my hand around the base of my dick to keep myself from coming before I got inside his tight hole.

His teeth sank into his bottom lip. I wanted to be the man who caused that look on his face. I rubbed the lube around my fingers to heat it up and pressed my hand down, batting away his. My fingers caressed his crease, feeling the slick path to his entrance.

I circled his hole until he begged me to penetrate him. "Do it," he cried out.

Careful not to hurt him, I slid my first finger up to my knuckle. "Fuck, you're so tight. I'm never going to fit in there without splitting you in two."

"You will," he panted. "Now move your finger slowly, in and out."

I did as he told me, pushing deeper each time I went in. He began to bear down on that single digit and all I could think was this was the hottest thing that had ever happened to me.

"Give me another one and scissor them when you pull out."

The next time I slid two fingers inside. The snug fit was more than I could imagine on my dick. I separated my fingers as I pulled out and quickly shoved them back in. His lower body shifted.

"Crook you finger."

I didn't understand what he wanted until his ass bucked off the bed. He fisted one hand in the sheets and gripped the base of his cock like he was holding on for dear life.

"Are you okay?"

"Mmm...that was my prostate. Pleasure central."

Loving the blissed out expression on his face, I thrust my fingers in and out a few more times, then did it again.

"Oh fuck. If you don't stop that, I'm going to come before you get inside."

He held the condom out to me. Besides Sawyer telling me no, nothing would have stopped me from rolling that condom on and burying myself deep within his body. I tore the package with my teeth and pushed the latex down my shaft.

"Do you need to turn over?" I asked when he still lay on his back facing me.

"No, I want to see your face while you're fucking me."

My dick twitched. Showed you how much I knew about gay sex. Was there a book I could read to catch up? I had to admit, it was even more exciting knowing that I could take him face-to-face. Sawyer wrapped his hands under his knees and pulled his legs to his chest, giving me the perfect view of his ass. I lined my cock up and looked at Sawyer.

"Now," he mouthed, gripping my ass and forcing me forward.

I pressed into the tightest, hottest hole I'd ever been in in my entire life. If I could have, I would've stayed there forever. Slowly, I pushed forward, hoping not to hurt him.

His fingers dug into my ass cheek. I looked down, afraid I'd caused him pain. "Are you okay?"

"Yes," he breathed. "Too slow. I told you I wanted you to fuck me."

"My pleasure."

Without any other warning I slammed into Sawyer, our identical groans echoing off the walls. I froze. Who knew I could feel this way? If I wasn't careful, I'd end up coming before I got to really have him.

"Move, damn it."

I leaned forward, resting my elbows on either side of his head. "Give me a minute. Otherwise, I'm coming before I'm ready."

"You better not," he warned.

When I felt like I had my body back under my control and the shock of the moment wore off, I pulled back and shoved my hips forward. Sex had never been like this. Sweat beaded on my back as I kept thrusting into Sawyer's body, taking my pleasure and giving him his own.

"Harder," he begged, taking hold of his dick and stroking feverishly.

"As you wish."

I sat back on my knees and holding his thighs against my shoulders, I pounded into his body harder than I'd ever had before. He jerked his cock even harder, leaking everywhere. I lifted his hips slightly and thrust. And holy shit, Sawyer erupted. White jets of fluid landed all over his chest and stomach. That wasn't the only thing I noticed. As his ass clenched around me, all my attention was centered on my own dick. A tingling sensation ran down my spine. My climax hit out of nowhere. I had orgasms before.

Not like this.

My entire body shuddered. Pins and needles ran down my arms and legs. Black spots danced in my vision. Unable to hold my weight, I collapsed onto Sawyer's chest, his arms banding around me, holding me tight as we both panted for breath.

"I've never come like that in my life."

Sawyer chuckled. "That's the point, isn't it?"

"I don't think I can move," I said, my body still tingling.

"Then stay here. I don't mind."

The tone of his voice had me lifting my head to look him in the eye. It was different than the moment before. More serious. The experience of being with Sawyer had eclipsed every other sexual experience in my life. Hearts pounded against each other, syncing together. My connection with Sawyer grew in that moment. With my sex-addled brain, I almost let three words slip that I didn't think either of us was ready to hear or say. I bit my tongue and kept them to myself.

As our breathing settled and my dick softened, I pulled out of Sawyer, missing the heat of him immediately. I tossed the condom in the trash next to the bed. When I turned back, Sawyer had moved to one side of the bed, his arms behind his head. I lay down next to him and gave in to the impulse to cuddle up next to him. His one arm came down, holding me tight to him.

"Is this okay?"

"It's better than okay."

As I lay there curled up against Sawyer's side, reality began to settle in. Tonight had changed things with Sawyer. Whether or not he realized it, the time had come for me to admit maybe for the first time to myself that I was bisexual. Not really an epiphany. I'd been with Sawyer for weeks, but lying there with my head resting on his chest, I knew the time had come to admit that to more than me.

Sawyer's fingers drew light, lazy circles over my back.

"I'm bisexual."

His fingers stopped moving and I felt the slight vibration in his chest. "Yeah, I'm pretty sure I figured that one out."

"I know, but that's the first time I admitted it out loud."

Sawyer hooked his knuckle under my chin, lifting my face to his. His eyes held mine. "Are you okay with it?"

I reached up and cupped his cheek. In no way did I want Sawyer to think my own inner turmoil was a reflection of him. "I really think I am."

"Okay, so what's wrong then?"

"I'm not sure I can keep hiding from the world, living in secret."

Sawyer's entire body went rigid. "You know I can't. I mean, I wish I could, and what about your—"

I covered his lips with a finger. "Relax. I don't mean I'm ready to tell the world. But I think my parents should know the truth, especially since we're together."

He let out a breath on a rush, like he'd been holding it from the moment I mentioned living in secret. A shy smile, something very rare from Sawyer, came across his face. "You really want to tell them?"

Leaning up on my elbows, I pressed my lips softly to Sawyer's. "I do. I think they deserve to know." He nodded and I took advantage of his encouragement, asking for something he didn't need to do. "Would you come with me to tell them?"

He cupped my face and brought it to his, our mouths connecting in a kiss full of so many promises. God, I never imagined how much he could mean to me. Those three little words floated through my head again. Not that I was anywhere close to ready to say them. But they were there anyway, waiting for the right time.

"For you I'd do anything."

I didn't need to hear the sincerity in his voice to know the truth. Sawyer would do anything for me just like I'd do anything for him.

"We can go this weekend, unless you have a last-minute show."

He brushed the hair from my forehead. "Actually, we have nothing this weekend."

"You don't?" I couldn't remember the last time the band didn't have something on a Friday or Saturday night. "How did you manage that?"

Suddenly, Sawyer's expression dropped. "Well, Tom came to see us today."

Tom was the band's publicist. Other than that, I knew nothing else. I'd never met the guy. I held him tighter to me, wanting to absorb whatever bad that happened today and protect him from it. "What's wrong? What happened?"

He covered my hand with his. "Nothing's wrong. It's just they want to send us on a PR tour for the next two weeks. Hit all the major broadcasting markets on the East Coast."

I sat up so fast, I dislodged his hand from my face. "Really? That's awesome."

"It is, but I'm torn. I really don't want to be away from you for two weeks."

I hadn't thought about that. If it pushed his career further, it would be worth it. "That will suck. It's not like that couldn't happen if they decided to send you on tour and that would be much longer."

He groaned. “I don’t even want to think about that.”

“Okay, so let’s focus on this one. We can get through two weeks. It will be a good practice run for later. Besides, you can video chat me.”

“Oh, so now you’re into phone sex.”

I winked. “Maybe. I’m into a lot of things you don’t know about.”

He rolled so I was under him. “Well then, I guess it’s time to find out.”

He lowered his head and did his best to figure out what other things I might like and I wasn’t going to complain.

Reagan

For the hundredth time today, I thought about telling Sawyer to pull over so I could puke on the side of the road. My stomach was twisted into knots and bile burned the back of my throat.

What the hell am I doing?

Every time the question popped into my head, I forced myself to really look at Sawyer and remember all the time we spent together the last month. The fear made it easy to forget how quickly I was falling for my best friend. We'd told the band about our relationship. Outside of the public finding out, there was still one hurdle left to climb.

My parents.

Sawyer had gotten the call last week that Jaded Ivory would be heading out on a PR tour for their upcoming album. The buzz the single Midnight Dream had already created led the bigwigs at the recording studio to believe the album would sail up the charts once it was released, making Jaded Ivory a household name. With my new case heading to trial, I needed to stay and get work done. Not to mention we didn't want to give the press wind of anything they didn't need to know.

The band had the weekend off before getting on the road Monday morning. Even though I had no idea if I was doing the right thing, I convinced Sawyer to take a trip home with me. We could tell our parents about our relationship. Since his parents already knew he was gay, I had a feeling they'd be a little shocked the two of us ended up together, but in the end I knew they would be happy for us. They knew Sawyer leaving had a lot to do with his feelings for me.

My parents, on the other hand, were about to be blindsided with the fact their son, after twenty-six years of being straight, was now in a relationship with a guy. No matter which way I tried to say it, I couldn't think of a way that wouldn't give my parents the shock of a lifetime. Although, telling them was the only fair thing to do. Especially after I almost forced Sawyer to tell the rest of the members of the band.

Now faced with my own reveal, I understood his choice to keep it under wraps for so long.

I shoved my hands under my thighs to keep them from shaking. Sawyer must have noticed the move from the corner of his eye. He reached between my thighs and extracted my hand, lacing our fingers together and bringing it to his lips for a kiss.

"What can I do to help you relax?"

"I don't know that I can find a way to relax."

He ran his thumb along my knuckles. "I'd help you relax the way you helped me, but then I'd have to pull the car over."

I rolled my eyes at his joke. "Your mouth may not be available, but your hands seem to be." I shook the hand he held for emphasis.

He released my fingers and ran his hand down the front of my jeans. "Is this what you mean?"

When his fingers slid over my denim-covered cock, I had a hard time not thrusting up into his hand. "Mmm, I think you want that." He slowed to a stop at a red light and leaned over to trace the shell of my ear with his tongue. "How about I promise that tonight I'll make you forget about everything that happens today?"

"I'm holding you to that. Not that it helps me here and now." My stomach was tied in knots as the light changed to green.

"How about we go to my parents first? Since they already know about me and my feelings for you, you can be the one to tell them about us. It will give you some practice to face your own parents."

It wasn't the worst idea. "I haven't seen your parents in years. I didn't bother once they refused to tell me why you left."

He lifted my hand to his lips again and pressed a kiss to the back of it. "I have to take the blame for that one. I begged them not to tell you anything."

"Doesn't mean they even like me anymore. I caused you pain for a lot of years."

"That wasn't your fault either. I kept the truth from you. They know that, and they'll understand."

I quirked a brow at him, but he continued.

"Honestly, they're going to be thrilled that we're together. They want me to be happy and I'm guessing that's all your parents want from you."

"I hope so."

I really did. The difference between me and Sawyer was he had the advantage of knowing he was gay and watching his parents for signs about the way they might react. I, on the other hand, was about to throw a grenade in their laps and hope the explosion didn't cause too much damage. Unlike Sawyer, my parents were all I had. There were no siblings to help me through this like he had with Julia. I'd be gutted if they couldn't accept our relationship.

"When did you tell your parents? You said before you ran from them, so I guess it wasn't right before you left."

He shook his head. "No. I had so much to work out in my head when it came to my feelings for you. Plus, I was scared to death of what they would say." He rested his hand on my leg. "I knew my parents loved me, but this was a game changer. That's how I know exactly what you're feeling, but I promise everything is going to be okay."

As each day passed, I fell a little bit harder for the man next to me. It might have seemed fast, but I knew him almost as well as I knew myself. His likes, his dislikes, his favorite food and movies. I even knew every one of his pet peeves. He was a slob to my neatness and a night owl to my early riser, but there was nothing about Sawyer I'd ever change. If my parents made me choose, even after raising me for the last twenty-six years, I'd still choose Sawyer. The realization smacked me in the face like I walked into a door.

I love Sawyer.

I was 100 percent, hands down in love with Sawyer. And nothing anyone said or did was going to change that. I'd stick by him no matter what and glancing at him out of the corner of my eye, I knew he would do the same for me.

The closer we got to Sawyer's childhood home, the more my hands started to clam up. Lines of perspiration ran down my temple and neck. Deep down, I recognized that Sawyer was right about his parents. Didn't make the thought of telling them everything any less terrifying. When Sawyer pulled into the drive, my heart slammed into my chest.

"I don't know if I can do this." Each breath seemed hard to draw in.

Sawyer turned to me, taking both of my hands in his. "I would kiss you and promise you can, but I don't want to give anything away. Please just trust me. You can do this and everything is going to be okay."

He searched my eyes. Maybe trying to find my confidence, my sense of calm? I had a good feeling I threw them both out the window and left them on the interstate on the way here. Something deep in his gaze made me nod and suck in a breath. He rubbed his thumb over my knuckles and waited for me to release the breath I'd been holding. I blew it out and reached for the door handle.

You can do this. I chanted it in my head over and over again, hoping it might give me the strength to face the next twenty minutes. By the time we reached the front door I had a hard time staying upright. Even my knees were shaking, threatening to drop me to the floor.

Sawyer wasted no time pushing the door open and gesturing for me to step inside. I did, just a little happy his parents hadn't greeted us in the foyer. It gave me a few more minutes to calm my racing heart.

"Sawyer?" a soft female voice called from the top of the stairs.

"It's me, Mom," he shouted back, then leaned over to whisper in my ear. "Breathe, Reagan. Breathe."

My eyes darted to his and for the briefest of seconds, I thought about begging him to take me home and forget about telling anyone. We could keep it between the two of us and his bandmates. No one would ever have to know. But how fair was that to Sawyer? I didn't want him to think I was ashamed of being with him, but I also didn't know if I could face the reality of my parents pushing me away.

"Hey," she said, walking across the top balcony that led to the stairs. "What are you—" She froze at the top of the stairs, her eyes staring directly at me. "Reagan? Is that you?"

"It's him, Mom."

She raced down the stairs and wrapped her arms around me in a tight bear hug that practically cut off my ability to breathe. "Oh my God, I haven't seen you in forever."

Awkwardly, I patted her on the back. She'd been like a second mother to me growing up, but that had been a long time ago. "It's good to see you again, Mrs. Alason."

She leaned back and stared me down. With a little more than a foot on her, she still happened to be one of the most opposing figures I'd ever crossed. "Don't start with that Mrs. Alason crap."

I smirked. "Sorry, Charlene." The tension in my body started to flow from me with the familiarity of being in her home.

"That's better. Now, tell me what you're doing here." She turned to Sawyer. "And why are you here with Reagan. You haven't seen him in years."

"Where's Dad? Do you think we could all sit down and talk?"

She watched him closely. "You're being very mysterious."

"Mom, please. I..." Sawyer glanced over at me. "*We* have something to share with you."

She didn't move. Didn't blink for a few minutes before she threw her hands up in the air. "He's out in the garage. Let me get him and we'll meet you in the family room."

"Thanks, Mom." He bent down and kissed her on the cheek.

"Yeah, yeah, yeah. I want to hear what you have to say."

Charlene left us standing in the foyer. Sawyer took my hand and squeezed it when she was out of sight. "Want a drink? My dad still hides the good stuff in the cabinet above the stove."

One thing we knew about sneaking liquor from Sawyer's parents' house was to leave the stuff in the top cabinet alone. His dad always managed to catch us when we did that. I laughed. "No, I'm not sure it will help right now. I may definitely need one when the day is over, though."

He led me down the hall to the back of the house. The only things that had changed in the years since I'd last been there were the pictures. Many of the frames now held pictures of different graduations and some of Jaded Ivory's successes.

The couch still sat along the back wall, with a chair on either side. Sawyer pulled the chairs closer and sat down on the couch. It felt like my whole body trembled as I paced back and forth in front of him.

He placed his hand on my arm, stopping my movement. "Would you sit down? Everything will be fine. Remember, I've been here before."

I sat down and rested my arms on my thighs. Sawyer rubbed his hand along my back.

"Hey, if you want me to tell them, I'll do it. I don't mind."

That brought my head up and I stared into worried eyes. He cupped my face in his hand, bringing me closer to cover my lips with his. I stopped for a brief second before I realized we'd hear the door to the garage close when they were on their way back inside. Our lips connected and the room around us faded. All I could pay attention to was Sawyer's tongue as he drew it across the seam of my lips. Every time we kissed it was like the rest of the world no longer existed. I didn't think I'd ever get enough of feeling his mouth on mine.

A door slammed in the background. Sawyer and I jerked away from each other, facing forward and trying to pretend the last few minutes hadn't happened. At least until they knew everything.

Sawyer's dad stepped through the door first, followed closely behind by his mom, crossing the room with his hand extended. "Reagan, it's so good to see you again."

I stood and returned his handshake. "It's good to see you, too, Mr.—" At that his dad's brow lifted. "Sorry, Derek."

"Much better." He smiled and practically yanked Sawyer off the couch, tugging him into a hug. "Glad to see you finally called Reagan to work things out."

Sawyer laughed and the sound traveled straight down my spine, setting my blood on fire. I loved his laugh. "Not exactly, Dad. Reagan hunted me down at a meet and greet."

He looked over at me. "Good for you, son. I wasn't sure this guy would ever get his head out of his ass."

"I didn't expect him to either, so once I heard they were playing at the arena near Hayward, I decided to go see him."

Sawyer glanced back and forth between his parents. "That actually has a little bit to do with what we wanted to talk to you about. You guys mind sitting down?"

They glanced at each other warily before moving around to take their seats.

"What did you want to tell us?" Charlene asked.

Sawyer looked over at me, waiting for a sign that I was ready to do this. I'd probably never be ready, but it was now or never.

SAWYER

Reagan looked like a deer in headlights. I knew that feeling all too well. The way my stomach clenched. Hearing the pounding of my heart in my ears. Exactly how I felt walking into this house the night before I left for college and laying it all at their feet. I'd never understood how much my parents loved me before that moment.

It was unconditional.

But Reagan's fear was real. Many times, people expected their parents to understand and the opposite happened. Most of me believed that of Reagan's parents. However, there was a small part of me that worried about what would happen if they couldn't or wouldn't understand.

He gave me a slight nod and turned to face my mom and dad.

"Mr. and Mrs.—"

"Reagan," my mother warned. Her eyes flashed to me and quickly back to Reagan. A sparkle brightened her gaze.

She *knew*. Somehow she already knew about our relationship. Another reason my mom was the best. She didn't say a word. I knew exactly what she was doing. She wanted to give Reagan a chance to practice saying it all and getting that first time acceptance. Right then, I wanted to jump from my seat and hug the shit out of the woman. Instead, I kept my ass planted to the couch and waited.

"Sorry. Charlene and Derek. Sawyer and I have, uh...we, uh, have...something we need to tell you."

A small smile tugged at the corner of her lips. Not the megawatt one I knew she wanted to use, but encouraging nonetheless.

This time I gave *him* the nod of encouragement. He sucked in a breath, slowly letting it out. I could see the way his hands trembled in his lap and I had to stop myself from reaching out and taking hold of them.

"Well...um...Sawyer and I...have been, uh...dating for the last few months," he rushed out on a breath of air.

My mom paused for all of about a half second before she launched herself at the two of us. Out of the corner of my eye, I saw Reagan brace himself as she wrapped her arms around our necks, pulling us into a group hug that stole my breath. And I mean literally stole my breath. Her arm was so tight I couldn't suck any air into my lungs.

"Oh my God," she squealed. "I'm so happy for the two of you."

"Charlene, love," my dad said from somewhere behind her. I couldn't see where he was standing, Mom's hair blocking my line of sight. "I think you need to let them go now so they can breathe. Their lips are starting to turn blue."

Mom's grip instantly released. "I'm sorry. I'm just so happy. I never thought Sawyer would find anyone who could meet his standards."

"Mom," I warned. Reagan and I had come a long way, but that still didn't mean he knew the depth of my feelings for him. The right time hadn't come to give him everything.

She pressed a kiss to both our foreheads and moved back to her own seat, giving my dad a chance to stand up and shake my hand, yanking me into another tight hug. At least this time I could breathe. He did the same to Reagan, patting him on the back, telling him how much courage it took for him to tell them.

My parents were amazing even if deep down their words made me a little sad. Not for the way they accepted Reagan without batting an eyelash, but for the fact he had to be brave or nervous. I hoped for the day where no one had to *come out of the closet* so to speak. We were just all people living our lives any way that made us happy. I knew having Reagan in my life that my happy had already started.

Reagan dropped down onto the couch, a sigh of relief blowing past his lips. I rested my hand on his thigh and his eyes flew open. For one brief moment, I thought he might protest. Outside of the band this was the first time I'd touched him as more than a friend in front of others. Almost like his mind had to catch up, he glanced at my parents, who were still smiling, and laid his head back against my sofa, enjoying the simple touch.

"You are so cute together," my mom cooed.

I rolled my eyes and glanced at her. "We try our best."

Reagan took a few calming breaths, then sat up to face the rest of us. "Sorry, I needed a minute."

Dad nodded. "We understand. What you just did isn't easy."

"You're right. It's not."

A sheer line of sweat covered Reagan's brow. Only his first adrenaline dump of the day. I had a feeling he'd put telling his parents in the back of his head until it was time to head over there. Mom got up and moved to the other side of Reagan on the couch. "Have you talked to your parents yet?"

At least if my mom hadn't brought it up.

"Not yet. Sawyer thought it would be good practice to tell you first."

She took his hand in hers. "I think that was a very smart move. Your parents love you no matter what you decide."

"I hope you're right."

She covered his hand with her other one and gave it a squeeze. "Don't worry, I am."

"Thanks, Charlene."

I cupped Reagan's jaw with my right hand and turned him to face me. "I told you everything would be fine." I didn't give him a chance to protest, just pressing my lips to his, hoping to ease his tension of the last few hours.

We broke apart, but he pressed his forehead to mine. "Thank you for being here with me."

"I wouldn't be anywhere else."

Once it seemed as Reagan calmed down, we sat and talked with my parents for a bit. I gave them all the information about the PR tour I was about to head out on. Reagan filled them in on his time working as a lawyer. I noticed the way his leg bounced up and down as he told them about the types of cases he handled. He hadn't even given them a true accounting of how much time he put in at work. My mom must have noticed it as well.

"Reagan, honey, I'd love to hear more about your job. Believe me, I find what you do absolutely fascinating."

"Thanks a lot, Mom," I said, letting the sarcasm bleed into my tone.

"Don't start, Sawyer. I hear about the band every other day. This is something new." She turned back to Reagan. "I can't help but notice the way your leg is shaking and the way your gaze keeps traveling around the room like your mind is somewhere else."

"I'm so sorry."

She shook her head. "Don't be sorry. You have a lot on your mind. Why don't you let Sawyer drive you over to your parents? If you and your parents feel up to it afterward, we can all have dinner together and catch up some more."

"I think that sounds like a great idea," I chimed in.

Reagan slowly stood. "You're right. My mind is definitely elsewhere. I need to get this off my chest. No matter what their reaction might be. I can't keep hiding from them."

"I promise." Mom held up her one hand. "They are going to be fine with all of this."

"Mom, you talk like you have some kind of inside knowledge."

"Absolutely not. I just know how Kathleen and Tommy are. They'll love you no matter what your choices are."

He gave her a half smile, one that didn't reach his eyes. The color slowly drained from his face. He needed to get this over with so he could breathe easy again. Even if they hurt him, he wouldn't have to worry about the unknown anymore.

I stood and reached out for his hand, lacing our fingers together. "Ready?"

"As ready as I'll ever be." He looked at my parents. "Hopefully, we'll see you later."

"Even if you don't do dinner, you're always welcome back here."

I waved to my parents on the way out the door, wanting to get Reagan to his parents before he threw up or worse, decided not to tell them. That this was all too much for him to deal with.

We climbed in the car. Reagan didn't make a sound on the short ride there. He sucked in short, shallow breaths and for one minute I thought he might start to hyperventilate. I put the car in park and faced him.

"If you want me to, I can stay in the car."

He shook his head emphatically. "Absolutely not. You may not be able to hold my hand while I tell them, but I want you as close to me as possible. I need you to be my rock, no matter what happens."

"I'll be anything you need me to be."

We got out of the car and I followed a short distance behind him, trying to not stare at his ass, making everything more than obvious. He lifted his hand like he was knocking on some strangers' door. Just as quickly he lowered his hand and blew his hair off his forehead.

"What the hell is wrong with me?" he whispered under his breath and pushed the door open.

"Mom? Dad?" he called.

"In the den," his dad called out to us.

He gave my hand a brief squeeze before starting toward the back of his parents' house. The TV blared in the background as we took the three steps down into the room. In the years since I'd been there, they'd replaced some of the furniture and the TV. A large U-shaped sectional took up the middle of the room on one side. The wall to the left still held a ton of pictures of Reagan throughout his life. Looking at that wall, I understood what he was afraid of losing.

"Hey, Reagan, what are you—" His mom stopped mid-sentence, her gaze flying to me. "Sawyer?"

"Hey, Mom. It's him."

She stood and like my mom, rushed over and pulled me into a hug, rocking me back and forth. "Where have you been hiding? We've been keeping tabs on your band since Reagan pointed out it was you behind the drums."

"Awww, thank you."

She stepped back, holding me by the shoulders, her gaze examining every inch of me. "That doesn't explain where you've been."

I glanced at Reagan out of the corner of my eye. It was now or never. Sweat formed on his brow, but he straightened his shoulders.

Now.

"That's kind of what we're here to explain."

She took each of our hands and led us over to the side of the sectional couch. She sat on one side of me with Reagan on the other. "Talk to us. What's going on? Does it have something to do with your band members?"

Reagan shook his head. "Nothing like that, Mom. We need to talk about why Sawyer left."

His mom's gaze shot to me. "Did something happen to you? Were you okay? What can we do to help?"

"Mom," Reagan groaned. "Would you stop asking a million questions and listen?"

She pretended to zip her mouth shut and folded her hands in her lap, like a schoolgirl who'd just been given a detention for her excessive talking.

"Well...uh...Sawyer...uh, and I...um...have something to tell you."

His mom moved closer to the edge of the couch. "What is it?"

Reagan looked at me and I could see his Adam's apple bob as he swallowed hard. And again like at my parents' house, he let it out on a rush of air. "Sawyer left because he's gay and he thought I might not be able to accept that."

Fiery eyes moved to Reagan. "You better not have given him that indication. We don't choose who we love."

With those words, I noticed Reagan's shoulder start to relax. Kathleen had crossed her arms over her chest, waiting for his answer. I think a part of him was so relieved she wasn't upset, that he forgot to answer her. One of her brows winged up to her hairline as a sure sign she might lose her shit on him in a matter of seconds. Belatedly, he realized how close his mom was and rushed to reassure her.

"No, Mom. I would never push him away because of who he loves."

If only Reagan knew he was that person. He had been the only one.

She looked back and forth between us, her stance relaxing as she waited for us to continue.

"Well..." I started, but Reagan shook his head, stopping the flow of words.

He turned back to his mother. "There's more to it than that."

Her head tilted to the side, probably running through the million scenarios that could make me being gay different. I would have been willing to bet the reality was nowhere near what she expected.

"What else could there be?"

Reagan opened his mouth to speak and at the same time quietly slipped his hand in mine. Her eyes followed our hands. "Sawyer and I are in a relationship."

Tommy was staring at our joined hands, and I braced myself for their reaction. I saw Reagan do the same thing out of the corner of my eye. "So you're gay?"

There was no animosity or hatred in his voice, just curiosity. Just a parent trying to understand what his son was telling him. His mom still hadn't said a word.

Reagan looked at his dad. "No, I wouldn't say gay, maybe bi. I didn't suddenly start not finding women attractive. I'm just more attracted to Sawyer right now."

He squeezed my fingers. While it felt good to hear the words, there was a part of me that couldn't leave out the *right now*. Would he eventually get tired of me, push me away for a woman? Someone who society would be more willing to accept? Digging deep, I shoved those thoughts away. Reagan was with me and I wouldn't let the what-ifs of the future ruin that.

His dad nodded and stood from the couch, holding his hand out to Reagan. He took it and let his dad pull him to standing. Reagan's dad wrapped his arm around him, hugging him tight. Reagan began shaking from head to toe.

"You have nothing to worry about. You are my son and nothing will change that. I'll always love you."

Reagan's whole body relaxed against his dad, letting him absorb some of the shaking from the adrenaline dump. A tear glistened in Kathleen's eyes as she wrapped her arms around my shoulders and kissed the top of my head. "Tommy's, right. We love you both no matter who you're with. All we want from either of you is for you to be happy."

I hadn't noticed the tension in my shoulders when we'd left my parents' house, but those words made it seem like I could breathe again. Reagan turned around and hugged his mom.

He watched me over his shoulder and winked. I loved having my Reagan back. "He makes me really happy."

"That's all I care about."

Reagan sat next to me, closer than before, and laid his hand across my thigh, resting his head on my shoulder. "Thank you," he whispered.

I set my hand against his cheek. "Anything for you."

The room was silent for a moment while Reagan's parents came to terms with the new reality, but that didn't stop them from also asking us to stay for dinner. In the end we decided to take both of our parents out. We talked, laughed, and joked. Things were looking brighter every day. If only the rain cloud of telling my secret to the world would have disappeared.

It was something we still needed to face, but until the time came, I planned on enjoying my little piece of happy.

Reagan

Time seemed to stand still. No earth turning on its axis. No cycles of the moon. Each day blended into the one before it.

When Sawyer mentioned the PR blitz tour, I thought nothing of it. We'd spent years apart. Two weeks would be a walk in the park.

Boy was I fucking wrong.

Those years passed in the blink of an eye. After the first few months, I stopped waiting for Sawyer to walk through the door and apologize for bailing. What I should have realized in that time was his feelings for me and maybe even my feelings for him. It would explain why I felt so lost and abandoned when he first left. This time couldn't have been any more different.

This time I knew what it felt like to have his lips on mine and his fingers electrifying every part of skin he touched. My cock ached at the very thought of being buried deep inside Sawyer or his delectable mouth on my dick. I spent many nights keeping myself company with my right hand, but it wasn't the same.

Honestly, I couldn't wait for him to be home.

Unfortunately, there was still an entire week to go. They were flying almost every day as they hopped from one major city to the next, doing interviews or playing live on the radio. Earlier I'd watched the video of them playing in a studio. Things seemed to be going really well for them. Every time they stopped in a city, their single moved farther up the charts.

A quick glance around my living room and I was a little lost. Thankful that Harrison was on a business trip for a week, but still lost. I spent so much time at Sawyer's place, mine no longer felt like home. The stuff was all mine, it just wasn't the place I wanted to be. I leaned my head against the back of the couch. The words on my laptop blurred as my focus strayed from the brief I'd been working on to Sawyer. Or more accurately, everything I wanted Sawyer to be doing to me at the moment. My eyes crossed with just the thought.

I slammed the lid shut and made my way to the kitchen for a beer. If I couldn't get any work done, the least I could do was drink and watch a game. I'd just sat down and reached for the remote when my cell phone rang. I picked it up from the coffee table. The name on the screen had me answering instantly.

"Hey, sexy."

Sawyer growled into the phone. "What if it wasn't me on the other end of the line?"

I rolled my eyes. "And who else would it possibly be?"

He sighed. "Ugh. I have no idea. I'm just cranky."

"Aren't things going well?"

"Things are going extremely well."

I placed the beer bottle on the table in front of me. "Then what's the problem? I thought you were most excited for touring."

"That was before I had you in my bed every night."

Something squeaked into the receiver. "Are you guys at a hotel?"

"Yeah," he said on a sigh. "I'm lying on this lonely bed with no big, warm body to snuggle up to."

I chuckled. "I'd give you shit about that, but I can't seem to get you out of my head tonight either."

"Oh, really? Thinking about my mouth on your cock?"

Visions of the way he swirled his tongue around the tip made every ounce of blood that could possibly be in my head rush south. My dick hardened in an instant. Since Sawyer and I first hooked up, it had been a long time since I'd gone without sex. And my body craved his.

Soft moans sounded over the phone that sent a shiver down my body. "Are you jerking off?"

A louder groan hit my ears. "Yeah. The sound of your voice makes me hard as a rock."

"It does, doesn't it?"

"Oh God, please don't stop talking," he begged.

If Sawyer was going to get himself off while on the phone with me, I wanted to do the same. Lying across the couch, I tugged down my basketball shorts and boxers, freeing my cock from its confines. With visions of Sawyer's naked body in my mind, I wrapped my hand around my dick, pulling off one stroke.

"All I can think about is fucking you until you can't walk the next day."

"Oh fuck." That thought made my balls pull tight to my body.

I moved my thumb over the slit, spreading the pre-cum, using it as lubrication over my already aching dick. My hands slid up and down faster. The sounds coming from the phone grew louder. I knew Sawyer was close. So was I. My balls pulled tight to my body. The moment I heard my name shouted from his lips, I lost it. Come shot out all over my chest. Good thing I hadn't bothered with a shirt earlier.

My breathing slowed and I grabbed a tissue to clean myself up. Even without Sawyer touching me, orgasms were explosive. What else did I expect from the man, when his voice made me hard as a rock? I tucked myself back into my pants and imagined Sawyer doing the same.

"I miss you," I said, almost hating the sound of vulnerability in my voice.

If we couldn't make it two weeks how were we supposed to make months at a time when he toured. It wasn't like I could go with him. No one but the band knew about us and I certainly couldn't give up my job. I didn't want to make Sawyer feel worse about the choices he made. This was the career he'd always wanted and I wouldn't make him feel guilty when it took him away from me.

"I miss you, too."

"How many stops do you have tomorrow?"

He sighed. "Just one."

"You'll be home before you know it."

"Yeah, but for how long?"

I may not have been able to see him, but I could hear the defeat in his voice over the phone. "Why do you sound like your mom took away your drumsticks?"

He was quiet for a long moment. The silence stretched on, prickling over my skin. I didn't think his intention was to freak me out. He was only trying to figure out how to put whatever he wanted to say into words.

"Sawyer, talk to me. I will always be here to listen to you. Just like I've been for most of your life."

"I..." He trailed off and for one brief moment I braced myself.

Was I ready to hear those words?

Could I return them?

At that moment, with so much distance between us, I didn't think it was the right time. Not that I could stop him if he did say it. And yeah, I was feeling it, but I wanted us to be face-to-face when we said it.

"I," he started again. "I don't want to be apart from you for this long again."

I shook my head, even though I knew he couldn't see me. "We've been over this. We'll deal with a tour when it happens."

He scoffed. "That might be sooner than you think."

I sat up straight on the couch. "Did they offer you a long-term tour?"

"They said if the success of this PR tour continues, they'll start looking into dates for a solo tour when we return." Melancholy laced his voice.

"That's awesome news."

"Then why do I feel guilty for only part of me being excited about it?"

I ran a hand through my hair. Sawyer hadn't given me the whole story and without it I couldn't figure out how to help him through whatever he was feeling. "Why aren't you excited?"

"'Cause." In my mind I could see him sitting on the bed shrugging. "I'd rather not spend nine months having phone sex with you."

My eyes flew wide-open. "That's what you're worried about?"

"The thought of spending nine months apart doesn't upset you?" The sadness had been replaced with a bite. Sawyer was pissed.

"Slow your roll, babe. That's not what I said. Being apart for that long will be hard, but the tour wouldn't start tomorrow, would it?"

"No. It takes months to plan."

I dropped my head on the back of the couch. "Then what are you worried about? We have months to figure out a way around not seeing each other. It gives me time to save money to fly out to you when you're not playing too far."

"And how will we do that when no one knows about us?"

I rolled my eyes. "Don't be ridiculous. We'll make sure we have adjoining rooms, then no one will see us."

"I never thought of that," he breathed.

"That's 'cause you're too busy looking at the negatives. I'm the optimist, remember?"

"Fuck you." Sawyer laughed.

It was good to hear my Sawyer coming back to himself. I really liked the way that sounded—*my* Sawyer. Made it very clear that no one else could have him. "Don't I wish, but I have to wait until you get home."

Sawyer stopped laughing instantly. I heard him swallow hard. That was when I realized what I said. I'd been thinking about it, but hadn't told Sawyer yet. I wanted to be able to give myself to him in a way no one had me before. Something only for him. The one thing holding me back was the fear of the pain.

"Are you serious?" he whispered.

For Sawyer, I knew I could get past it.

"Dead serious."

It was the phrase we'd used growing up when we were joking around, but we needed the other person to know at that moment we were telling the truth. Any time someone said it, you had to listen because it was important.

"Holy shit, you are serious." Sawyer growled. "Of course you have to mention this when I'm hundreds of miles away and can't do a goddamn thing about it."

"You can dream about it."

"Fuck, you're making me hard."

I knew the feeling. It didn't matter we'd just come, the conversation alone was making my dick hard and ready. "It'll give you something to look forward to for the next week."

"Look forward to? You've got to be kidding me. That's all I'm gonna think about for the next seven days."

"Focus on the music and you'll be fine."

"I doubt that," he mumbled.

A loud pounding came through the phone.

"What was that?"

"Monty being an ass and beating on my door. They want to go to dinner."

I heard the chain fall from its lock and the sound in the room grew.

"I'm starving," Monty whined. "Can't you talk to lover boy when we get back?"

"Ow," he yelled a moment later. "Fuck, Mari, stop slapping me."

"Then stop being an ass. Hi, Reagan, ignore his cranky ass. He's hungry," she shouted into the phone.

A chorus of hellos sounded into the phone.

"Babe," I said. "Go get dinner before they drag you out of there kicking and screaming."

"Not really hungry for food right now." And he didn't have to say what I knew was on his mind. He wanted something else for dinner.

"I'll be here when you get home in seven days."

"Fine, but you can't blame me for what happens when I get there."

"I want it, so come get me."

We said our goodbyes and hung up the phone. What had I gotten myself into? True, I'd been thinking about it, but was I really ready to face all that it meant? What if I couldn't take it? I glanced at the date on my phone. Promises made would be kept, which meant I had seven days to get myself ready.

SAWYER

The equipment was set up for our very last stop. For seven days, I'd lived in a perpetual state of semi-arousal. Maybe it made me a dick, but I could think of little else except getting my hands on Reagan and sliding my dick into his tight ass. I dreamed about it. Daydreamed about it. It was one of the only thoughts occupying my brain.

Heath bumped against my shoulder, yanking me out of another fantasy. "Jesus, get a grip. You can see him tonight after we get home."

I rubbed the back of my neck. "I know. I know. It feels like forever since I've seen him."

"Seriously? It's only been two weeks. What are you going to do when they schedule the tour?"

"We don't even know if that's happening." Not because I didn't believe, more that I wasn't ready for it.

His bows arched over his eyes, waiting for me to see the stupidity of my statement. They'd all but told us we'd be scheduled within the next six months.

"All right, I'm just not ready to think about that yet." It was much more pleasurable to think about Reagan bent over the side of my bed.

He narrowed his eyes. "You know what, I don't want to know what you're thinking about with that dreamy look all over your face."

"I'd make your head spin."

The door opened and the radio host stepped in. We shifted our focus to her and introduced ourselves. She led us through the routine of the show, which ironically was pretty standard up and down the coast. She'd play a few songs, then introduce us and ask some questions before handing over the mic. We'd play and thank her and the audience for being there. The sooner we got through that, the sooner I could get home to Reagan.

Everyone tested their equipment one last time before we took our seats in front of her. She warned us it was the final song in the playlist and we'd be up next. The final notes of the song played and the on-air light lit up the window.

"Good morning. Welcome to the Marian Daye show. It's been a blast so far this morning as I got the opportunity to spend some quality time with the members of Jaded Ivory. You guys wanna say hello?"

She nodded to the mic directly in front of Heath. We all leaned and said hi. Told them how excited we were to be there.

"Okay, well, what an enthusiastic response. Before they play their newest single Midnight Dream, I want us to get to know each other a little better. So, I'm going to let you guys call in and ask the band some questions."

Well, that was new.

In the end the questions were pretty basic.

How did you meet Cole?

What's it like when he travels?

Did the piercing in your lip hurt? Always to Monty.

These were questions we answered over and over again for the fans. We knew the acceptable answers by heart. Ones that would not cause controversy from the start. At least I thought so.

"Good morning, Ashley. What would you like to ask the members of Jaded Ivory?"

"OMG, I can't believe I'm talking to you guys. Well, my question is for Sawyer. Sawyer, are you single? If you are, you can certainly come home with me."

Yes. I knew I was supposed to answer yes. The PR department was happy having four of the five members of the band being single. And I was supposed to say yes. *Of course, you haven't seen me on the streets alone 'cause I'm damn good at hiding my relationships from you.* The words stuck in my throat. I couldn't bring myself to deny Reagan, or suddenly out myself. The band must have noticed me struggling with the answer.

Heath wrapped an arm around my shoulders. I'd never been so grateful to have such supportive friends. "No, he's not going to give that up. If he did, he wouldn't have any secrets left. I don't even know who it is." He laughed. The five of us knew it was forced. Didn't mean the audience would.

Another landmine and another crisis averted.

The reality was, these kinds of questions were going to come up more often and I needed to be able to give the right answer without choking on it. The biggest problem I had was not talking to Reagan about it first. In my head I knew he would understand considering the circumstances. It was more the heart that was having trouble dealing with it.

"All right, that's all the questions we have time for. I don't know about you, but I'm dying to hear them play." That was our cue to get to our instruments. "Here's Jaded Ivory with Midnight Dream."

Ten more minutes and we'd be on our way home. I played through the song on autopilot. Each beat fell in time to the thud of my heart as it sped up the closer we got to leaving. I hit the last beat and practically jumped from my seat.

"Oh my God, I loved it," Marian gushed into her microphone. "Thank you so much for coming and playing for us today."

"Thanks for having us," Mari said, a smile on her face, the same one that had to be on mine. We both had a reason to get home sooner rather than later. I had no idea how she handled Cole being gone every other weekend.

"Ladies and gentleman, make sure you check out our pages for the link to download Midnight Dream. When we come back, I have news about our super listeners contest. Don't go too far."

Marian flipped a switch, turning off the light and starting the next song simultaneously. She pulled Mari into a hug. "Seriously, guys, thank you so much for being here. That song was fucking awesome and I look forward to hearing it live in concert one day."

That compliment stopped me from running to the drums and putting them away. Things were changing for us, faster than any of us ever expected.

The success was exciting and frightening all at the same time. We were about to be given a solo tour and were slowly becoming a household name. The least I could do was take five minutes out of my time to thank the people who helped us on our way up. I turned and gave Marian the proper thank you instead of being a selfish asshole and blowing her off for my boyfriend who still happened to be at work. I'd be happy with getting home the same time he did.

After packing up and stopping for lunch on the way home, we pulled into the studio lot a little after five. Long before Reagan would be home from work. So, I rode home with Heath, trying not to think about all the things I wanted to do to Reagan. Not an easy feat when you knew you were finally going to get the chance to do some of those things. I packed a bag for Reagan's place. His roommate was out of town. Thankfully, we wouldn't have to deal with the little shit for the night. I also wanted to give Heath the chance to have the house to himself. He'd been great about Reagan staying there, not complaining once. I owed him for that.

"Would you stop pacing and just go over there? I'm sure he's home by now," Heath said a few hours later. "And if he's not, just call him and tell him you're waiting."

"But—"

"Jesus, you're that nervous about seeing him that you forgot about this great invention called a cell phone." He picked mine up off the table and threw it at me. I caught it right before it hit the floor.

"Don't be an ass. I don't feel like going out to get a new phone tonight."

Heath rolled his eyes at me and turned back to the TV. "Call him."

He didn't understand. I wasn't nervous about seeing him. I was nervous he'd changed his mind. While I loved having Reagan inside me, fucking him changed things. He'd already admitted to recognizing his bisexual side, but this was different. This was trusting someone enough to let them into your body. There'd be no going back afterward. And that didn't even scratch the surface of my worries. What if he hated it and never wanted to do it again? Would I be okay with that? For Reagan, most likely.

My fingers began flying across the keys when I decided, fuck it. I didn't need to warn him before I showed up on his doorstep. He already knew I'd be coming over tonight. The whole situation messed with my head. It was time to go over there and see what happened.

The ride to Reagan's was a blur of green lights and stop signs. My mind was still buried deep in questions about tonight. I had no idea if I was pushing him too fast. Then I started to wonder if he was doing this for me, because he thought I wanted it. Or if this was something he really wanted to experience. I rode the elevator up, stuffing my hands in my pockets when I couldn't stop the shaking. The ding of the door opening practically had me jumping out of my skin. With measured steps, I walked the long hall to his door. I felt like Alice in Wonderland, trying to find the end of the hall.

The things this man did to me apparently extended to my brain turning to mush when faced with the prospect of taking him the first time. I lifted my hand to knock when the door in front of me flew open. Reagan stopped dead in his tracks.

"Where the fuck have you been? I've been waiting over an hour for you to get here." He waved his keys in his fingers. "I was on my way over to get you."

I took the keys from his fingers and backed him into the apartment. Reagan's back hit the wall of the hall and I tossed the keys in the general direction of the table by the door before kicking the door shut with my foot.

I took his lips in a kiss so fierce it sizzled along every one of my nerves. We could talk later. Right then I needed to taste him. His hands came up to rest against my chest. The heat of his body penetrated the cotton of my shirt. I couldn't stop my body from trembling when his thumbs lightly grazed my nipples, the fabric adding to the sensation.

My cock hardened in seconds. If I didn't say something now, I'd have him naked and under me before we got another chance to speak. I tore my mouth from his.

"You were coming to get me?"

His eyes glazed over and he blinked several times to regain focus. "Yeah. You didn't answer any of my messages."

I took the phone from my pocket and sure enough, at least fifteen messages, almost since the time I left my place. I shrugged. "My phone was in my pocket."

He took a step forward, forcing me to take one back. "That doesn't explain why it took you so long."

"Let's just say I was being an idiot." I took hold of his hand and placed it over my dick. "Doesn't matter anymore. All I want right now is to be naked with you."

Without a word, he took my hand and led me the rest of the way down the hall and into the living room. Reagan didn't bother stopping, walking straight through the door of his bedroom. Then we were kissing. He sucked my tongue into his mouth and it was heaven. I'd missed being able to touch him more than I could remember. Needing to feel his warm skin against mine, I broke the connection of our lips just long enough to divest us both of our shirts. We fell onto the bed in a tangle of limbs.

I found the waistband of his sweats, sinking my hand below the fabric to take his hot, hard cock in my hands. Pre-cum already leaked from the slit and I used my thumb to spread it around the head. If this was going to be Reagan's first time, I wanted his body good and ready before I sank balls deep inside of him. I wanted him to enjoy everything I was doing to him.

His hips bucked up when I pulled off the first stroke. "More," he begged, fumbling to undo the buttons of my jeans.

I reached down with my free hand to help him. Once I had them free, I sank my other hand into his hair and held his mouth to mine, plunging my tongue inside mimicking what I wanted to do with my cock in a bit. I thrust my hips forward, groaning as our erections rubbed together through the fabric of our clothes. Reagan stroked my cock and pulled his mouth away.

"You know how much better that would feel if we didn't have any clothes on?"

I took the waist of his pants and yanked them down to his ankles, letting him kick them to the floor. "Aren't you the tease tonight?"

"The only tease tonight is how slow you're taking things."

"Slow?"

He slid his hand around to the back of my jeans, shoving them down as far as he could reach.

"Yes, slow. I haven't seen you in two weeks and I just want you to fuck me."

My hand froze midair as I was reaching for his nipple. Suddenly, making his first time perfect didn't really matter anymore. As long as he enjoyed it, it didn't matter how perfect getting there was. I stood and kicked off my shoes, dropping my jeans and boxers to the floor. Reagan naked was a spectacular sight. Strong, rippling muscles in his chest and arms, not to mention the deep V at his groin, pointed exactly where I wanted to go.

"Lube and condoms?" I asked. Once we got started, I had no plans on stopping.

"In the top drawer." He pointed to the table next to the bed.

I grabbed the things I needed, happy to see that both boxes were new. In the back of my mind, I knew Reagan had been with women, but I didn't want to think about them. He was with me now. I climbed back on the bed and lightly ran my hand down his chest until I reached his hard, waiting shaft. The head was slightly purple and he looked like he was ready to explode.

"Tonight," I whispered against his lips. "I'm going to take care of you."

"Please." He thrust up, trying to get closer to my hand.

I slid my hand down past his balls to the crack of his ass. I hadn't bothered with lube yet. We'd get there when I was sure he was ready to take it. Slowly, I ran my finger over his puckered entrance, feeling the way he clenched at the lightest touch. With a small amount of pressure, I kept rubbing, forcing him to relax. The way this was playing out, I'd end up coming before I ever got inside of him.

Reaching down, I squeezed at the base of my shaft, calming me enough to get Reagan ready for me.

I opened the lube and poured a generous amount onto my fingers. Reagan's eyes stayed on me the entire time. Once again, I ran my hand down past his balls. This time when I reached his asshole, I pushed one finger inside. The tight ring of muscles clenched around it.

"Relax, baby," I said, taking his dick in my hand and stroking it. "I need you to relax. You've done this before. I don't want to hurt you."

"Feels weird."

"I know it does, but the moment you let me in, I'll make you feel all kinds of pleasure."

He nodded and closed his eyes, trying to relax.

I could see his shoulders lower to the bed, and the sharp, shallow pants from before slowed. The only thing that wasn't relaxing was the one thing I needed to. I removed my finger and leaned up to press a kiss to his lips. "Try something for me, okay?"

"What do you want me to do?"

"I want you to clench your ass and hold it for a few seconds."

One eye popped open. "Okay."

"Trust me, just do it."

His face scrunched in concentration. After a few moments, he shook his head. "I can't."

"Just a few more seconds."

He held his breath for those few seconds, until I watched his whole body relax beneath me.

I slid my fingers between his crack, and this time when I slipped my finger inside, it went all the way in without a problem. To reward him, I crooked my finger, rubbing the sensitive bundle of nerves. His whole body trembled below me.

"Holy shit," he cried out. "So good."

"I told you. Stay with me."

I moved my finger in and out of him until his body was pressing down, trying to get more, and I added a second finger. It slipped in easier and a moan left Reagan's lips. I scissored my fingers, loosening up the muscles even more. By the time I added the third Reagan was bucking against my hand. If he wasn't ready by then, he never would be. I let my fingers slip from his body.

I tapped his hip. "Roll over and put a pillow under your hips. It'll make it easier for you the first time."

His eyes were darkened with lust. Without question, he rolled to his stomach and took one of the pillows from the top of the bed and pushed it beneath him, angling his ass up to me. For the first time, I had the perfect view of Reagan's ass and I wanted inside more than I wanted my next breath.

I ran my thumb along his pucker. "Ready for me?"

"Fuck yes. Feels like I've been ready forever."

I grabbed a condom and rolled it down my length. Lining my dick up, I slowly pushed forward until the head of my dick breached that first tight ring of muscle. And I was thankful for all the time I'd spent getting him ready when it slipped in easily.

"Fuck," he growled.

I ran my hand down his back. "You're doing so good, babe. Just a few more inches and all you'll feel is pleasure."

"Do it." He started to thrust his hips back, but I held them still. "Easy. Let me do this so I don't hurt you."

He lowered back to the bed and I pushed the rest of the way in. He was so hot and tight, I gripped my thighs to keep from coming to soon. "You feel so good. I could stay here forever."

I slid back and thrust back in, this time angling the head of my dick to hit the perfect spot. His back bowed.

"Holy shit, do that again."

"My pleasure."

I lay down on top of him, slipping my hands beneath his shoulders and holding on as I began to thrust in earnest, my balls growing tight with each pass. There was no way I was coming without Reagan. The noises he made every time I hit his prostate could have put a porn star to shame. And I loved it. He seemed to love everything I was doing to him.

The tingle started down my back and I knew this couldn't last forever. I sat up and pulled his hips toward me. He kept his head lowered to the bed, giving me the perfect angle. Reaching around, I took his cock in my hands. Using the hand already covered in lube, I slicked him up and stroked him at the same pace I thrust into him.

"I can't hold on anymore. I'm gonna come," he moaned.

I picked up the speed of my thrusts and was rewarded with warm sticky fluid running through my fingers. His ass clenched so hard, it ripped the climax from me. I'd never experienced a whole body climax before. Then again everything with Reagan was different. Tingles raced along my limbs and black spots danced before my eyes. My body slipped from his and I collapsed onto the bed next to him. Reagan's eyes were screwed shut and his breathing was rapid.

I rolled over, discarding the condom in the trash can near the bed. When I looked back, Reagan had managed to face the ceiling. He hadn't said much and I started to get nervous.

"Man, I've been missing out."

I crawled up beside him, resting my head on his chest and pressing a soft kiss there. "Yes, you have, but I'm glad you waited for me."

"Me too." Reagan yawned. "I'm not moving until the morning. Hit the light, would ya."

I leaned up and hit the switch on the light, quickly lowering back down to where I was. Reagan wrapped his arm around my waist and I'd never been so content to fall asleep.

The light seeping in the windows pulled me from sleep. I ran my hand along the bed, only to find cold sheets. My eyes flicked open. Where was Reagan? I glanced at the clock where a paper sat blocking the time. I picked up the paper and saw it was well after ten in the morning. Reagan was at the office. I opened the paper.

Sawyer,

I didn't want to wake you. I figured you had enough jet lag. Let's see a movie tonight. I had Madison pick me up and brought a change of clothes. Come get me after work and we'll go right there. Oh, and make sure you come upstairs so Madison doesn't kill me. Apparently, she's a big fan and that's her payment. The movie starts at 7. Maybe we can have a repeat of last night after it.

Reagan

That wouldn't be a problem. My heart soared. Everything seemed to be falling into place with Reagan. I wanted so much to tell him how much I loved him. We were getting close, but I wouldn't say it until I knew he was ready.

I'd gone home for a few hours. Jackson and Monty came over and we finished up the last bit of the song we'd been working before we left. By the time they left I still had at least an hour to burn before I had to leave to get Reagan. I watched a bit of TV, then jumped in the shower to leave. It was twenty minutes to seven when I arrived at Braddock & Minetti. Like the first time, I took the elevator up to the floor and went to introduce myself to the receptionist.

"Hello again, Mr. Alason. Mr. Setton is expecting you and asked me to show you right back."

It seemed weird to have someone call me by my last name, but I went with it and followed her down the hall to an office door. Reagan's head popped up the moment the door opened. "Hey. Let me change real quick and we can get out of here."

Reagan grabbed the bag and left the room. I sat down at Reagan's desk and looked around his office. It wasn't large, but it kept him from being stuck in one of the cubicles in the hall.

"Well, hello again."

I looked up to see the woman I remembered as Madison.

"Hi." I stood and reached out my hand to her. "Madison, right?"

"You got it." She sauntered into the room and sat on the edge of the desk. "I love your latest single." She ran her finger along the desk innocently, but I'd seen that look before. It did nothing for me, but most men would be falling at her feet. She was beautiful, with long brown hair hanging loosely to her shoulders.

"Thank you."

"Stop flirting with him." Reagan walked back into the room, ignoring the way she was perched on his desk.

"You take away all my fun."

"Yep," he said, shutting down his computer. "That's my goal in life, ruin Madison's fun." He came back around to the front. "Night, Madison. See you in the morning."

When the elevator doors closed behind us, I turned to Reagan. "Thanks for the note. And thanks for saving me. She comes on strong."

"Madison's bark is worse than her bite. I'll be honest, though, it took everything in me not to kiss you and mark you as mine in front of her. It kills me how bad she wants a shot with you."

"Well, you and I both know that's never going to happen."

The doors opened and we walked out to the almost deserted lot. Only a few cars remained. I'd parked in the back. Even in the open air, Reagan's cologne surrounded me. I wanted to touch him so badly. My brain short-circuited when he bent down to put his bag in the backseat. Not thinking where we were, I pressed my lips to his. His eyes widened and he jumped back out of my reach.

"What are you doing?"

Fuck.

I ran a hand through my hair. "Goddamn it. What was I thinking?" I glanced around and noticed Reagan doing the same. There didn't seem to be anyone. "Get in the car."

Reagan said nothing, just climbed into the passenger seat. I threw the car in drive, peeling from the lot. About a mile down the road I pulled into another parking lot and slammed my hand against the wheel.

"I fucking know better."

Reagan rested a hand on my arm. "Relax. No one was out there. It's fine."

The sincerity in his eyes went a long way to calm my racing heart. “You’re right. I don’t know why I’m getting so worked up. Let’s go to the movies.”

Everything was going to be fine.

At least I hoped it was.

SAWYER

A loud bell sounded from somewhere near me. I tugged the pillow over my head, hoping to drown out the noise. It wouldn't stop. Whoever was calling better have had a good fucking reason for waking me at the ass crack of dawn. I reached for Reagan and my hand only encountered cold sheets. Waking up that way was getting old. That's when I remembered he'd gone back to his apartment late last night since he had a meeting this morning.

Without opening my eyes, I smacked my hand around on the table, trying to find my phone. Finally, my fingers touched the edge and I brought it over to lay on my chest. I tried cracking one eye open. Fuck, it was bright in my room. The phone started ringing again. With a groan, I dropped my arm over my eyes and brought the phone to my ear.

"'Ello."

"How the fuck are you still sleeping?" Mari's voice was shrill coming from the other end of the line.

Squinting, I pulled the phone away from my ear to see the time. A little after eight. "It's eight in the morning. What the hell else would I be doing?"

"Shit. Shit. Shit." Something about the tone of her voice melted away the last bit of drowsiness.

"Mari, what's wrong with you? Are the paparazzi up your ass again?"

"No, but they're onto yours."

I lurched straight up in bed, no longer worried about how bright my room is. That wasn't right. It couldn't be. Reagan and I didn't do anything to give ourselves away. "What did you just say?"

"Jesus Christ, Sawyer. Look at the picture I sent you. They know about you and Reagan. Well, they don't know his name yet, but it's only a matter of time."

With trembling hands, I lowered the phone and opened up the text from Mari. My heart slammed into my chest. There on the screen were pictures of me and Reagan, holding hands, kissing.

"Holy fuck." I had no idea how long I sat there, frozen, staring at the evidence that had the potential to not only destroy my career, but Reagan's as well.

"Sawyer," Mari shouted.

"What?" I answered in a daze. My brain couldn't process all that I was seeing.

"You need to talk to Reagan."

Unable to sit still, I stood and started pacing the room. Talk to Reagan. No. I needed to save him from the shitstorm that was about to rain down on us. He worked for one of the most prestigious law firms in the city, who also happened to have a few very homophobic partners. Being in the closet was the only thing keeping him from having problems there. There was no reason he had to stay on board my sinking ship.

My chest ached. He could forget about all of this. Think of it as some kind of sexual experiment gone wrong and find himself a girl to settle down and have a family with. Bile burned as it rose up my throat.

I loved that man more than I ever thought possible. In twenty-six years, I'd never met someone who understood every part of me without question. Letting him go would be one of the hardest things I'd ever done, but I had to do it. He deserved to have the happy, carefree life that being straight afforded him. Mine was now destined for turmoil, something I wouldn't wish on my own enemy. My stomach cramped just thinking about the words I needed to say. No matter what it took, I'd say them.

"No. I need to talk to Tom."

"Why the hell do you need to talk to Tom?" Her voice rose with each word. Best guesses, she was also wearing a hole in her own rug.

"I want to set up a press conference."

"I don't think you can deny this."

I glanced at the picture. There was no denying what was right there for anyone to see. Didn't mean I had to feed Reagan to the wolves. "I know I can't deny what they see in the picture. Doesn't mean I have to give them what they don't already know."

"You're not making any sense," she said.

"They may know it's me and that I was with a guy, but they don't need to know who that guy is."

"Are you kidding? Of course they're going to figure out who he is. They're going to have cameras all over your ass trying to figure out who the man that made Sawyer Alason go gay is."

I threw the sheets off and moved to the side of the bed. "That's fucking ridiculous to think that Reagan made me go gay."

"Doesn't matter. They want a story and will do whatever it takes to get one."

Cleanup time, but I didn't have to put into words what I knew I needed to do to fix this mess. I sat silently on the phone and waited for Mari to reach the truth. A few minutes passed and I waited.

"Oh my God. You're aren't going to do what I think you are?"

I sighed. "And what is that?"

"Break up with him before the media drags him through the mud."

I paused for a second. "You know me too well."

"That's the dumbest fucking idea I've ever heard. Do you plan on telling him before or after you let the whole world know it's over?"

"Don't start, Mari. I won't ruin his career because I can't keep my hands to myself around him."

"Ugh...you've lost it." There was shuffling and a sound of jingling keys. "Don't you dare do anything rash until after I get there. I'm leaving the house now."

"Mari," I warned, but she didn't answer. When I looked down, she'd hung up.

I paced my room for a few minutes, planning out my next move. There were not good answers when you were stuck between a rock and a hard place. Either way I needed to get the ball rolling before I lost my nerve. I sat down on the bed and began to dial Tom's number when my bedroom door burst open. I expected to see Mari, thinking she drove fast as hell to get there. I was surprised to look up and see Heath, who swiped the phone out of my hand before I could finish dialing.

"What the fuck?"

"Don't start," he snapped. "Mari told me to take your phone until she got here and the two of you could talk before you do something stupid and rash."

I swiped at my phone. "There's nothing to think about. Nothing to talk about. I will not let Reagan go down with me."

He sat on the bed next to me, keeping the phone firmly out of reach. "Who says you're going down? And even if you are, you need to let Reagan support you in times of bullshit like this."

"It's not fair to him."

"Dude, that doesn't even make sense. He's in this just as much as you are."

"Not if I can keep him out of it."

"You're going to ruin the best thing that's ever happened to you so you can play the martyr card? That's absolute bullshit."

I sighed. All the plans I had for Reagan and myself came crashing down and shattering like glass on concrete. No matter what anyone said, the decision was made. My stomach churned and for a bit I thought I might throw up. That all changed when the door flew open and this time Mari swooped in like an avenging angel. For at least an hour we argued back and forth over the right thing to do. Eventually, I'd won and called Tom to set up a press conference for a few hours from now.

If I thought time with Reagan flew by in the blink of an eye, time away from him seemed to drag on forever. I paced the small room, tuning out Mari's pleading and begging for me to not do this.

My heart was on her side.

My head was not.

The sound of my heart echoed around the room with how loud it beat when Tom came back to bring me into the room. A bead of sweat formed on my brow as I walked toward the door. He opened it slightly, stepping through and giving me a good visual of what awaited me on the other side. The crowds for our PR tour were very large and this had to be twice the size.

"Thank you all for coming today."

Tom stood at the podium ready to call me up to the stage. My hands were shaking so hard I could barely hold the paper in my hand. Not that I planned on using the speech they prepared for me. I knew the gist of it, but I had no intention of coming off like an insensitive robot. A machine who had no feelings about what he was saying.

Mari took my hands in hers. "Are you sure you want to do this alone? You know if you called—"

I shook my head so hard, it hurt. "No way. I will not put him through the bullshit the press and the paparazzi are about to rein down on my ass."

She squeezed my hands tighter. "You love him, do you not?"

Bile raced up my throat. "There are no words for how much I love him."

"Then don't shut him out," she pleaded.

My eyes burned. "I have to. I won't ruin his career because I'm selfish. He can still be happy with a wife and kids."

"But where does that leave you?"

I shrugged, trying to stop myself from puking all over the waiting area. "Alone with my drum kit. How it's always been."

"Sawyer Alason." That was my cue.

Swallowing back the bitter taste in my mouth, I climbed the stairs to face the music. No pun intended. Flashes went off in every direction, practically blinding me. It might have been dumb, but it distracted me enough from my misery to start talking.

"Hello, everyone. As you know, pictures were uploaded sometime yesterday of me holding another man's hand and kissing him. I won't lie to you or try to cover up what's going on in those photos. The reality is that I am gay. I've known it since I was sixteen years old. Honestly, I didn't think it was anyone's business who I'm in a relationship with. That being said, the time to clear the air has come."

A reporter in the middle raised her hand. "Who is the man with you in the picture?"

I knew exactly who stood so close to me, our lips connected at every point. My heart pounded in my ears and my stomach lurched. But I held my ground and did what needed to be done.

"No one of importance."

"Do you have a boyfriend?" someone shouted from the back.

This question was even harder to answer than the first. "No, I do not."

Out of the corner of my eye, I could see Mari wiping the tears from her face. If I didn't have to keep it together, it was guaranteed I'd have tears of my own. Somehow, by some sheer force of willpower, I was able to hold them back.

"So there's no one special in your life?"

I shook my head. "Nope. Just me and the band."

Like it had always been and probably always would be.

Another hand. Another question.

It went on like that for the next thirty minutes. I stood at the podium trying to protect

Reagan's identity. I would do everything in my power to protect him from the hell my life was about to become. By the time we were finished, I had nothing left. It took every ounce of physical and mental strength to survive ripping my heart out. All I wanted was to be alone.

Heath texted me that news vans surrounded the house. Not long after Mari received the same text from Cole. Seemed they gave everyone the same warm welcome treatment. A quick bend over while I ruin the rest of your life and career kind of treatment. For everybody's sanity, I thought it best I get a hotel room for the night. At least there, I could be miserable all on my own without bringing everyone else down, especially as they should be celebrating the number one ranking of our latest single.

Mari tried repeatedly to convince me not to go to the hotel.

"They have enough security to keep the people out and no one will have to deal with them. Once they figure out I'm not there, maybe they'll leave me alone."

She wrapped her arms around my waist. "You shouldn't have to be alone at a time like this. Cole and I don't mind dealing with the paparazzi. We've dealt with our fair share."

"I know, but I can't do that to you. Plus, right now, I really need to be alone."

I could tell she wanted to keep arguing, but something made her close her mouth and keep it to herself. She nodded.

"Fine, but if you change your mind, call me, you know I'll be there."

I pressed a kiss to the top of her head. "I know."

The back of my throat started to burn. I knew it was time to get out of there before I lost it in front of the others. Without a word, I stepped out of her arms. Slinging my bag over my shoulder, I walked out the back door to the car service Tom had set up when he made the hotel reservation and scheduled the news conference.

The door of the hotel room closed behind me. For the fiftieth time, my phone lit up. Another message from Mari.

"Enough," I screamed and chucked my phone across the room, watching with satisfaction as it shattered against the wall.

Unable to keep my emotions at bay, I leaned against the wall and slid to the floor, letting the tears come.

Reagan

My desk had papers lying everywhere. A pretty good indication I had too many things on my plate. But I would not let my first solo case be a failure when I knew I could win. The pieces were all there. All I had to do was put the puzzle together. I ordered lunch an hour ago thinking food might help. It still sat in a bag on the corner of my desk.

Two years at the firm and I'd been waiting for this moment. The time when I would have a case and not have to completely rely on one of the senior associates to guide me through. I grabbed my sandwich from the bag, taking my first bite, when my cell phone rang. Setting my food down, I wiped my hands on a napkin and pulled my phone from my pocket. A quick glance at the screen told me how late it was.

I hadn't heard from Sawyer in hours. Not completely surprising. I knew his publicist wanted to talk tour dates with the band today. They'd probably just finished up. I opened the message to see that it wasn't from Sawyer, but Heath.

Heath: Watch this

The next message was the link to the news website. My stomach dropped. Not that it stopped me from clicking on the link. A video opened up and that one bite of sandwich turned sour in my stomach. Sawyer stood behind a podium, his gaze focused on the people seated in the chairs in front of him. Whether he realized it or not, his fingers lightly tapped out a rhythm on the top of the podium.

He greeted everyone. I wasn't listening to a word that came out of his mouth, too busy trying to figure out what in the hell he was doing up there. Then he let the bombshell drop and you could hear a pin drop in that room. "The reality is I'm gay."

My ass flew out of the chair, but I couldn't stop watching the wreck happening before my eyes. Sawyer had mentioned a picture of him kissing another man.

Oh, fuck.

He'd kissed me when we were getting into the car last night. When he realized what he was doing he backed away quickly, looking around to make sure no one saw what we were doing. The place had been deserted. We thought we were in the clear. Apparently, we'd been very wrong. I held my breath, waiting for the question I knew was coming.

Was Sawyer seeing anyone?

I had no idea whether I was ready to be outed publicly, but the time to worry about it had come and gone. My reality had changed. For Sawyer's sake I had to accept it with grace and move on. Sawyer would need me by his side when he faced down the media. And even if it tanked my career, I would be right next to him, holding his hand and doing everything I could to shield him from the bullshit.

"Who's the man in picture?" Not exactly the question I expected, but still the same answer.

"No one of importance."

No one of importance? I had to be hearing things. My nerves had taken control of my brain. Then he answered about having a boyfriend. The moment he said no, I knew exactly what he was doing and I had no plans on letting him. He figured if he pushed me away, I'd be safe from dealing with the hoard of paparazzi about to descend on his life. And at the same time be able to keep my job at the firm. Which wasn't even close to what I wanted. If he had to face the masses, I'd face them with him. I wasn't delusional enough to think we wouldn't face hurdles. Plenty of people would hate us for loving each other, especially my boss.

Suddenly, I wanted to slam my head against the wall. I still hadn't told Sawyer that I loved him. In his mind, I could find a woman and fall in love with her without any of the damaging consequences to my career. I glanced around my office. The simple desk and chair. A picture of my parents on one corner. Papers strewn everywhere. Would I be able to give this up if they couldn't accept the fact I was in love with a man?

For Sawyer?

I'd give up anything.

Ignoring the mess on my desk, I grabbed my keys and went in search of my assistant. If I wanted the firm on my side through all of this, I needed to give them the courtesy of not running out without an explanation. Not that I had high hopes for that, but it was worth a shot. Bridget was seated at her desk amongst the multitude of cubicles.

“I have a family emergency to take care of. Let anyone who’s looking for me know I’ll be back tomorrow.”

Her eyes widened. Leaving halfway through the day didn’t really fit my style. I worked late. “Okay.” She nodded slowly. “I’ll take care of everything.”

“Thank you, Bridget.”

“My pleasure. I hope everything’s okay.”

“Me too,” I called out on the way out the door.

My steps ate up sections of pavement on the way to my car. The first thing I needed to know was where he went. I texted Heath.

Heath: The Homestead Hotel

Why would he go to a hotel? In the end, it didn’t matter. I knew I needed to find him and soon. There was no way I planned on letting him push me out of his life. Not without a fight.

I slammed my foot on the gas, the smell of burning rubber filling my nostrils as I peeled from the parking lot. My phone rang and I hit the button on my steering wheel to answer it. My mom’s voice filled the car.

“Reagan Michael Setton, you better start explaining why I just saw Sawyer standing up there all alone to tell the world he’s gay. Why wouldn’t you stand up there and face it with him?”

My hands tightened on the wheel. Normally, I’d be more sympathetic of her ability to jump to conclusions. Not tonight. Not when I needed to find Sawyer.

“That’s not what happened, Mom.”

“Well, that was sure what it looked like happened.”

I held on tighter, doing my best not to lose my temper on her. "I didn't even know Sawyer was giving the press conference. Heath sent me the link when it started. I would never leave him to the wolves like that."

"You didn't know he was going to announce that?"

"No. I would have gone with him. Whatever happened it has something to do with the photo he mentioned. He kissed me in the parking lot of my office last night. We thought we were alone. Turns out we weren't."

"Oh my, poor Sawyer. Do you know where he is?"

"Yeah, Mom. I'm on my way there now."

She was quiet for a long minute and I was curious about what might be going through her head.

"Are you going to be okay when all of this comes out?"

"I love him." The answer was so simple in my mind, no other words needed to be said.

"Then go to him and call us if you need anything."

"I will. Thank you, Mom."

"Anytime, sweetheart. We love you."

I disconnected the call when I pulled into the lot of the hotel. I'd call her back after I talked to Sawyer. Heath texted me with his room numbers and I made my way immediately to the bank of elevators on the right and took one up to his floor.

I stepped up to his door and lifted my hand to bang on it.

No more hiding. It was time for both of us to come clean.

SAWYER

Something slammed into the door over and over again. I ignored the sound. I didn't give a shit who was on the other side of it. At the moment, there was only one person I wanted and I couldn't have him.

Pound. Pound. Pound.

"Sawyer, you better open this goddamn door right now before I kick it in."

His voice drew me from my misery if only for a second when I remembered all the reasons he couldn't be there. I stood on the other side of the door. The pressure in my chest made it hard to breathe. But I forced myself to not reach for the handle. Not drag him inside and press my body against his to remind him who he belonged to. I clenched my hands into fist at my sides and stood my ground.

"I'm not opening the door. You need to go."

"Open the fucking door," he yelled loud enough that I was sure the people in the rooms next to me heard him.

"I...I can't." Two words. Only two words and they felt like they were being ripped from my throat.

"Yes, you can." His voice was softer this time, but still held a slight edge.

I shook my head, even though he couldn't see me. I had no words left. Hearing his voice, knowing he was on the other side of the door, was like the dagger was back in my chest and being twisted for fun. Why did the cosmos need to torture me that way?

I heard another thud against the door, much heavier than the previous sounds.

"Sawyer, please open the door."

I told myself to be strong. To tell him I didn't want him anymore, but I couldn't make the lie pass my lips. Instead the truth came stumbling to the surface. "I won't ruin your career too."

"Is that what you think?"

Think? "It's what I know. I can't have you suffer for me."

"Open the door so we can talk about this."

"No."

He was quiet for such a long pause, I thought for a moment he left. "Sawyer?"

I took a step back from the door. "Go," I begged. "You can find a nice girl, settle down, and have a family. No one knows it's you in the picture and they never need to know."

I could hear the scoff through the door.

"Is that what you think? I'm gonna leave after all we've been through and find a woman to stick my dick in?"

I was hoping he could. At least a part of me wanted him to be happy. The other part I was doing my best to keep buried, so I said nothing, afraid of what might come out of my mouth next.

He sighed. "Sawyer, I'm not going to go find a girl. I don't want them anymore. I don't love *them*."

My heart stuttered in my chest as he continued.

"I want you. I love *you*."

Three simple words and nothing could have stopped me from reaching for the door this time. I yanked it open and fisted my hands into the front of his shirt, dragging him into the room.

My lips were on his in an instant, our tongues tasting each other like we'd been separated for months, not hours. I had to make sure he was real before pulling away. Positive, I pulled back and gazed into his eyes. "Say it again."

"I love you, Sawyer."

My eyes burned as moisture rushed forward. It seemed like I waited my entire life to hear him say those words. It was everything I ever wanted and never thought I would have. His green eyes held mine and for the millionth time I saw the small flecks of gold inside that brightened with desire. I knew that walking through that door tonight took miles and miles of courage. There was no way I could push him away now. Time for the whole truth. All of it.

"I love you, Reagan."

He opened his mouth to speak, but I covered his lips with my fingers. There was so much more he needed to know.

"I've loved you since I was sixteen years old. I know that's a long time to keep a secret like that. When you found out I was gay, you asked if that was the reason I left. A small part of it was, but mainly I left because I wanted you and knew I would never have you. It hurt too much to admit I was gay and that I was in love with you when I thought that love would never be returned."

I swallowed past the lump in my throat, forcing myself to continue. "You once accused me of keeping secrets from you. You're right, I have, because not telling you the truth was so much easier than the risk of hearing you say you would never love me. I'm sorry I hurt you."

This time, Reagan wrapped his fingers around my wrist and pulled my hand away from his mouth. "Now it's your turn to listen."

I wanted to protest, but instead I waited.

"I will never leave you alone to face this mess. When two people love each other, they don't abandon each other when things get tough. They hold on tighter and face the challenge together. And that's what we are going to do. No matter what it takes to save your career, we'll do it together." My knees weakened and I slowly lowered myself to the floor, unable to stop the single tear from tracking down my cheek. "Nothing is as bad as the thought of losing you again. I'm sorry I walked away."

Reagan reached a hand down and pulled me to my feet, dragging me over to the sofa in the center of the room. He cupped my face in his hand and used his thumb to brush away the tear. "I know you are. I forgive you as long as you promise to never do it again."

"You have my word. I have never felt so sick as I did the moment I told those reporters you were no one important when you are the most important person in the world to me."

He lifted a brow. "I wouldn't worry about that, because we are going to fix that little bit of information tomorrow morning."

"How?"

"Heath has already been on the phone with Tom setting up an interview with Joni Taylor so you can introduce your boyfriend to the world."

I shot to my feet. "Absolutely not. I will not let them make your life a living hell too."

He grabbed hold of my shoulders, forcing me to stay still. "You think my life is better without you in it?"

"You've spent the last few years working your way up in the firm. I won't be the reason you lose everything you worked for." My chest ached.

He took my face between his hands and captured my lips in a kiss so sweet, it seared itself in my memory. I wasn't sure I could survive without it.

When he pulled back, he kept hold of my face. "If I lose anything it will be because people are narrow-minded bigots. If the firm can't accept me for who I am, then I'll find a place that will. Braddock & Minetti isn't the only law firm in town."

"But—"

He took my lips again, silencing me. This time, he didn't let go, backing me toward the wall. Right before we reached for it, I spun us and shoved him face first against the wall.

I needed him. I didn't want to think about pictures or press conferences. I didn't want to think about being without him. What I wanted was to fuck him until I didn't have to think anymore.

I ran my tongue along the shell of his ear and watched the shiver run through him. "I wanna fuck you right against this wall."

"Do it."

I popped the button on his dress pants and yanked them down to his thighs. We could undress later. Right then, I didn't give a fuck. I ran my finger through his crease. He was so dry, there was no way I wouldn't hurt him. There was one way to fix that. I dropped to my knees behind him, spreading his cheeks. At the first swipe of my tongue, his ass bucked back toward me.

"Oh shit, I had no idea that could feel so good."

I kept at him, getting his ass nice and slick. His hands gripped for purchase on the walls. I added one finger, then another, loosening him up. The sounds coming out of him almost made me come. When I knew he was wet enough and ready to take me. I stood and grabbed a condom from my wallet. After rolling it on, I lined up my cock and with one sure thrust I was balls deep in Reagan.

"Fucking move," he ordered.

Normally I'd argue with him about topping from the bottom. Not tonight. I needed to come with this man and I'd do anything to get us there. I pulled back and slammed back in, setting a rhythm I wasn't sure either of us could survive. Reagan reached down and began stroking his cock.

"Make me come."

"My fucking pleasure." I moved faster, if that was even possible. Two thrusts later, he erupted all over the wall, shouting out my name. I joined him in ecstasy, thankful we were close enough to fall on the bed. There was nothing sweet or romantic about what we'd just done.

It was rough and carnal and perfect.

Reagan

"Are you sure you want to do this?"

We sat in the greenroom at the studio, waiting to be called to the set. The thought of being on television had never crossed my mind before. Yet, there I sat waiting to admit to the whole world that, not only was I Bi, but that I was in a relationship with the drummer of one of the hottest up and coming bands. To say my nerves had gotten the best of me was an understatement. I had to concentrate to keep my whole body from trembling.

I glanced over at the man seated beside me, the way our hands looked laced together, and I knew no amount of fear would keep me from standing next to this man forever.

"Yes."

"You can change—"

I squeezed his hand, hoping he'd look at me. "Would you stop trying to talk me out of this? I made up my mind and we're doing this."

The last few days hadn't been easy for either of us. While I didn't think it was the partners' business who I decided to have in my bed, under normal circumstances, I would've kept the information to myself. This wasn't a normal circumstance and I wasn't dating an average guy off the street. The next day I went to work and spoke with the assistant of the partner who had hired me. The meeting went almost exactly like expected.

Not good.

He told me my personal life was a reflection of the office and he wouldn't force the clients to be represented by someone like me. I had to choose, the firm or my perverted lifestyle. If I chose Sawyer, I'd be stuck in the office with shit cases. Never seeing the inside of a courtroom again. With a smile on my face, I thanked him for the chance he'd given me in the beginning and walked out the door to clean out my office.

After I left, I stopped by Madison's office. Of all the people I'd worked with in the last two years, she'd been the one I'd grown closest to. She deserved to hear the news from me, not on replay of our interview. Well, Sawyer's interview. I had a feeling they wouldn't care much about what I had to say. She was shocked and a little disappointed that she wouldn't get to work with me anymore, but she was happy for me.

Sawyer had a few bumps in the road. Thank God the first night he'd had no access to social media. I was able to censor most of the hatred shoved his way. Not that there was a lot of it. Most people had been really supportive of his decision to come out. At least they made it sound like it was his decision. No one seemed to want to mention that an asshole with a camera and no moral compass forced him to make that choice. I knew if he saw it, he'd focus on the five negative comments instead of the thousands of good ones. Seriously, it seemed to be a one to one thousand ratio.

At least Heath had been thinking at the time and gave Monty control of the social media accounts. Monty was already known for his 'I don't give a shit' attitude. Once the naysayers got a taste of their own medicine with Monty's quick wit, they gave up pretty quickly. Unfortunately, my ability to keep him from it ended with his replacement phone. After that I did my best with Mari's help to make him focus on the positive.

Mari had to be one of the most amazing women I'd ever met. While I went to look for a new job, she made sure to keep Sawyer from freaking out all over again. I was there to stay and he needed to remember that. Easy when I was with him. Not so easy when I wasn't and he'd start thinking about all the ways a wife and kids could make me happier.

No one could make me happier than him.

"I feel like you're sacrificing everything for me."

"For fuck's sake. What am I sacrificing?"

"Your job for one."

"No, I had the choice to stay and never practice in a courtroom again. I made the decision to leave. I'll find another firm to work at. I want my Sawyer back." I gestured up and down at him. "Not this broody man who always sees the glass as half empty."

He sighed and leaned his head on my shoulder. "I'm trying. I always thought I'd do this my way."

I rested my head against his. "Would you have ever come out if you didn't have to?"

One beat.

Two beats.

His silence said it all. It made me a little angry to think he would have hidden our relationship forever. Then again, maybe I would have been able to change his mind. Either way it didn't matter. Here we were whether we were ready or not.

"Look at it this way. You don't have to hide who you are anymore."

"If only it didn't come at the expense of the people I care about."

I opened my mouth to answer when my phone rang. Pulling it from my pocket, I smirked. I'd been waiting for her to call.

"Who is it?" Sawyer asked and I held up a hand to him.

I hit answer and lifted the phone to my ear.

"Hey, Charlene."

His eyes snapped to mine. I ignored his reaction and kept talking to his mom.

"Hi, Reagan. How's he holding up? He won't answer my calls."

I kept my gaze on him as I answered. "He's sitting here brooding, thinking he's taking us all out in the blaze of glory."

"That's ridiculous. Did you tell him that's not true?"

"I tried. He's not listening."

Sawyer narrowed his eyes at me.

"He can be anyone he wants to be as long as he's happy."

"*I* know that."

"Put him on the phone."

I reached the phone out to his ear, but he shook his head and pulled away. "You better take it," I warned. "Or I'm going to put her on speaker phone. And you'll still have to listen to what she has to say."

He yanked the phone out of my hand and lifted it to his ear. I couldn't wait for this interview to be over. Hopefully, then he'd see most people were on our side and the few narrow-minded ones who weren't didn't matter.

"Yeah, Mom."

I couldn't hear what Charlene said to him. Best guess, it was a lecture that people's opinions didn't matter. Him being happy did.

"I know, Mom." He looked at me, a small grin lifting his lips. "I will. I love you, too."

He handed the phone back to me and I lifted it to my ear.

"Good luck today. And if he starts moping again, kick him in the butt."

I laughed. "I will."

"Good. We both love you, boys."

"We love you, too."

I hung up with Sawyer's mom and swiveled my whole body to face him. "She told me—"

"I know. She told me the same thing." He brought our joined hands up to his lips. "You know how much I love you, right?"

"That I do know. Now please trust me. Everything is going to fine."

"I'm trying to believe that. I am."

A light knock sounded on the door. It opened a crack and a woman with long curly blond hair popped her head in. "Mr. Setton and Mr. Alason, we're ready for you."

I nodded and stood, holding my hand out to help Sawyer up. He took it and for a moment, we stood there, face-to-face, neither of us moving. The reality of what was about to happen settled over each of us in our own way. It was also hard not to notice the way the black T-shirt stretched across the muscles of his biceps, or how his shaggy hair fell over his forehead and into his eyes. My fingers itched to reach up and brush it from his face. More than that, I wanted him to feel our connection as we walked onto that stage. I wrapped my hands around his waist and cupped his ass, drawing him closer to me.

"You know how sexy you are in a T-shirt and jeans?" I flexed my fingers to make my message loud and clear.

"Mmm..." He nipped at my lower lip. "About as sexy as you are in this shirt and tie." He ran his hand down the front of my shirt.

"There's my Sawyer. Now let's go announce to the world that you're mine and everyone else can keep their hands off."

Sawyer was still chuckling as we followed the woman who came to get us through a few halls and to the door of the set. One of the stage hands attached a microphone to my lapel and I watched as they did the same to Sawyer. Being with him meant that the cameras, the videos, it was all part of my life now too. Jaded Ivory had quickly become a household name and with that came the part where you lived in a fishbowl. People paid attention to what you did. And from now on, they'd be seeing me doing it all with Sawyer.

The stage hand caught our attention, counting backward from five on one hand before opening the door. The heat of the lights hit me as soon as I stepped out onto the stage. What I didn't expect to see was the entire audience on their feet, clapping and cheering. Some of them even held up signs saying 'Sawyer, we love you' or 'All the hot ones are gay.' The best one was 'I'll be your Grace to your Will BFFS.' Sawyer practically stopped in his tracks and I could see the tension leave his shoulders. This was exactly what he needed.

Joni stepped forward. "Sawyer. Reagan. I'm so happy you could join us today."

She must have noticed Sawyer's moment of surprise and guided us to the couches in the middle of the studio. I sat down, not leaving an inch between Sawyer and me. People needed to see us together and that was exactly what I'd give them.

Sawyer seemed unable to find his voice, so I answered for him. "Thank you. We're thrilled to be here."

That snapped Sawyer out of his daze. "Definitely. This was pretty awesome of you."

"Well, boys, let's get right to it 'cause I have a little surprise for you later. Sawyer, the last time we saw you, you mentioned there was no one special in your life, so who have you brought with you today?"

Sawyer settled back into the couch and took my hand in his. "Joni, this is my boyfriend, Reagan. I wasn't trying to mislead anyone. To be honest, I didn't know how the world would accept me as a gay rock star. It's why I stayed in the closet for so long. Once it was out, I didn't want to ruin everything Reagan worked for in becoming a lawyer." He turned to look at me. "You see, I've loved this man since I was sixteen years old and I would do anything to protect him, even if that meant giving him up."

A chorus of 'awws' sounded throughout the room. I brought his hand to my lips and pressed a soft kiss to it.

"Reagan?" Joni asked, drawing my attention. "I'm guessing you changed his mind."

"That's an understatement." Good thing neither of us were blushers. I knew Sawyer's mind was remembering the hot coupling against his hotel room wall. "I practically kicked down his hotel room door when I saw the press conference."

Her jaw fell open. "You didn't."

"I did. He wasn't getting away from me that easily."

A smirk lifted one corner of her lips as her eyes darted to our joined hands. "I can certainly see that. Can't we, ladies and gentleman?" she asked the audience over her shoulder. Another round of cheers went up.

"Well, I have to say you two make one hot couple." She pretended to fan herself. "Sawyer has his own fan club, but I'd be willing to bet in no time, you'll have one too." That comment garnered a bunch of catcalls and whistles.

"I'm starting one when I get home," one of the audience members called out.

Sawyer let go to lift both his hands. "Whoa, whoa, whoa, ladies and gentlemen. You can look all you want, but he's mine to touch."

Joni and I laughed with the crowd joining in. And just like that the tension broke. I knew everything would be okay. Joni asked us about how we met. She was shocked to hear we hadn't seen each other in seven years before finding our way back to one another. Eventually, the conversation turned to Jaded Ivory and their new album and upcoming tour. It gave me the chance to watch the audience, see how they reacted to Sawyer. In it, I saw nothing but excitement and acceptance. They were excited to get to see a member of one of their favorite bands. They didn't care who he slept with as long as he kept making music.

"Okay, Sawyer, I have a favor to ask. And I'm sure the audience would really appreciate it." She looked over at them, giving them an exaggerated wink, which caused them to start clapping. When it reached its peak, Joni quieted them down with her hands and turned back to Sawyer.

He laughed. "How can I say no to that? What's the favor?"

She folded her hands in front of her. "Would you please, please play one of the songs off your new album? Something we haven't heard yet."

"Well..." He trailed off. "Joni, I'm a drummer. I'm not sure how much of a song it would actually be."

She stood and gestured to a part of the stage I hadn't noticed before. It moved to the side, revealing the rest of Jaded Ivory. "Good thing the whole band is here then."

Sawyer's head whipped around. The chanting started for Mari immediately. The crowd loved her.

Joni Looked at Sawyer. "What do you say?"

He shook his head, laughing. "How can I say no to that?"

"I'm hoping you can't," she said with a smile.

Sawyer leaned over and pressed a soft kiss to my lips and the crowd went crazy. "I love you," he whispered against my lips.

"I love you, too." I gave his shoulder a shove forward, pushing him off the couch. "Now go show the world what Jaded Ivory can do."

His entire face lit up as we walked over to join the band. Mari handed him a set of drumsticks as he pulled her into a tight embrace. He stopped to give each of them a hug for their support before climbing behind his kit and counting them in.

Everything was how it should be.

Sawyer

I stared at the menu, unable to decide what I wanted for dinner. “I can’t choose.”

Reagan rolled his eyes. “It’s not that hard. What do you feel like eating?”

I grabbed my stomach with both hands. “I’m starving. Right now, I want everything on the menu.”

Things had been a nonstop whirlwind of activity. More interviews. More time in the studio. More interviews for Reagan to handle. He had plenty of offers, but he chose the one I’d been most excited about. The studio wanted to hire him for their legal department. Our popularity as a couple was so high, they wanted us together at shows. I should have been pissed at the cheesy PR move, but I couldn’t be. Not when it meant Reagan would come on tour with us and still get paid.

The last two months had been absolute chaos. Even though Reagan and I were out, it seemed that lately we saw less of each other than before the world knew about us. I couldn’t remember the last time we had the chance to sit down and have dinner together. Most of the time we had takeout, unless I got home early to cook before crawling into bed together. It didn't matter whose place we stayed at. Especially after the fucker who lived with him moved out.

We came home after the Joni Taylor show to find him packing all his stuff up. The ironic part was he didn't give a shit if we were gay, he was more worried about the paparazzi that surrounded the building and how they were interfering with his foreign film blog. Whatever. The guy was completely insane and neither one of us was sorry to see him go. Reagan had been paying the entire lease and I knew he was worried about finding a roommate. I had another idea and I thought a dinner out with just the two of us would be perfect.

Not that it was ever just the two of us anymore. Like Mari and Cole, each of us found ourselves being regularly followed by the paparazzi. We both ignored them since no one had pushed too far yet. If they did, Reagan talked about filing injunctions, whatever that meant. I'd leave the legal shit to him.

"Now you're being dramatic. Choose a burger. And I'd choose it quick 'cause we're about to have company."

His eyes moved to the left and I followed his line of sight. A group of three teenagers were walking slowly toward us. One had a marker in her hand. That was another thing I'd had to get used to. No longer could I hide behind a hat and mostly get away with it. Ever since being on the Joni Taylor show, everyone recognized my face and they had no problems asking for autographs when they saw me. I didn't mind it in the least. It proved how far Jaded

Ivory had come, but more than that, it showed me that these people supported me no matter what my sexual orientation.

"Fine. When the waiter comes, I'll have the bacon double cheeseburger."

Reagan lowered his menu. "See, was that so hard?"

"Very funny."

I turned just as the girls reached us.

"Oh my God, it really is you," one of them practically shouted. "You're Sawyer Alason."

Out of the corner of my eye I could see Reagan's shoulders shaking. He found it amusing when they had to tell me who I was.

"That's me. How are you ladies today?"

Two of them turned a bright shade of pink, while the other stepped forward, marker extended.

"Would you mind signing my shirt?" She gestured behind her at the other two. "They're hoping you'll sign something for them too, but they're too shy to ask."

"Amanda!" One of the girls in the back smacked the other one.

I held out my hand and smiled. "I'd be happy to. Do you have a favorite song?" I asked when she turned around, and I scribbled my name across her back.

"I love Midnight Dream."

I nodded when she turned back to face me. "One of my favorites too." The other two handed over their cell phone cases to sign. I handed them back when I was done, loving the smiles on their faces. Reagan took a picture of the four of us with Amanda's phone.

"Thanks," Amanda said, shoving it back into her pocket. "I'm so glad we got to meet you. I have the ticket sale set in my calendar. There's no way I'm missing your show."

"I love hearing that. Thanks for coming over and enjoy your dinner."

I waved as the girls walked back to their table, practically bouncing up and down on the way there.

"You're good at being a rock star," Reagan said, drawing my attention back to him. He lifted the bottle of beer to his lips.

"Oh, really. Do you think I'm good at being a roommate?"

He set the bottle down and narrowed his eyes. "Are you having a problem with Heath?"

"No, no, no. Nothing like that. I know you're worried about the rent payment on your condo and it seems stupid for us to keep two places..."

He reached across the table and covered my hand with his. Something that three months ago would have made me yank my hand back in fear. Now I could enjoy the feel of his touch.

"Are you asking me to move in with you?"

"What would you say if I was?" As much as I knew Reagan and I were forever, I also had a healthy dose of fear of rejection, which happened to be sitting at the surface for the moment.

He leaned back in the booth and rested his arm along the back. "I don't know. I guess you'll have to ask me to find out."

I sighed. "You aren't going to make this easy on me, are you?"

He scoffed. "When have you ever made anything easy on me?"

"Fair enough." I turned my hand over, allowing us to hold hands. "Would you move in with me?"

"What about Heath?" The two of them had become closer the more time we spent at my place. I knew he wouldn't want to do anything to hurt that friendship.

"Well, we've been looking at new places. Bigger places. I figured you and I can move into one room and Heath into the other."

"And Heath's okay with this?"

I shrugged. "I figured we could talk to him tonight, if you said yes."

"I don't know, Sawyer."

My heart dropped.

"I would love to live with you and come home to you every night, but I don't want to mess up the plans you were making with Heath."

"So, you're saying you want me to live with another man?" I used the joke as a deflection.

"Don't do that. You're only making jokes 'cause you think I'm saying no."

I shouldn't be surprised how well he could read me, but sometimes I was. "You're not saying no?"

"What I'm saying is, if Heath's okay with it, then I'd love living with you."

"He'll be fine with it. He asked me not long after Harrison moved out if I was moving in with you. At the time, I don't think either of us was ready, but we are now."

The corner of his mouth lifted. "Look how far you've come. Hiding who you are to talk about moving in together."

"Don't tell anyone. I'd only do it for you."

"It better be only me."

"It's only ever been you since I was sixteen."

Heat lit his eyes and I couldn't stop myself from leaning over the table and stealing a quick kiss.

Paparazzi be damned.

Reagan

"Goddamn, you need to clean up your shit."

I glanced around the piles of papers and drumsticks lying all over the floor. The bus had been clean this morning when I got up. *How in the hell did Sawyer make this big of a mess in such a short time?*

"It's just a few things," Sawyer called from the bedroom.

"A few things?" I glanced around at the aftermath of a tornado. "You've got to be kidding me. You're not allowed to let our place get like this. What makes you think the tour bus is different?"

A few months ago when Sawyer and I decided to move in together, ground rules were set. Heath and Sawyer had already been looking for a bigger house. One with almost two wings to the place, giving them each their own space. More shows meant more money. Not that I could blame them. A house was an investment.

Sawyer and I had gotten tired of having two of everything, or wondering at which house our stuff could be. We talked and sat down with Heath. Neither one of us wanted to ruin the plans they already started making. In the end all three of us decided to get a larger house, with enough room that Sawyer and I, as well as Heath would have their own space.

It took us a while, but we found the perfect place. All the communal areas were in the center of the house. Living rooms, kitchens, dining rooms. On each side of those rooms there was a hall that led to a set of bedrooms. Each side of the house had three of its own bedrooms, for a total of six. On our side I'd turned one of the rooms into an office, while Heath and Sawyer were working on having the basement remodeled into a sound studio. Heath and I even sat Sawyer down and explained that his nasty ass ways had to go. No more leaving shit out until someone else cleaned it up.

It worked at home. Apparently not so much here.

"Get out here and help me."

I bent down and started shoving papers into a pile. Sawyer only really got this bad when he was close to finishing a new song. Something he hadn't done in a while. Almost like his brain completely shut off to everything but the music.

"Fine," he said, emerging from the back in just a towel.

Instantly, my dick went hard. Nothing about that had changed in the time we'd been together. One look at him and I was hard enough to pound nails.

"And you couldn't get dressed before you came out here."

He wiggled his hips. "Like what you see?"

I groaned and looked back down at the floor. "Don't start. You have a show tonight and I have paperwork to file before that happens."

He stood behind, grazing his fingers along my back. "You're no fun."

I batted his hand away. "Quit pouting, would ya."

"Whatever." He bent down and started picking up drumsticks.

"That's the last one," I said a few moments later as I threw an empty energy drink can into the trash.

Sawyer came up and wrapped his arms around my waist, letting his hard dick rub up against my thighs. *Oh, hell yes!* "How's the venue looking for tonight?"

We'd been on the road for a few weeks, hitting city after city for the band to play. The crowds grew with each show they put on. I was so proud of how much they'd accomplished in such a short time. Another benefit happened to be my new job. It was honestly the job of my dreams. As a lawyer for the studio it was my job to make sure everything at each venue went smoothly and according to the contract they'd agreed to. I'd been shocked the first few days at the things the venues tried to sneak by when no one was looking.

The best part was I got to spend all the time in the world with Sawyer, traveling, seeing the sites, listening to them play and not being separated for months at a time. Everyone watched at how hard it was on Mari when Cole had to be on campus, which thankfully wasn't often. Even though we spent years apart, now I couldn't imagine not seeing each other for that long.

Sawyer bent over to grab a pencil that had rolled under the couch, and I couldn't help but notice the way the towel stretched across his firm ass. Moving up behind him, I placed my hands on his hips and brought his ass back so it cradled my dick. He glanced back at me, fire in his eyes.

"I guess you do like what you see."

I hummed in the back of my throat. "I like it a whole hell of a lot."

He stood up and let the pencil slip through his fingers. I reached down and adjusted the erection in my pants, thinking about all the places I wanted to put it. Sawyer covered my hand with his. "How about we take care of that instead?"

I took a step closer. Our mouths mere centimeters from each other. "What do you have in mind?"

"Anything that requires us both to be naked."

I took his hand, leading him back to the bedroom. My fingers slipped into the knot of the towel, letting it drop to the floor. Our mouths connected and all I could think was how lucky I was that I had this man in my life. The road was rocky, but every misunderstanding and secret along the way made us stronger people. That strength helped us to stay together when so many others would have given up. Somehow in all the years, I hadn't seen it, may never have expected, but Sawyer was the one for me.

Every day I thanked the heavens for him kissing me that night. Sawyer was my one and only.

ALSO BY REBECCA BROOKE

Forgiven Series:
Forgiven
Redemption
Healed
Acceptance

Letters Home Series:
Letters Home
Coming Home
Just Once

Traded Series:
Traded
House Rules
Taken

Jaded Ivory Novels:
Rock Me
Ride Me

Stand Alone Titles:
Beautiful Lessons
Ryder
Second Chances

The Folstad Prophecies:
Twin Runes
Elemental Runes

With Brandy L. Rivers – The Pine Barrens Pack Series:

Cursed Vengeance

Vengeance Unraveled

ABOUT THE AUTHOR

Rebecca Brooke grew up in the shore towns of South Jersey. She loves to hit the beach, but always with her kindle on hand. She is married to the most wonderful man, who puts up with all of her craziness. Together they have two beautiful children who keep her on her toes. When she isn't writing or reading (which is very rarely) she loves to bake and watch episodes of Shameless and True Blood.

Facebook

https://www.facebook.com/RebeccaBrookeAuthor/

Twitter

@RebeccaBrooke6

Website

www.rebeccabrooke.com

Join My Mailing List

https://www.subscribepage.com/RebeccaBrooke

Made in the USA
Middletown, DE
06 October 2018